THE UNHOLY MOTHER

Enya Wolf

Connlaswell Publishing

Copyright

FAMILY

1 - Kim

No mother should ever lose her child. I'm sure we can all agree on that. And the way I lost mine, no woman should even know about, never mind read about. So if you're the sensitive type, cut your losses and read *Gone Girl* instead. And if you're pregnant, STOP RIGHT NOW. You shouldn't even have picked up this book. Go wash your hands and forget about it. A few Hail Marys wouldn't hurt either.

"JAMIE!"

I'm not a screecher, but that's how it came out.

He looked from me to our son William who was spreadeagled on the floor, not so much wailing as whining, old enough by now to feel the indignity of a fall as much as the pain of it. I scurried over and picked him up before bustling back to my guard station at the luggage cart. Jamie shrugged as if to say ... *what?*

Well, here's what, my beloved husband.

While you were amusing yourself at the car rental booth, tickling our son for the entertainment of the girl behind the desk, I was putting myself into a trance. That sounds strange, I know. But my heartbeat—thump, thump—was slamming me between the eyes like a chainmail fist. Another headache from hell. I'd woken up with it on the plane coming over from Miami, and I was trying to get rid of it with this self-hypnosis thing I'd picked up online.

First, note the color of the pain and its intensity on a scale from one to ten. Then put the pain in a box and lock the box with a key. Finally, remove the box from your head.

And at precisely that moment, you decided you needed both hands to complete the paperwork. So you dumped William on the floor. Point of information: why not sign with one hand? You have ten years of college. Didn't they cover one-handed writing at some point? And by the way, that ugly crunching sound echoing around the airport terminal is the aftermath of our son's elbow hitting the deck as he ran over to his mom. So now I have a purple headache—a number eight—in a green plastic box, sticking half in and half out of my head, plus a screaming three-year-old.

That's what!

Jamie smirked his remorse and turned back to the cute twenty-something who was taking care of him at the desk. Her eyes lingered on me, blazing scorn.

I nestled William on the luggage, kissed him, and soothed his scuffed elbow with a mother's touch.

So this was me on a bad day in paradise.

Our big day. Me and Jamie.

Okay. Jamie's big day, the launch of his new adventure reality TV show, and we were hours away from a PR gig in some ritzy hotel. Soon we'd be guzzling cocktails and putting on a dazzling show of togetherness for the assembled media. I closed my eyes as I hugged William. It was going to get better. It had to.

And so it did when we made it to our rented villa where we got the warmest of welcomes from the housekeeper, Beth. She was a real charmer and no doubt an island pinup in her day with a complexion the color of amber rum and all the sweetness and warmth that goes with it. Her eyes lit up when she saw William. She scooped him up and he soon added Granny Beth to his burgeoning lexicon. The house was called *Paradise Found,* but it rated a lot better than its clichéd name. Beth gave us a tour with William still perched on one arm. Up the spiral staircase we went and out onto the terrace of each of its three floors. The views were spectacular, nothing but ocean and sky trimmed with an empty white sand beach.

After the tour, I was in the kitchen with Beth going through our schedule when Jamie's phone rang. He was splashing around in the terrace pool with William, against my advice, in deep water. So I picked it up. It was his TV producer, Sydney Kingston, the Svengali who had turned him from a geeky archaeologist into a ballsy adventurer and thinking woman's pinup. She wanted to know how the house was and I gave her all the right answers as I walked the phone out to the pool. She was being polite, and so was I. I wondered if it was as hard for her as it was for me. I gave Jamie the phone and took William, wrapping him in a towel and drying him before leaving him with Granny Beth and heading upstairs.

The master suite, with its king-sized bed and his and hers bathrooms, occupied the entire top floor. I went out onto its terrace and slumped against the wall, my eyes scanning the beach and the seascape, and my ears tuning in to Jamie's voice. I could hear it, but I couldn't make out the words. He was tucked out of sight in the shade somewhere down by the pool. So all I got was the muffled, warm tone of it. Jamie had told me more than once that he had a lot of respect for Sydney and that he admired her. I'd never asked him what he thought of her. But he'd told me anyway. I wondered about that—why he talked about her unprompted—as though she was always there on his mind. And what about that word *admire*? I was a writer by trade. I noticed words, and every passing day that one was getting more and more slippery and extremely suspicious.

2 - Jamie

"You're not going to drown. I promise."

I was teaching William to swim, but we'd hit a snag.

Fear.

At three years old and three feet something, learning in a pool that was three foot something plus made trusting your dad a big ask. He was spluttering and coughing and shaking his head, just about ready to quit. So I pulled him up out of the water, rocking him against my chest, my eyes trailing back and forth across the beach and the turquoise ocean beyond it. Maybe I was pushing him too hard. Kim had warned me about that. According to her, the correct age for swimming lessons was four, and before then splashing around in a few inches of water was enough. She was right, of course. She always was when the subject was kids. She'd had all sorts of problems becoming a mom, and by the time she'd made it, she was a certified black belt in motherhood and everything that goes with it. But I was sure he was ready.

"Say, Will ... do you want to play with dolphins like they do at *SeaWorld*?" He nodded, still rubbing his eyes with bunched fists. "So after we finish daddy's business stuff here, I planned for us to play with dolphins. But you can't swim yet, so I guess I'll have to cancel." His face dropped. "If you can do a couple of strokes, I won't have to..."

"And Mommy?"

"Mommy too. The three of us. What do you say?

One more time?"

It took him a minute. Then his eyes hardened with determination. Real commitment. I was so proud of the little guy. I held him afloat with one hand and off we went, his arms and legs churning the water in a jerky breaststroke. Then, two yards out from the edge, I let him go, and this time, he didn't flap and flounder.

He swam.

I grabbed him out of the water and whooped it up, splashing his legs around and making a big fuss of him. But Kim cut our celebration short. She emerged from the villa, her face tinged with a scowl. I wasn't sure if that was because of her headache, or my playing with William in the deep water. She was holding my phone in one hand and shielding her eyes from the sun with the other.

"The lady of the hour." She rattled the phone.

That was Sydney, and her call was another likely candidate for the black look Kim was giving me. They used to get along. Or so I'd thought. But lately, their contact had been spikey. Still smiley. But spikey.

Kim put down the phone at the edge of the pool and took William with both hands, wrapping him in a towel. I clambered out of the water, picked up the phone, and headed towards the other end of the pool where I could chat overlooking the ocean. But then, with Kim's lady of the hour comment ringing in my ears, I went back to the villa and nestled into a chair on the shady part of the terrace where she could eavesdrop on the conversation.

No secrets in this marriage.

At least, not yet.

"How's it going?" I said. Syd was at some star-studded hotel in downtown Nassau organizing the promo event. "Did they all show up?"

"Sure. Wouldn't you?"

No doubt about it. There's nothing like a freebie trip to the Bahamas to clear space in your calendar.

"And are they all suitably schmoozed?"

"Not yet. But they'll get there. The open bar kicks off in an hour. Full attendance guaranteed. So how's the villa?"

"Fabulous. I've been splashing around in the pool with William."

"Don't get too relaxed. This is our big day."

"Don't worry. I won't let you down." She must have heard the flatness in my voice. I didn't mean it to come out like that. But faking it is not one of my talents, and a rendezvous with the media ranks better than a trip to the dentist as my least favorite way to spend the day. "I'm going to clean up now. Kim's already started."

"She's coming too?"

"Sure. The housekeeper agreed to babysit."

"That's great news." Now it was Syd's turn to sound flat.

We said our farewells and I went into the house. Beth was in the kitchen, pouring a juice for William.

"Can I get you anything?" she said.

"I'm okay. I was wondering where Kim was."

"She's upstairs getting ready." Beth paused, fussing with William. "We ladies need our time, you know." She inflected it with a charming island lilt. She was a young-looking grandma with a husband called Bubby who drove a city bus. William entered the conversation in his usual commanding fashion by knocking over his glass and spilling juice across the table and floor. "Good work, young fellow." Beth went to the rescue.

I checked my watch. I had time—not too much— but enough to check out the beach. I was already planning William's next swim lesson and nothing beat learning in salt water.

Leaving William in the capable hands of Beth, I slipped outside and headed down the stairs at the side of the terrace. At the foot of the steps, paddleboards stood in a rack next to a picnic area with a comfy-looking hammock shaded by coconut palms. I headed past it, my feet sinking into the soft white sand. The beach was private. And with the neighboring villas showing no signs of life, it looked like it was all ours. At one end, the beach tapered to a rocky headland, its verdant green littered with rooftops of yellow, red and purple. At the other end, it snaked in a gentle curve and disappeared. I stopped when I was ankle deep in foaming wash, shallow water with a gentle slope, the perfect venue for a budding swimmer like William. On the horizon, the Atlantic bled into a cloudless sky in endless shades of tropical blue, and every one of them a treat for the eyes. I kicked around in the shallows for a while, then turned back towards the shore. The serenity of the place was working its magic on me already, and even the prospect of an evening in the company of media types—all handshakes and smiles to my face while sharpening cutting comments behind my back—was not enough to dampen my upbeat mood.

"Jamie!"

Kim was bouncing around on the terrace, flailing her arms. I was rooted to the spot, my mind racing. She had cracked some remark earlier about the villa being *grotesquely child unfriendly* with its winding staircase, terraces, and unfenced pool.

William?

3 - Kim

When Jamie rang off, his whispered words with Syd concluded, I watched him head down to the sea, then stepped back into the welcome shade of the master suite.

Where are those painkillers?

I soon gave up the search. I'd packed my bags in two sessions, and obviously, the ibuprofen had fallen through the crack. I went downstairs and tucked my head around the kitchen door. Beth was making sandwiches and my hungry son was sitting close by, his eyes on the breadboard. He glanced up and I waved a *hi*, then said to Beth, "I don't suppose there's a first-aid kit in the house with a few aspirins in it?"

"Headache still bothering you? You poor dear." She stood up. "There's one with a few basics. Band-Aids and such. Definitely no medications."

"That's what I thought. But it was worth a try."

I was heading out when Beth said, "Is it really bad?" I spun around and made a gun with my hand, pointing the barrel at my temple and miming a boom sound. "I probably shouldn't, but ... I have something." She disappeared into a utility room and returned with a box. "I found these, cleaning up after the last guests." She gave it to me. "My Bubby had these same pills after his heart surgery. The owners would kill me if they knew I was giving them to a guest. I'm not worth suing, but they are. I planned to flush them down the toilet."

I checked the label and flipped open the box.

Tramadol. Synthetic opiates.

"They were young people, too," Beth said. "And they didn't look in pain to me."

"They just left them?"

"In the drawer of the nightstand. People often leave things there, but usually it's a book or a sleep mask. Those pills are very strong. You shouldn't take one if you're pregnant."

"I'm not pregnant."

I didn't so much say it as snap it, and the look on her face told me as much. I was fumbling for an apology when she said, "I didn't mean..." She waved her hands vaguely at my body, then patted her own midriff. "Look at me. You're—"

"It's not that. I had a miscarriage three days ago and—"

"Three days! You shouldn't be traveling on planes."

"That's what my doctor said."

Beth's face wrinkled, and she reached up to touch my face with her fingertips. "You poor dear."

"I should be used to it by now. It's not like it's my first. This headache too. It's all part of the package. I wanted to stay home and cry me a river. But here I am, doing my duty." Beth was a born empath, and I could see my pain written in the softness of her eyes the moment I said it. I checked the contents of the box. There had to be fifty pills in it. "Not exactly a doctor-recommended remedy for a headache. But thanks anyway. I'll try to pick up some ibuprofen on the way to the hotel. If I can't, and it gets worse..." I held the box up and rattled its contents.

The elevator whisked me up to the master suite where I put the pills on the dresser in the bedroom. Theoretically, that made them out of Williams's reach although he was such an adept climber that nowhere fit that category anymore. I wandered out onto the terrace, staying in the shaded part, and sucked at the sea breeze, getting it deep in my lungs. Maybe that was all it would take to calm my throbbing brain. Jamie was alone at the water's edge, up to his knees in swash and splashing around like a kid. I let out a sigh with the faintest shake of my head.

That man will never grow up.

When we were dating, he took me sailing and we ended up on a deserted cay, real *Pirates of the Caribbean* stuff. We barbecued a fish, killed a bottle of rum and made out all night in the sand. When I woke up, the sun was way up and Jamie had built a sandcastle with a moat running down to the sea. I thought it was odd. Bear in mind, this man has a PhD. When I asked him if he wasn't a tad old for that type of construction project, he wriggled like a stuck worm, telling me it was a metaphor for life, a Zen thing. I fell in love with him that day. My new boyfriend was all man, smart and sexy both. But it was that goofy boy that got to me. He just stared at his castle as the tide washed it away, and when it was gone, he said, "Will you marry me?" That was it. No ring. No bended knee. But impossibly romantic.

My Sandman.

"Mrs. ... Mrs. Steiger." Beth was hurrying up the staircase, getting to the top as I dashed in from the terrace. She was carrying William with one arm and steadying herself with the other against the handrail.

"What is it? Why didn't you take the elevator?"

I took William and she put both her hands on her heaving chest.

"Bubby, my husband, he's had a heart attack. He's at the hospital ... in surgery."

"You must go there. Right away."

She nodded, still gulping air, her eyes widening.

"Thirty-five years ... thirty-five."

"He'll be okay." I put William down and hugged her. "It's fantastic what they can do these days. Come on." As we hurried out of the room, I turned to William. "Do not go on the terrace." I pointed towards it and gave him my *or else* look. "And don't climb anything. I'll be right back."

Downstairs, I called for a taxi, but that was going to take too long. So I gave her the keys to our rented SUV and ordered a taxi for Jamie instead. This called for a change of plan. I'd have to stay home and take care of William.

I comforted Beth on the way to the car, or at least I tried to, but I doubt she heard a word. She was hunched over the steering wheel as I opened the garage door, her eyes blank, focused on some fearful inner vision.

Thirty-five years.

The garage door was taking forever to open. I choked back tears as I reached through the open window and pulled her close enough to kiss her cheek.

"God bless."

It was all I could think to say.

She glanced up at me, the wisp of a smile brushing her cheeks.

4 - Jamie

When the taxi finally came, I slumped in the back and we roared off, my somber thoughts riding roughshod over my driver's jolly shtick. There was an insurance convention in town, he said, excusing his lateness.

The town's full of Brits. Go in that conference center and shout out Nigel. Four hundred people gonna say "yes".

He had a good laugh about that one, and it even squeezed a smile out of me. But my thoughts soon drifted back to the daily news. There's nothing like a heart attack to get you focused on what really matters.

When I got to the hotel, Sydney rushed me to my front-row seat and the show kicked off. She had just enough time to drop a few words in my ear, soft and cajoling.

"Be nice ... try to be liked."

I kept turning it around in my head as my eyes followed my own swashbuckling adventure unfolding on the screen.

What a strange thing to say.

I thought I was nice. I thought people liked me.

My attention drifted back to the screen. A close-up of a man's hand. Tanned, physical. A hand that knew the outdoors, a hand that had worked but never toiled.

My hand.

It was holding a silver crucifix against a tropical blue sky.

"Fingers crossed." Sydney whispered it in my ear, leaning so close I could feel the heat and wetness of her breath. I flashed her a nervous glance. I wanted to ask her about that *be nice* stuff, but now was not the moment. I dragged myself back to the screen where my voice began the intro.

Look closely.

The camera zoomed in on the crucifix, a silver cross with a unique corpus, its features embellished with stones, corals and shells.

... this is not Jesus Christ. This is no Christian crucifix. Behold, the naked body of a woman, her belly fat with child, her breasts ripe for suckling. Symbols of life. But her arms and legs defleshed. Her skull skeletal, its eyes bottomless pits, its jaws agape and raised aloft as if to swallow heaven itself. A grotesque vision of voluptuous sexuality. Procreation showcased in the persona of death. A woman's corpse—nailed to a cross—yet burgeoning with life. So who is this most Unholy Mother? Some crazy biker's acid nightmare? A Black Sabbath album cover that didn't make the grade?

A calculated pause. I was getting better at those stage mannerism. I'd picked that one up from the host of a well-known TV talent show.

This was handcrafted five hundred years ago by so-called Christians. By a people who embraced the God of their Spanish invaders, but not at the cost of their old gods. By a people railroaded at the point of a sword into a religion they barely understood. New World Christians who fused ancient beliefs and rituals into a vision of Christianity where Eternal Life fed on death and sacrifice—

Suddenly, it hit me.

Walgrave.

That was why she'd said it.

Be nice.

Walgrave or Walgreave or whatever his goddamn name was. I remembered seeing the little shit a few rows back when I took my seat. Walgrave had carved himself a career out of hurting people. His specialty was acidic soundbites and caustic critiques and he'd grown his blog, with its *Toxin du Jour* column, into a serious career.

Yes ... Walgrave.

Be nice.

The little shit was always up for an unfounded rumor, and a photo of me and Sydney cozying up together in a restaurant had broken on his blog. It was just a kiss. A peck, really. She grabbed my face and laid it on me. Two seconds. Nothing to it.

What was I supposed to do?

Punch her in the mouth?

Kim had brushed it off at the time, dismissing my groveling excuses with a joke. But I could see she'd been hurt. Not much. But enough for me to remember the little shit.

Be nice.

In other words, *don't smack Walgrave.*

The camera pulled back, and there I was in all my makeover glory, standing on the deck of a yacht, blue linen shirt open at the chest, hips in white chinos shifting rhythmically with the waves sliding under the boat.

Not bad for forty-two.

Yes. I did think that. I admit it. I'm not a vain guy. But I'd been hanging around TV types for a long time by then and passing a mirror without sneaking a look was getting harder and harder. Ruggedly handsome. That was how they described me in the handouts, although I figured there was more *rugged* than *handsome* in that. Even so, Syd's makeover guys had done a great job—everything short of cosmetic surgery.

It was fifteen years ago when I found this crucifix washed up on a beach on Worthless Cay.

I perked up. I liked this bit.

I am Dr. Jamie Steiger. And this is the story of how I found the missing links between this crucifix and those who worshiped it, how I followed the trail of a militant priest from his fiefdom in the jungle to a cabin on a Spanish Galleon, and how this crucifix led me to the wreck of that ship—to the richest treasure ship of all time—La Capitana, the flagship of the 1564 Fleet of Juan de Mendoza. Join me now on this great adventure.

The credits rolled and I sat back and stretched out my legs. I had a rumbling concern that Walgrave might try to provoke me, so I decided not to drink too much. These sessions are awash with booze and the last thing we could afford was a scene on a day like this.

My hand reached up to touch the *Mendoza Crucifix* hanging from my neck. From the moment I'd found it, my life had shifted gears, the years since a storybook transformation from rags to riches. Predictably, my PhD thesis had kicked off a storm of controversy. But then I'd turned it into a bestselling book, although, in reality, Kim had done most of the actual writing part of the book. From then on, the roadmap to success had rolled out before me. My life, according to the TV bigshots, had all the ingredients of compelling reality TV. Lost civilizations, mysteries, hi-tech equipment, exotic locations, and a ruggedly handsome adventurer with the brains and balls to bring it all into the living room. Or at least, that was the hype. And until this night, that had been the way the story had played out, beat by beat perfect.

We all know the rules of life. One thing follows another. You study hard, you pass the exam. You forget to lock the door, a burglar calls. All our expectations are built on this premise. But looking back, it doesn't look so simple to me. I read somewhere that when you hear a bird sing, you write a romantic poem. In other words, life flows from one thing to another according to a mystical rulebook, rather than logic or a scientific paradigm. It means that alchemy is intrinsic to life's DNA, and at any point along the predictable path of cause and effect, magic can intercede. The bird's song becomes the lover's inspiration. Base metal becomes gold. And on that day, life's alchemy was afoot. Unbeknown to me, the death of Beth's husband had rolled the dice. My fate. My family. It was all in play, and my life was about to be transformed beyond all recognition. But it was a far cry from a lover's poem or a chest of gold doubloons.

5 - Kim

"Died? ... Oh no!" I pressed the phone tight to my ear to stop my hand from trembling. Her name was Grace. Beth's daughter. Her mother was not coming back to work. That was the gist of it. But she couldn't make the call herself. So her tearful daughter had stepped up to the plate. "Of course I understand. For God's sake, I..." That was where I lost it, the verbiage tumbling out of my mouth broken by sniffs and sobs. The dead dad I could deal with. I'd already had one of my own. But Beth's concern for me—a woman she'd hardly met—her reaching out on such a day, that cut me up. Grace went on, talking about her father and how her mother was coping, or mostly not. Maybe it helped her to talk. But what do you say to a woman you've never met whose father has just died? Words gushed out anyway. Words of sympathy, condolence. Useless words.

After the call, I pulled myself together and got William ready for bed. I always read to him at bedtime, but his storybook was still packed. So I improvised.

"I'm going to tell you a fairy tale called *The Rose of Béroche*. That's a town in Switzerland where mommy grew up. My daddy used to tell me this story every summer when the roses came out in our garden."

So I told him about the girl called Rose who had magical healing powers given to her by the Lady in White. How one day, a jealous evil witch tricked Rose into swimming in the lake where she drowned her. And how the Lady in White transformed her dead body into a beautiful rose and forever blessed the roses of Béroche.

I loved that story as a child, and its theme of innocence transformed into beauty never failed to enchant me and bring out tears of joy. It was my first lesson in life. Nothing dies. It just changes. But all that was lost on William. His face was wonky on one side, like it always gets when he can't figure me out. And if I had any doubts about that, they were soon cleared up when he said, "Call the police?"

That really brought it home. Bedtime stories were not one size fits all, and times changed. My son was not into fairy godmothers and witches. He was more of a Special Ops guy. I scurried off to dig out his storybook, finding a more appropriate tale of a sheep who couldn't fall asleep like the other sheep. So he had to do all these funny things to get tired. We were soon back on track and Will's face glowed with giggles at all the funny bits. I felt blessed and oddly guilty to have the schadenfreude shadow of Beth's loss light up the dusk on this strangest of days.

When we finished the story, we said our prayers and I kissed him goodnight. My head was still throbbing. So I went up one floor to the master suite and sat on the bed holding the box of painkillers and wondering if I should. I was no doctor, but I was the next best thing, a hypochondriac. Or so Jamie had told me. And I knew plenty about pills, having popped a few in my day, although I'd been careful to avoid opiates, aware of their potential for addiction and abuse. This wasn't abuse though, misuse maybe, but that was something I could live with. So I washed down two with a San Pellegrino. Greedy that. But I craved normal, and that meant killing this pain. Down in the kitchen, I checked the fridge. Plenty of food, stocked up in advance of our arrival by Sydney or one of her lackeys more like. I checked a few labels. Top brands every one. Fresh fruit and salad in the drawers and every low-fat goddamn thing you can think of. Except for that tub of foie gras of course, one of my European habits following me across the ocean and through the years. Jamie and Sydney would be dining on lord knows what at the gourmet buffet. Why shouldn't I spoil myself? I could have it later with some crackers and...

Mm-hmm.

I'd hit an awkward moment.

Wine?

Not a drop had passed my lips for over a year, not only the time I'd been pregnant but also while trying to conceive. A debate ensued, culminating in a heated argument, which I both won and lost. The issue now was not pregnancy, but pills. Painkillers and alcohol don't mix. Everyone knows that. But foie gras is indigestible without wine. Everyone knows that too. In the end, it came down to *what's the worst that can happen? I get sleepy, or maybe a little high? So what? I'm not driving.* My plan was to do absolutely nothing but nurse my aching head. So I took a glass out of the cabinet, not a wimpy wineglass, but a highball cocktail glass. I filled it halfway with Chardonnay, then topped it to the brim with ice cubes. I sipped it as I wandered outside and settled down on a poolside chair. The ocean breeze caressed my body like cool fingers laced with a healing balm. I slipped off my top, and as the ice in my glass melted and my makeshift cocktail reached the right balance of wine and wet, my sips grew into lusty gulps. The opiate fire blanket I'd swallowed kicked in soon after, and the heat in my head died, my purple headache fading into gray as if an eraser were being dragged back and forth across it.

Should I message Jamie to tell him about Beth?

Jamie had all sorts of theories about death. When you're an archaeologist, death is your office. The Mexica—that's the Aztecs to you and me—believe that our lives end up embedded in objects. He told me that once and I never understood it. But sipping white wine on the terrace with an opioid drip muddling my mind's eye, it made sense. Beth had lived through years of marriage with all the baggage that comes with it—love, birth, pain, and death. Now it was all buried in objects—their wedding rings, his armchair, the pen he used to write her love notes. I fetched another glass of wine and went back to my seat on the terrace where I sipped it deep in thought, although that's too sharp a word for what was going through my head. Images, ideas, feelings. They were all slipping and sliding on the pills and the booze, oozing into each other, edges all blurred. My head felt better but still tender, and I had this sense of being trapped, dragged in a downward spiral. Another miscarriage had to be a big part of that. There came a point where it was hard not to take it personally. And Bubby's death too, all that family grief washing over me. I wandered back inside and checked on William. He was still awake, pretending to be asleep. I can always tell. I sat on the bed and picked him up. He slid his arms around my neck and slumped his head on my shoulder as he whispered in my ear.

"Where's your daddy now?"

He was still thinking about my fairy tale.

"He's in heaven. Where God lives."

I rocked him side to side. I'd been stupid to tell him that story. Death and drowning. He was way too young.

"Can dolphins drown?"

"I don't think so. Maybe when they get old and weak." I laid him back on the bed and tucked him under the sheet. "Why don't you forget about Rose and think about Billy the sheep instead? Remember all those funny tricks he knows? Why don't you try some of those?"

He closed his eyes and his face eased into a smile. I kissed his forehead and sat watching him until he fell asleep.

A lake of ice.

In truth, that was where my daddy was, or at least where I'd lost him. And sitting there, my hand on Will's chest, feeling the rise and fall of his breath, the link from my dad's death to my son's life came to me as a sudden recollection that made my stomach heave. My father and I had been hurrying to the airport to pick up my American mother when he'd swerved to avoid a truck and the car had skidded down an embankment through clouds of snow toward the lake. In that split-second, I saw us crashing through the ice and dying together as the car sank to the bottom of the lake. But that didn't happen. We hit a rock instead. It stopped the car, breaking my dad's neck. It took them six hours to rescue me. I spent it looking at my father, his head hanging against his chest like a puppet waiting for its master, his face twisted towards me, floodlit by moon and snow, his eyes a blank stare. We moved to the US after that and I was parachuted into a new school, a thirteen-year-old girl with a funny accent and no friends and no father. So my life continued to skid downhill until I hit my own rock.

The gas range in our kitchen.

I have an idea that we all consider suicide at some point, if not during our troubled teens like me, then later as our bodies rot in old age. I walked for miles that day, sweeping tears from my cheeks, and I ended up in a library. On the day I was checking out of life, I wasn't interested in checking out a book. But I had to kill time until my mother went shopping, and the air-conditioned library was a welcome relief from the summer heat. I browsed the bookshelves and I was soon thumbing through a book about yoga. Not the Hollywood yoga they sell on the internet. This was the real thing, a weighty red tome translated from Sanskrit more than a hundred years ago. I learned that self-survival is the most powerful human instinct and it comes from a chakra located between my anus and my vagina. That stopped me dead. I didn't even know I had a location there. I dug deeper, learning that our second most powerful instinct is survival of the species, or sex, centered in a chakra between my navel and—once again—my vagina. So there it was. The keys of life. Not sublime, but gross. Self-survival and sex. And all of it spinning around a single axis ... *my vagina.*

Back home, I stood at the gas range and turned on the taps with my mind racing ahead. I could see my mother cradling my dead body, blaming herself—and with good reason. Mothers reap what they sow, and my dead body would be an appropriate harvest for a mother who had abandoned me emotionally after my father had died.

So that was the final curtain.

Her lamentations would be the last vestige of my existence, and when she died, there would be nothing left of me, not a single trace.

That stuck in my craw.

No trace.

I turned off the gas taps and rushed up to my room, my body raging with heat. I launched myself onto the bed and tore off my jeans. *I will not disappear without a trace. I'm going to leave an indelible track, a living-breathing human being.* I slipped my hands into my panties and explored my chakras. In the ornate words of the big red book, my lotus flower was about to unfold, its soft wet leaves beckoning for a suitor.

So my grades improved and my school attendance record became perfect. I made friends instead of enemies and organized my life into achievable goals. I became a model student. And in turn, a model wife. It was only when I got to the model mother part that things fell apart. Evidently, *Eve*, I was not. There were endless tests. And finally, I was diagnosed with endometriosis. This ushered in years of laser surgery and hormonal injections, all leading to abject failure and our last option. IVF. The silver bullet. Or so we'd thought—until the first miscarriage. But whatever the cost in money, pain or time, from that day on, my motherhood had never been negotiable. William was the lifeline that had rescued me from the abyss.

I kissed him on the forehead and went downstairs, where I topped up my Chardonnay and wandered out onto the pool terrace and down the steps to the beach. There was a table with some chairs and a hammock slung between two palms. I hitched my butt up onto the hammock and parked my eyes on the night sky. There was plenty going on up there with palm leaves waving and puffy white clouds scudding around in the moonlight. But it was all wasted on me. The ice lake had brought me down with a thump, and although my thoughts had moved on, they'd carried the downer with them. All I could see up there was the bad stuff in my head. Jamie and Sydney *schmoozing* at the preview, working the crowd and working each other.

I started swinging the hammock aggressively, feeding the glass up to my mouth, my arm keeping time with my increasingly sour mood like a metronome heading towards a crescendo. Something was bound to break and in the end it was the glass. It got caught in the hammock strings and went tumbling down to the beach. That could have worked out better too. On powder-fine sand like this, you might expect to get lucky. But I'd found the only rock on the beach and the glass didn't so much as break as explode. Now I'd have to clean it all up. If I didn't, my clumsy husband would step on it with bare feet first thing in the morning.

I checked my phone. There was no message from him. I slumped back in the hammock, cursing him, cursing Sydney, and finally cursing myself to sleep.

When I came to, I struggled to pull myself up, the world around me seeping unreality. Disoriented, my foot caught in the hammock, and I pitched out onto the sand, landing on my hands and feet like a cat. But not quite. A cat would have picked a more judicious landing site.

A snap of glass.

I yelped, rolled onto my back and grabbed my ankle, twisting my foot to check on the damage. A curved chunk of glass was hooked into the sinewy flesh on the ball of my foot.

Now I was plenty awake.

I sat there holding my ankle, looking around as though some passing Samaritan might lend me a hand.

"Jamie." I hollered.

But the house and the beach were silent beyond the lap of waves.

Where the hell is he? What time is it?

That beautiful tropical night was gone, the deserted beach unsettling me now, no longer the romantic setting for love in the sand, but something sinister, a scene in a noir thriller with me cast as the doomed heroine, an injured woman with her tits hanging out like an invitation mat for the nearest available rapist.

Get a grip!

I took a breath and reached for the glass.

"Hey you!" A man's voice, loud and strong.

I fell back in the sand, holding up my hands. He was standing with his back towards the terrace lights, so I couldn't see his face. But I could make out his body. Big. Huge shoulders.

"Holy shit." He stepped closer, reaching down towards me.

6 - Jamie

Applause.
The final credits were rolling and the vibe was good. I turned towards the audience as the lights faded on. Syd was holding up her hands as if to hold them all back. "Before the stampede to the buffet, Jamie will take a few questions. Ten minutes max."

I stood up and perched myself nervously at her side, running through my checklist.
Be nice. Don't smack Walgrave.

I smiled. Syd had hired a coach to help me with this media stuff, but I was still shit at it. Seeing the problem I'd had forcing a smile, he'd suggested I imagine tiny car jacks in my cheeks and when I needed to smile, I should turn an imaginary jack handle to hoist up the edges of my mouth. He was proud of that nugget, calling it a visualization technique.

The first question was from a man in the front row with a bony face and enormous glasses. His name was Charles. Sydney dropped it in my ear as she gave him the floor with a pointed finger.

"I'm seeing a gap here between your book and the TV show in the details of the cult. I know some people got uppity about those religious points. Did you get pushback from the network on that?"

"Good question. Uppity is a nice word, and a lot more family-friendly than others that come to mind." I paused for a few snickers. "The truth is that no one knows the fine print on the cult's beliefs. They were into rituals, not scriptures. In the book, I had room to speculate. But for TV we stuck to the big picture. When I found the crucifix, it was hidden in a sheath of clay. But inside was something remarkable—the Aztec Queen of the Dead, a pagan goddess, pregnant and sacrificed on the Christian symbol of Eternal Life. Who worshiped her? Why was it concealed like that? And how did it end up on that beach? It's a detective story, not a theology lesson."

"You said speculate. Don't you mean stir the pot?"

"I never went out of my way to offend anyone." I glanced at Syd, eager to cut that topic short. She pointed out the next questioner, a lady in her late fifties, a round smiling face floating in the middle of the room.

"Jamie, you're such a likable guy—"

"Well, thanks."

"So how come everybody hates you?"

"Everybody? That's a bit harsh. Syd likes me." I gave her a one arm hug. "And so does my wife."

"But you're so controversial. And it's not just the trolls. Even your peers get in on the act. I've got some quotes here ... *fake science, wobbly research*. And those are the good ones. Here's my favorite, *that popular archeolojock.*"

I stifled a chuckle.

"I'm sure their opinions have nothing to do with the fact that I've got a *New York Times* bestseller and none of those guys can sell a book except to their own students when it's a mandatory part of the syllabus." I pointed to another hand, eager to change that topic too. "Next question. You, Ma'am."

"Hi, Jamie. I'm Suellen." She was young, urban, her head shaved bald on one side and what was left of her hair lacquered into a gimlet point. "I loved it to death." That was a good start, but I was hearing alarm bells. In my experience, a compliment is a setup for a sucker punch. I tightened up the jacks, wishing I'd spent more time going over the list of attendees. Suellen looked way too young to be an opinion maker. But Syd had handpicked the guest list. So she had to be someone. "I have a spin on that last question."

"About people hating me?"

More snickers.

"Sort of … you brushed it off as academic jealousy. But your book kicked up a storm way beyond that. You got death threats, right?"

"The world's full of crazies. Religion is a touchy subject."

"But you're implicating Jesus Christ in human sacrifice by calling this a Christian cult. That's inflammatory."

"*So-called* Christian cult. I was sensitive about that."

"So-called or not, they were chopping up bodies in the name of Christ. Why wouldn't people be shocked?"

"I just found the crucifix. I didn't dream it up. Besides, this is the twenty-first century and religious fanatics are still sacrificing humans in the name of God."

"You mean Islam?"

"I'm just saying that some of my critics need to watch more CNN news."

"The beheadings? You're talking about Islam, right?"

I had dug myself a good size hole here and I was teetering on the edge. The last thing I needed was a fatwa top-ten rating. Syd always told me I was great to work with, except that whenever I opened my mouth in front of a journalist, my guts fell out. I had the feeling that they just did.

"I don't mean Islam. I mean so-called Islamic terrorists. When Cortes conquered Mexico, Christianity was the same age as Islam is now. Holy Wars were ripping the heart out of Europe like they are now in the Middle East. So, in an age of extremism like that, imagine the fault line between the Spanish Inquisition and the Mexica. On the one hand, the pious pretensions of Christians cloaking immense brutality and greed, and on the other, the sacrificial harvesting of humanity concealing a sophisticated cosmology and a startling innocence. So suddenly, they're in bed together. And guess what? *El Culto de La Madre Impia*, the Cult of the Unholy Mother, was their ugly child."

I glanced at Syd. She was eager to close and so was I. But I wanted to lighten the mood first and end on a high note.

"Can I pitch another question?" Suellen was still on my case.

"Okay. One more, last one. But only because you're having such a good hair day." That line just popped into my head and the crowd loved it. Evidently, I was not the only connoisseur of scary coiffure and urban chic.

"Are you really good at what you do? Or is it blind luck?"

"I'll take luck over smarts any day. But my real good luck is to have a job that I love, colleagues that I admire,"—I gave Syd another one arm hug—"a darling of a son, and"—it took me a moment to pick out Walgrave in the third row and catch his eyes with a fuck-you drill bit—"a beautiful wife whom I adore. As for finding relics under the sea, I rely on research and science."

"What about your nose, Steiger?"

Another voice. Harsh like a bark.

"What?"

"You said you could smell truth."

It was a man's voice from way at the back, full of anger and thrown at me like an iron-studded gauntlet. I felt the jacks under my smile give way with a snap.

"Yes, I believe I did." I was deliberately vague, but I remembered it exactly because the interviewer was my wife. Kim was my girlfriend at the time, a rookie TV news reporter who had begged her producer to squeeze in a segment about me. How could I forget? It was the launchpad of my celebrity career. "You have an excellent memory, Mr.?"

"Excuse me, sir." Syd edged in front of me. "What's your—"

"And another thing." He bawled it out, shutting her down. "You're a fucking liar. You didn't find that crucifix." He pointed at my chest. "It found you. The only question is *why?*"

The audience turned as one with a gasp, whipping out smartphones like gunslingers at the O.K. Corral. I was forgotten. There was a new show in town, and this one was a lot more interesting than a wrecked Spanish galleon and a creepy old crucifix.

"So what makes me a liar?"

I felt Syd's restraining hand on my shoulder pulling me back as I stepped towards him. Eamon, her PA, was standing at the door waving an invitation card. So evidently, this guy had one. She flicked her hand at him and he got the unspoken message, slipping out the door to get security.

How did we miss this guy?

It was so obvious he didn't belong. And it wasn't just the mothballed jacket and sawn-off denim shorts. There was that face. All the others—male and female, young and old—were at least at home in the twenty-first century. But this face was from another age, like a profile chiseled on an ancient coin.

"You're a ghoul, Steiger. The Unholy reap the living. You rape the dead. Now it's payback time. They're knocking on your door." His face twisted into a lopsided grin. "I'm the messenger. *Ding-a-ling.*" His chair skidded back as he sprang into the aisle and charged.

Syd leaped in front of me and the audience spun their smartphones back towards us. "We're getting security." She held out her hands to stop him, but I shoved her aside.

Nobody is going to video Jamie Steiger hiding behind a woman.

The double doors burst open and Eamon came through with two security guards. Smart white uniforms, but no guns. "Sir!" One shouted as they ran towards the old man. But it was too late. I keeled over as he hit me, my head smashing into the floor. He was on top of me, clawing at my throat. He stank of putrid sweat and a sickening sweetness that made my stomach heave. His thumbs crushed into my windpipe. I slammed the butt of my hand against his nose and felt it break. He screeched and pulled back, blood spraying down on me as the guards dragged him off. Syd wrapped her arms around me as I pulled myself up, sucking down air in raucous gasps. The guards wrestled the man and pulled out cuffs. Syd stroked her hand through my hair and showed it to me.

Blood.

"It's okay," I said.

My eyes went back to the old man, limp now, his bolt shot, a guard on each arm. His right hand was cuffed already, and he feebly held up the left in compliance. But before the guard could cuff him, he spun and slammed his knee into his groin. Then he drove his elbow into the midriff of the other guard and both men staggered aside as he ran for the door.

I launched myself in pursuit.

"Jamie." Syd's voice was a shriek, pulling me up like a chain. "He's not worth it."

The man disappeared through the door with one guard giving chase. The other one was still wriggling on the floor. Some guests helped him up into a chair. The rest were still in video mode. I checked the back of my head and inspected my bloody hand, then raised it to the audience.

"Now that's reality TV, folks."

There was a ripple of laughter as we all did our best to resume normal service.

"Couldn't have put it better myself." Walgrave's voice piped up above the murmuring crowd. "And it's already online." He was waving his smartphone like a winner's trophy.

The little prick.

7 - Kim

I was shuffling backwards on my butt in the sand, one arm covering my breasts.

"For Chrissake, Dave." A woman's voice. "You're scaring her." She was standing behind the man, as tiny as he was big.

"I'm trying to help her."

"She don't know that, does she?"

The man edged closer, his eyes on the chunk of glass sticking out of my foot.

"How'd you do that?"

"She stepped on it, stupid." The girl pushed him aside and crouched next to me. She was young, barely out of her teens, with swathes of tousled blond hair. "We heard you scream."

"Where were you?" I dropped my guard arm, my raging heartbeat easing back to normal.

"Back there." She pointed along the shore.

"I thought it was a private beach." It was meant to be an excuse for sitting there with my tits out, but it must have sounded like a gripe.

"Oops." The boy finished fastening his belt buckle, whistling a few notes of something way out of tune.

I was getting the picture. The girl's bikini top was askew and one of her nipples had broken loose. His belt. Her bra. They must have crept onto the beach while I'd been asleep and been having sex in the sand when I screeched. The girl pointed to the resort, its flickering lights studding the dark spur of the headland. "We climbed the wall. They've got their own beach. But this one looked so special."

"And empty." The man added.

"Could you help me? I need to get back into the house."

"Sure. You want I should call a doctor?" A phone appeared in the girl's hand.

"I don't think so. Let's check it in the house." I went to get up, levering myself up with one arm while covering up my body with the other. I felt so stupid doing that, but it was a reflex. It certainly wasn't modesty. More like shame. I'm not so proud of my body these days.

"Pick her up, Dave."

I went to say *no*. I just needed someone to support me. But Dave had already plucked me off the sand like he was picking up a beach ball. There was something alarming about the way she said it and the way he did it with no pause in between. Like if she'd said, *Crush her skull, Dave*, then my brains would have already been decorating the beach. But it was too late for second guessing their intentions now. Dave had me cradled in his arms and was sashaying up the steps, swaying his body to keep my arms and legs clear of the rail on one side and the wall on the other. The perfect gentleman. He kept his eyes rooted on the way ahead, only once straying down to check out my breasts. Then he sat me down in a chair on the terrace and I slipped on my top while the girl turned on more lights.

"What's your name?" I asked the girl as she crouched to inspect my foot.

"Chris. We're Mr. and Mrs. Smith. Seriously. That's our real name. As of today."

"It's your honeymoon?"

"Yep." She held my foot up by the ankle and peered closely at the wound. "This is our first night of married bliss."

Now the picture was complete. A Bahamas honeymoon. A few cocktails. Then over the wall onto that deserted beach. Sex in the sand. It didn't get any better. Until a crazy, liquored-up bitch stepped on a wineglass and screamed.

"I'm so sorry."

"Don't worry about it," Dave said, as he peered into the lounge. "It's not like she's a virgin or anything."

"Shut up, Dave. Go get some hot water and paper towels." Dave dutifully disappeared into the house. Chris looked up at me. "Hold your breath." And with that, she plucked the glass out of my foot. Dave returned with a bowl of lukewarm water and a roll of kitchen towels. I dunked my foot and Chris massaged my calf until a pink cloud bloomed in the water around the cut.

"I think we got it all out," I said, as I pulled my foot out and dried it. I used a fresh paper towel to make a poor man's bandage and tucked the injured foot into a sneaker. Then Chris helped me to stand up.

"Jamie? Your husband, eh?" I looked at her blankly. "You called it out on the beach." I nodded. "So where is he?"

"He has a business thing in town. He should be back any minute."

"What kind of business is he in?" Dave was still eyeballing the place like a realtor doing a valuation.

Chris spun her head at him. "That's none of your business."

"It's okay. He's an archaeologist, a famous one."

"He must be." Dave said, still pricing the place. "It's kind of late for business, though. Archeology business."

That was what I was thinking too. How late I didn't know. My phone was still on the beach and there were no clocks around. I went to ask Chris, but I stopped myself. I was grateful to them. But now I needed them to go.

"Let me make it up to you." I went into the kitchen and took a bottle from the fridge. "Here." I offered it to Chris but Dave took it, virtually snatching it from my hands.

"Wow ... Roederer?"

"It's vintage champagne. French. Rosé. I mean pink."

"Check it out." He gave it to Chris.

She held the bottle with both hands like she was cradling a baby.

"We couldn't."

"I insist."

Jamie had brought it for us to drink after the preview, but I already knew that none of that was going to happen. I felt like wet mud about to ooze down a drain. Dave and Chris, my good Samaritans, were unintentionally triggering that. Their happiness was toxic. Their newly minted marriage, their togetherness, their love. I had inadvertently stumbled on a ruler to measure everything Jamie and I had lost. There was something so crude about their happiness that made it even more pure, and it was breaking my heart.

I walked them to the front gate, and I got back into the house and closed the door before my plastic smile erupted into tears. I marched onto the terrace and down onto the beach, ignoring the glass crunching under the soles of my sneakers. The preview had to be finished long ago.

So why hasn't he called?

Even on his busiest days, Jamie always messaged

me. I found my phone under the hammock, but there was no reassuring blinking message alert. I checked to make sure the signal was okay. Then I called him. I let it ring until it went to voicemail, but I didn't leave a message. I sat back in the hammock. But this time, I kept my feet firmly on the ground as I rocked back and forth.

So this was how the day that had started out so promisingly and turned out so badly got exponentially worse. I was sitting on the hammock, running video clips of the *Syd and Jamie Show* inside my head, and I knew from the opening credits that this would not be a story with a happy ending. Jealousy was not my style. Not normally. I trusted my husband. The problem was Sydney. Here was a woman with an agenda, and top of the list was Jamie Steiger. I'd always known that. It wasn't only the smooch in the blog photo. I'd read it off her the day we met. If she'd been a celebrity-besotted fan, I would have written it off. But she was his producer. They spent every day together. She was classy, American royalty, bred from the getgo to take what she wanted. She was Ivy-League smart too, and—as Jamie had pointed out more than once—an athlete who'd won the scholar-athlete cup in college four years in a row. This was a woman who had never set her eyes on a prize that she hadn't won, a woman with *triumph* tattooed on every strand of her DNA. So imagine my delight when her radar had locked on my husband. It was so obvious too. The tone in her voice, her body language, the way she touched him when she spoke to him. At first, I'd dismissed my fears. Sydney was not an obvious beauty—forgive my arrogance—not like me. In my TV news heyday, they'd called me *The Face,* and I still had that. But hers was nondescript, round like a dinner plate with lips and eyes painted on it with a magic marker. Although she had the body. I had to give her that. And everything she had, she knew how to use. Her sexuality was as much a part of her business toolkit as her MBA. I don't mean she screwed around. This girl was not cheap. I'm not talking about sex. I'm talking about sexuality. She didn't need to fuck men. They'd line up to eat crumbs from her fingers with no need for crude measures like that. A few hundred years ago in Salem, we could have sorted her out with a wooden stake and a box of matches. But this was twenty-first century America, where witches and bitches thrived. So every man she met was another rung in her ladder. As for my husband, I'd love to say he was the exception. Sadly, he was not. And he wasn't another rung either. He was her express elevator. I had always counted on his loyalty. He was not the playboy type. For some men, sex was a trophy cabinet. But for Jamie, it was a church. Sydney was smart enough to have figured that out. She'd know that all it would take was *one moment* to repaint the landscape of our lives, to recast our roles with me reduced to a bit part. The moment I am talking about here—in case you're slow on the uptake—is the moment she planted his cock in her cunt.

That moment!

Sorry to be so graphic and vulgar. But sometimes the urban dictionary is the only one that works, and Sydney's plan was as crude as it got. It wouldn't happen overnight. He wouldn't walk out the door the next day. There would be a long, drawn-out period of misery first. But from that moment on, he would change, becoming a stranger towards me. There would be lies, tears and promises. But none of that would mean shit. It would all be a symptom of a disease with a fatal prognosis.

A new word would pop into our conversation.

Divorce.

Maybe I'd even bring it up myself. My nuclear deterrent. But I'd be the one who got nuked. I'd had a DUI at college and they'd found coke in the car. There were other things too. A spin master like Sydney would sketch out a picture of me as a lot less than an ideal mother. They could take William from me. That bitch could hijack my whole family. That truth hit me with a jolt. I'd been in denial. *I should have exploded when I saw that blog photo.* Instead, I'd acted cool. Now it was too late. I knew it. I just did. I'd lost him.

I jumped off the hammock, struggling to breathe, my chest tight and twisted like a wet flannel wrung dry. I hate that word depression. It belongs in a weather forecast, not a doctor's diagnosis. I called my dark place *the swamp* because once I got lost there, if I tried to escape, I only got sucked in deeper. People who'd never been to the swamp often wondered about swamp folk like me, asking dumb questions like *why on earth do you want to kill yourself?*

Let me counter that with the view from the swamp.

Why on earth do you want to live? You're going to die anyway, and before then, your only guarantee is pain and loss. Welcome to the swamp. My name's Kim. I'm your tour guide.

I know what you're thinking.

She had a husband, a son, money. That spoiled bitch didn't know how lucky she was.

Wanna trade places?

You'd regret it in a heartbeat.

I slumped against the wall of the terrace, sobbing

my tears on the concrete. I had to escape. But where? There was only one surefire way out of the swamp. The emergency exit. That's a euphemism for the last choice you'll ever make. I was almost there, transported trancelike, my legs a magic carpet floating me over the sand and down to the waves. Water sloshed at my feet. I staggered a few steps, then fell. I pulled myself up and waded deeper, then plunged into the face of a rolling wave and swam out towards the reef. I was a strong swimmer, but it was much further than I thought. Stroke after stroke seemed to take me no closer to where the white tops were crashing over rocks. Beyond that reef was the open ocean, the Gulf Stream. As soon as I made it there, the current would drag me offshore. There'd be no going back then. I stopped and trod water, turning around and checking my distance from the shore. The beach was already remote, the lights of *Paradise Found* the only sign of life.

William.

His image. The moment I'd kissed him as he lay sleeping in the bed. The moment I'd left him. It hit me, racking my chest with a howl.

How could I even think of abandoning him?

It was a long way back, but I could still make it.

I struck out boldly for the shore.

8 - Jamie

Couples sharing intimacies, suits sharing war stories, all the usual suspects were gathering at the pool bar, the hotel's chic watering hole. I was a man apart, sitting at a table by myself, nursing a glass of rum and ice, twirling it, tuning in to its gurgling mantra, waiting for enough of the ice to melt. It was a meditation, something to occupy my eyes and ears while my mind raced back and forth over the day's events. Two stitches had fixed the cut on my head, and two pills had fixed my aches and pains. Syd was still dealing with the manager and the police, but with the event online already, statements were pretty superfluous. She had written off my attacker as a wacko, and maybe she was right. Maybe time would soften the edges of the night's events and reduce it all to a humorous anecdote. But I was doubtful. The old man was not just a freak. I could still smell him. That wasn't sweat. That was hate.

I needed a break. *We* needed a break, the whole family. I checked my phone. Kim had called. I'd missed it somewhere in this mess of a day. I went to call her back, then stopped. I didn't want to alarm her. Her day had been going badly enough already. So why make it worse? Besides, I was expecting an update from Syd momentarily. If they'd caught that crazy bastard, then I could call Kim and make light of it all. I was concerned about her. She'd taken that miscarriage like a punch in the gut. My wife had the habit of denying things she didn't like, as though reality was more of an opinion than a situation.

She'd insist she was okay when, in fact, she'd be anything but. That headache was a case in point. I'd asked her at the airport if we needed to drop by a pharmacy and she'd said no. But it had gotten worse. I hadn't seen her in a state like that since William had been born. He'd come months early while I was on a trip in the Indian Ocean. It had taken me days to get back. Meanwhile, Kim had freaked out when they'd put him in intensive care. It had gotten so bad they'd had to sedate her. She'd had headaches for weeks after that.

I checked Walgrave's site and played the video of the attack. I couldn't resist it. But then I played it again. Why? No idea. It was humiliating, the sight of me wriggling on the floor like a roach on its back with this guy squirming on top of me. It had all happened so quickly. I hadn't been afraid. Just confused. No one had ever attacked me before, and I'd never learned any self defense. I was physically strong. So in the end, my strength had carried the day. But I should have learned martial arts somewhere along the road. I imagined how things would have panned out then. I'd drop him to the floor with a triumphant *kyai* like Bruce Lee. Then I'd shrug it all off with a contemptuous glare as I smoothed a wrinkle in my shirt with a flick of the wrist like James Bond. That was what should have happened. Not the wriggling roach.

Before I left Walgrave's site, I lingered on the homepage. I couldn't resist that either. The smooch photo of Syd and me still had top-billing. That creep Walgrave was making a career out of me. But it was easy to see why he'd left it there. It was a great photo. A paparazzo had taken the perfect shot. Perfectly awful from my point of view. The way the bodies were turned towards each other, her hands on my face. It was like we were making out.

I moved on and checked my Twitter feed. #steigertheghoul was trending with links to dozens of video versions of the attack. I had to make some sort of statement. Something cool. Something smart. The best thing would be to post it on my blog. I went to my site. But I didn't make the post. I was hardly in the mood for cool or smart, and besides, Kim would do a better job of writing it. I hovered there, my eyes lazily scanning the welcome page and landing on a caption entitled My Vision.

T'is by more fiery winds our hearts are fanned. For the love of knowing what should NOT be known. We take the Golden Road to Samarkand.

That was spot on. Kim had found it in a poem by some 19th century British adventurer. *For the love of knowing what should NOT be known.* That was my road. *The Golden Road.* It was all about the mystery of where we came from and how we got here. How could anyone call me a ghoul? I closed the page. There was nothing cool or smart likely to come out of me today. I navigated back to Walgrave's site mechanically. That photo was still pissing me off, but I couldn't take my eyes off it. Syd had never looked better. The way she was twisting her body towards me, her breasts against my chest, her long legs bracing on the floor and sliding apart, and her hips swiveling up off the seat. If a Hollywood director had set up the scene, it could not have been more eye-catching. Then there was my hand. I'd never really noticed that before. As I recalled, I'd pushed her off me, but it looked a lot more like I was groping her tits.

"Make a good-looking couple, don't they?"

Syd was standing behind me, her hand on my shoulder.

"Not according to my wife."

I tossed the phone on the table.

She took the seat opposite, her hand trailing its fingers around my neck.

"Kim's a big girl. These things happen. She knows that." She snapped her fingers and the waiter scurried over. "She'll get used to it."

I wasn't sure what *these things* covered, but I let it go.

"So, who was that creep?"

"He got away."

"How did he get an invitation?"

"He had Jim Benson's invitation."

"Who's he?"

"Jim and I go way back. There's no way he would give his invitation to anyone, let alone a nutcase like that." She ordered a cocktail, and I finished my rum and ordered another. "God knows what happened. Jim's not answering his phone, so they're checking his room."

"What a pisser of a day!" I was only thinking it, but it came out of my mouth loud enough to be a PA announcement.

"It'll work for us. You'll see."

"No such thing as bad publicity, eh?"

"Marketing 101."

"Did you catch the look in his eyes? He hated me."

"Don't take it personally. At least you didn't get badly hurt." She reached across the table, squeezed my hand and leaned towards me. "You're a celebrity, a target for weirdos and wackos."

Our drinks arrived, and we hitched the glasses up in a half-hearted salute, but we left the toast unsaid. Syd drank thirstily, her tall glass looking more like a fruit salad than a drink. I sipped my rum as she continued to reassure me.

"As for the online trolls, they're a badge of success these days. You're no one without a dedicated band of haters trailing in your wake. Just remember, for every one of them, you've got a thousand fans. You're the new what-women-want man. Some sort of retro thing. We're all fed up with metrosexual gym bunnies with carefully cultivated stubble. Real women need rough diamonds now, not hunks of polished cubic-zirconia. You should check their selfies. You're getting at least ten pussy shots a day."

That had me chuckling. Syd knew how to buck me up.

"Comforting to know I'm appealing to intellectuals. I'd hate that PhD to go to waste." We shared a feeble laugh, making the effort. "I guess I'm just in the dumps. I had big hopes for this trip, and it's been screwed up from start to finish."

"It's not finished yet."

"That's true. And it can only get better. But I need to take a break after this."

"Why don't you stay over at the villa for a few days? I can fix it for you."

"I was thinking about a few months."

"You're quitting?"

"Hell, no." Syd's face was blank. She didn't believe me, and I'm not sure I did. "I don't want to be one of those assholes whose career is a stake through his family's heart. I'm working seven-day weeks and twelve-hour days even when I'm not on the road. I've been neglecting them. It's the truth." It was. But there was another truth too. I'd been spending too much time with Sydney. That long look at Walgrave's smooch photo had brought it home to me. Who was I kidding? That was no peck.

"How is everything ... with Kim, the family?"

"She had another miscarriage." It popped out as

though it was sitting there on my tongue waiting for the chance, but I regretted it before I'd even finished the sentence. Maybe I'm old school, but outside of declarations of love and clichés of that ilk, I believe that talking about your wife with another woman is something that a gentleman doesn't do. I'd already made that mistake once by giving Syd the blow-by-blow account of the problems we'd had with William's birth. That was an indiscretion that had gotten back to Kim, and I'd lived to regret it.

"That's tough. How's she taking it?"

"She's okay. We're okay. And don't worry about me taking a long break. There are plenty of secrets waiting out there for us. Plenty of bucks to be made."

"It's not the money. I just need you to be frank with me. I'm not going to lose you, am I?"

The rum was getting to me, warming, relaxing. She was eyeballing me, waiting.

"No chance of that." I raised my glass to make a toast. To what exactly, I don't know because I never got to make it. The hotel manager and an entourage of cops were scuttling across the terrace in our direction. They stopped a pace off our table, glancing at each other as though each of them was hoping for someone else to break the bad news.

9 - Kim

I never made it back to the beach.

No, that's not right.

I made it, but I never swam it. I got washed up there, saved by an incoming tide. I crawled in the wet sand, in water inches deep. I had to get out of the water and I'd almost made it when I passed out.

When I came to, I pulled myself up, my eyes scouring the waves. The world looked twisted out of shape, my mind a blank chalkboard with unfamiliar notions getting scribbled and erased. I swept the hair out of my eyes, tucking it behind my ears. Blood. I checked again, running my hand through my hair. That was blood all right, showing black in the half light. I must have cracked my head on a reef. I remembered the buildup, the broken glass and the good Samaritans, and the silent rage and terrible emptiness it had left in its wake. I looked out over the ocean as the aching truth of what I'd tried to do came into focus. I'd lost it. I'd flipped. I'd transformed this picture-postcard seascape into an updated gas range. I'd tried to kill myself.

Thank God I came to my senses.

I got to my feet, weak and shaky. There were lights on the second floor of the house. I was sure I'd turned them off. Jamie had to be home by now. He would have checked on William and turned them on. I set off, picking my steps, and when I looked up, I saw him. He was standing at the edge of the terrace. With the lights behind him, all I could make out was his silhouette. But that was Jamie, for sure. He was leaning on the rail, looking towards me, waiting.

"Jamie." I bawled it out, waving my hand.

But there was no response. He just stood there.

I'd left the house wide open. He had to be furious with me.

I set off, panting and rehearsing excuses. *I went swimming and thought a shark bit me. I panicked and nearly drowned. But it was only a rock.* No, that was crazy. Something simple, a lie built on truth. *I cut my foot on the broken glass and washed it in the sea. Then I lay back to rest in the sand and I must've fallen asleep.*

Better. More plausible.

Either way, I'd keep the truth to myself. I had never told Jamie about my *almost* suicide as a teenager and I didn't plan to do so now. This had been a random event like that. A weird cocktail of circumstances had knocked me off balance at a moment of weakness. It could happen to anyone. I was picking my way across the sand, wobbling on each step as my injured foot tested the ground, when I caught sight of movement in my peripheral vision. Jamie was waving back at me.

I stopped with a grunt.

Something about that was all wrong. I looked up, my fists sliding up to my cheeks.

The terrace was empty.

Jamie was gone.

Had he really been there?

I'd been so sure, but ... could it have been someone else?

I sprinted across the sand and hid in the moon shadow cast by the terrace wall. Someone could have climbed over the fence from the road or wandered in off the beach. Chris and Dave? Maybe not so innocent after all. I listened intently. But there was nothing to hear but the ocean washing against the sand.

William?

A tremor crept through me like a waft of wet fog. I'd left the house open.

I sprinted along the wall, then stopped.

Think.

The impulse to run up to William's room was overwhelming. But that was stupid. I had to protect my son, not lead a threat directly to him. What if an intruder was lurking up there on the terrace? I would be offering him two victims instead of one. He'd already seen me. I was done for. But William was still safe. I had to think smart. I had to steer the intruder away from William, like a plover faking a broken wing to lead the predator away from its nest. I ran up the steps and onto the terrace. The lounge lights were off, but the room was partially lit from the adjoining kitchen. The intruder could be anywhere. I was defenseless, the consummate victim, all decked out in bikini pants tied with bows on the hips like a present. I needed a weapon. There were knives in the kitchen if only I could get to them.

Then it came to me.

The bang stick.

I flung open the door of the pool house. Our diving kit was stacked against the wall at the back. I clicked on the light. A bang stick is like a spear. But instead of a point, it has a cartridge with no bullet. When you stab the target, the cartridge blasts a hole in it. Jamie's stick was leaning against the wall between our wetsuits. I grabbed it, removed the ball protecting the powerhead, unlocked the safety, and slipped my hand through the wrist strap. I'd seen Jamie blow a 12-foot Tiger Shark in two pieces with this stick. I spun around and headed for the door. If there was anyone inside that house planning on taking my son, they'd better have a thick skin.

The hotel manager hurried us away from the pool and into his office with the cops trailing behind. That didn't bode well, and we exchanged nervous glances as we were seated opposite a man in a crisp blue shirt. With the door closed, the manager hovering nervously in the corner and the uniformed cops bookending us, the man introduced himself as Detective Inspector Rolle.

"I'm sorry to tell you this," he said. "But Mr. Jim Benson, the man whose ticket your attacker appears to have stolen, was found dead in his room."

Sydney yelped and her body jerked back like she'd been slapped, her chair legs squeaking as they scraped on the floor. I reached out my hand and squeezed hers. I wasn't sure what I'd just heard.

"Died of?" I was fishing, but Rolle knew what I was after.

"Unquestionably, there's been foul play. Our preliminary report sees it as murder."

The manager hiding in the corner behind Rolle was trembling. Not much, but there it was, his hands twitching and tremulous. He saw me looking at them and tucked them behind his back. His mouth was half open, his eyes blank.

"They shot him? Stabbed him?"

"I can't get into the—"

"Unbelievable!" The manager barked it out. "I've never seen—"

"The manager here"—Rolle cut him off—"was with security when they went to the room. They found the body." He stood up and turned to the manager. "Sir, if I could use your office a little longer. You should take a break. The medics are still here. Maybe they could help you out with some…"

The manager nodded. All eyes were on him. So no one but me noticed Syd wobbling up off the chair. She grabbed her belly, doubled over, and hurled that fruit laden cocktail onto the manager's fine Persian carpet. Then her knees buckled and I caught her as she spiraled to the floor. I sat her back in the chair, medics were called, and we got her back on her feet. I escorted her back to her suite, guiding her with one hand on her elbow and the other arm wrapped around her waist. Once inside, she locked herself in the bathroom for an interminable amount of time while I sat on a couch, drinking rum and fretting.

"Syd?" I knocked on the door. I couldn't leave until I knew she was all right. I'd been planning my call to Kim. News like this was not something I wanted to tell her on the phone while she was alone in an empty house. So I'd make some excuse. But I had to call her, and soon. There was a mirror by the door and the odd sight of me dressed in a hotel waiter's shirt caught my eye. My own shirt had been splashed with blood in the attack, so the police had kept it as evidence. I noticed something else too. My hand lurched up to my scratched throat.

How could I have missed it?

He'd stolen the crucifix.

With the shock of it all, adrenaline raging, and dealing with medics and police, I hadn't even noticed. It was hardly a catastrophe in the light of the day's events, but it still hurt. That crucifix was my talisman.

"I'm okay." Syd's answer emerged from the bathroom, her voice crackling with emotion and sounding anything but okay. "I'll be out in a minute."

I headed into the lounge and called Kim.

There was no reply.

I left a message, soft-soaping the nightmare events by describing them as *a really serious issue* that was holding me up. I was out on the balcony watching the lights of Nassau shimmering off gentle seas when Syd appeared, dressed in a flimsy kimono. She was all washed up, but still sniffling, her wet hair draped in rat tails about her face. She indicated the bedroom with a vague wave of her hand.

"Coffee?" I said.

She nodded and I fetched two cups from the kitchen and joined her in the bedroom.

She was sitting on the bed.

I gave her the coffee, then pulled up an armchair so I could sit across from her. She was holding the mug with both hands, sipping it, elbows on knees, eyes focused on an empty space in front of her.

"You and Jim must have been really close."

She looked up, startled, as though she'd just noticed my presence. "He was my lucky break. My *Mendoza Crucifix*." I slid my elbows onto the arms of the chair and clasped my hands in front of my throat. She hadn't noticed it was missing, and I didn't want to trouble her with that too. "He interviewed me for a job fresh out of college. My first job. I didn't get it. But he suggested I try TV and he made a phone call. You know what I mean ... *this girl's okay*. So I got the introduction. Right at the top too. No HR bullshit. That was all I needed. Everyone needs luck in the beginning, someone to open that first door. For me, it was Jim. God only knows why. I thought I knew at the time. A successful older man. A young woman starting out. We've all heard that story. So I was expecting a late-night phone call down the road. Maybe I would have even paid him back. But that late night call never came. Gentleman Jim. Guys like that are pretty damn thin on the ground these days." Her face puckered and I thought she was about to cry, but she pulled it back. All sobbed out. "Did the cop say anything after I…?" She waved her hand, brushing past the barfing/fainting scene. "I don't know what got into me. I've never done anything like that."

"My attacker is a suspect. That's all. They have to check fingerprints, CCTV, DNA, forensic stuff."

Her face puckered up again. Maybe she wasn't as sobbed out as I'd thought. I sat next to her on the bed and looped my arm around her shoulders, pulling her close. She was in a space of her own by now, melting into me, her head nestling under my chin. It felt comfortable. Too comfortable. Alarm bells were ringing, but I had a finger stuffed in each ear. I was shaken up too. I wasn't a basket case like she was. But I felt like shit, and her body against mine made me feel a lot better. I had never seen this side of her, this vulnerability. There was something primordial about it, a rawness that was sublimely sexual. I'd always wanted her. I'd never had any illusions about that. But never so completely and irresistibly. That was why I'd been so angry with Walgrave. The little prick had gotten it so wrong and yet so right. There was nothing between us and nothing was planned.

But who could have planned this?

Shifting gears from business to bedroom was never straightforward. But now the stage had been set by the unexpected, and I was about to learn that gut wrenching trauma could open doors that no amount of candlelit dinners and romantic music ever could. My defenses were shutdown, my loyalty to Kim steamrollered by a chain of bizarre events. As if reading my thoughts, Syd ran her hand across my lap and pulled herself tight against me. This was it. Now she was ready to give herself to me like never before.

Submissive. Generous.

I could feel it already, erotic sensations charged way off the scale of normal. I lifted her head up to mine, her face a patchwork of longing track marked with tears. She gave it a wipe with her forearm like a little girl. I pulled her to me and kissed her, my lips chewing into her soft, wet mouth. She grabbed my head with both hands and pushed me back onto the bed. Our mouths fell apart, and for a moment, we were eye to eye, breathless. Hormones bristling. Two animals taking a breather after an initial skirmish. I took her in my arms and rolled on top of her, a rage of blood coursing through me. I ripped open her kimono, my mouth on her breasts.

But then it all went wrong.

I leaped off of her, stumbling backwards and falling against the chair.

Jesus.

Passion fled, replaced by something else, not quite awkwardness, but getting there, something tinged with guilt and more than a shot of regret. But was it regret that it had happened, or that it hadn't? I slumped into the chair and pulled at my clothes.

"Syd—"

She was sitting up, adjusting her panties and tidying her kimono.

"I know. We want to. But we can't."

She slipped off the bed and stood looking down at me. "Let's have a stiff drink. How about it?"

"Deal."

She fetched ice from the fridge and poured herself a bourbon and a rum for me. Then she sat back on the bed.

"To better days," I said as I raised my glass.

"My toast is to my dear friend, Jamie." She touched her glass to mine. "I guess Jim Benson wasn't the last gentlemen after all." She sipped her drink. "More's the pity. More's the fucking pity." The words opened a crack in her and the feeblest of sobs quivered through her body like tremors heralding some mighty seismic event.

I couldn't take it. I stood up and slipped away, cleaning myself up in the bathroom. I had to leave. Back in the bedroom, Syd hadn't moved. She was still sitting on the edge of the bed, those same feeble sobs trickling out of her. I didn't sit down. I wanted to announce my intentions. So I stood in front of her a few feet away.

"I have to go." I waited. "Are you going to be okay?"

She didn't look up. She didn't answer. She just continued to cry. Except that's too strong a word for it. This was a true whimper, like she didn't have the balls left for crying.

I sat on the bed next to her and put my arm around her. Her head eased towards me, resting on my shoulder and tucking up close against my neck. We sat like that for the longest while, not looking, not doing, just feeling. Some decisions in life you get to make for yourself, but some make you. We were sitting on a bed, and we were standing at a crossroads, but there was only one way we were ever going to go. I slid my fingers into her hair and lifted her head off my shoulder. Our eyes were shameless now, naked in their embrace, our mouths so close that each breath was a delicacy, a shared intimacy.

I wasn't going anywhere.

I slipped into the house through the terrace doors and flicked on the lights.

The room was empty.

I resisted the urge to run upstairs, to panic, to scream. I kept telling myself that I wasn't afraid. I was fearless, no longer a plover with a broken wing. Now I was an eagle. Now I had claws. Now I had the bang stick.

But could I use it?

A shark is one thing. But a human being?

Could I really kill a man?

The answer was yes. I would do anything to protect my child. What mother wouldn't?

"If anyone is hiding in my house"—I waited for my booming voice to get a reaction but there was none—"then now would be a good time to fuck off."

There was still no sound. Oddly, no sound from William. Surely my hollering had been loud enough to wake him.

"William." Louder yet, but still no reply, no sound of feet banging on the stairs, no squeaky half-awake voice calling out.

I hit the switch that controlled the terrace doors and they rumbled together, closing with a reassuring click. Now anyone outside was locked out. And anyone inside was locked in. It was a calculated risk. But I had to secure the house at some point. The man on the terrace was most likely some bum who had seen me dripping wet and naked on the beach. I was not the svelte beach babe I'd once been. But even so, that was a picture that might have come over as a tasty night's entertainment for the wrong guy.

But where had he gone? Had he chickened out? Or was he hiding, waiting to ambush me?

I had to get up to William's room. Once I was sure he was safe, I could set the alarm and call Jamie using the landline. I could find my cell phone out on the beach later when Jamie got back. There was no need for him to know anything about the swamp and my midnight madness. I headed for the stairs, checking every corner, my head spinning at shadows. Two steps up, I hit an invisible fog that cut through the tropical night with a chill premonition. Someone or something was waiting for me up those stairs. The bang stick shook. I couldn't stop it. Invisible arms locked around my ribs and squeezed tight. I couldn't breathe and nausea choked up my throat.

Then I heard William's voice.

To this day, I swear that.

I heard him.

He called for his mother. He called for me. That moment, when my hands trembled and the air in my lungs turned to pain, still haunts me. William cried for help. Something terrible was being inflicted on him, some unforgivable act. At a stroke, reality rolled over me with all its sharp edges intact, cutting loose my fear and bringing me to my senses.

"William." I ran up the stairs, screaming his name. There was a light coming from his bedroom but no sound. I didn't have to look inside. I knew already I was too late. The cold mists of premonition had told me as much. There was only one thing waiting for me in that room.

The unthinkable.

His bed was empty. The French doors to the

terrace I had so carefully locked earlier were ajar. A breeze rippled the lace curtain and waves rustled against a background of silence. I dashed onto the terrace and looked down at the pool and along the beach.

There was no one.

I stumbled back into the bedroom, emotions curdling and bubbling like live animals fighting in my chest. I was making sounds, not words, a symphonic soundtrack to the turmoil of heat and pressure coursing through me. Finally, a single word escaped.

"NO."

I whirled around, brandishing my weapon, stabbing at ghosts long gone. The dresser exploded in a shower of wood and I fell back on the empty bed, cracking my head against the wall.

When I opened my eyes, Jamie was holding me. His face was inches from mine.

"What happened here?" My eyes couldn't focus. They skidded off his face and skittered around the room. "Where's William?"

I tried to move, but it made me dizzy.

Jamie helped me to sit up. He snatched some tissues from the nightstand and wiped my face and my arms. There were smears of blood on the tissues. I saw the bang stick on the floor, and the dresser reduced to splinters and shards.

He said, "I called the police already. And an ambulance." But I continued to stare at him. "Kim." He seized my shoulders and shook me. "Where is William?"

"There was a man." The words came out of me, but they weren't mine, the woman I was replaced by an android. No human feelings, not even a trace.

"What man?"

"The man on the terrace. I was on the beach. I tried to save him, Jamie. I tried."

His face blanched as my head fell onto my chest and my body racked with sobs. Jamie didn't move at first. Then he sat on the bed at my side and cradled me in his arms. He said nothing.

STRANGERS

The Anniversary

<u>La Jolla, California - December 8, 2011</u>

The door was wide open. She'd left it that way.

Jamie stood in the hall, looking through the doorway at the empty drive. No car. Kim was gone alright, and she was not coming back.

Hell's anniversary.

Three years to the day since William. And nothing. Not a damn thing. Police, private investigators, global publicity and a seven-figure reward had yielded nothing. So what in God's name had they hoped to achieve by meeting on such a day?

Whatever it was. This was what they got.

The end.

He was sure of it. This was the real end. Not the fake end, like when they'd separated. The house, the family home, it was now officially on the market. There'd been papers to sign. At least, that had been the excuse for the meeting. But it was all about William really. It always was. About William, about failure, about them. Zero progress all around. So the house had become a token, the proverbial straw. But who could have anticipated that the camel's back would break so spectacularly?

He touched his cheek, checking the bruise she'd left there with probing fingers. No pain. But the whole side of his face was numb. He went into the guest bathroom and checked it in the mirror, eyes like murky pools deep in sodden black banks. He splashed cold water on his face and rinsed his mouth with a cupped hand, stopping when his eyes caught the blood he was spitting out. After washing it all away, he wiped his mouth with a towel.

The Sydney slap.

When Kim had dropped her name into the conversation, he should've seen the flashing red light. This was a showdown that had been brewing for months. His TV show had smashed ratings worldwide, its popularity fueled by the media frenzy following the bizarre attack, the murder and William's abduction. With so much money at stake, corporate pressure had forced Jamie to support the show on the road. That had meant quality time with Sydney, and after separating from Kim, that was only ever going to go one way. The sole blessing was that Kim had never found out when it had started, never asked him about that first night, never wondered why he hadn't answered his phone and gotten back so late. That crazy bastard's crimes at the hotel had swept aside any need for explanations.

Jamie went back to the hallway and stood at its center, the numbness in his face a creeping paralysis seeping through his body.

Nowhere to go now. Nothing to do.

He couldn't go back to Sydney. Not after this. She was too much a part of it all.

What then?

Las Vegas?

What did that have to do with it?

Nothing. That was the point. They'd never even been there. They had no friends there, no memories. It was the perfect destination. A desert drive, cold, sterile, and empty. Then boom. Vegas. Bright, buzzing, phony.

He exited the house, leaving the door wide open

just as she'd left it. And that was it. He was on the freeway, heading to Vegas. He was even looking forward to it, laughing about the craziness of it all. Zany with a capital Z. It was just what he needed. He flipped through radio stations looking for rock, something to pump him up.

Here's one.

He tuned the dial, catching it clear and loud. Some headbanging dance track. All beat. Perfect. He toed down, sweeping up tears between the laughs. They were supposed to be tears of joy, but they weren't. Then the laughs faded and he cut the radio, the sum total of his losses hitting him and twisting his guts from his throat to his bowels.

Should pull over.

He knew it, but he didn't.

Darkness. It had sneaked up unnoticed. How long had he been driving? The thick traffic was long gone, left somewhere back in the cities. He settled his eyes on the black asphalt zipping under his wheels. It was more like a tunnel than a road, pulling him into a tube of darkness lined with passing headlights, remote, otherworldly. He blinked, his eyelids heavy. And suddenly, he was at a funfair. It wasn't Vegas. That was still way ahead. It looked like somewhere up north, a county fair in a field of long grass shimmering to the swish of a breeze. He was offering William a cone of pink cotton candy, but his son just looked up at him like he was an untrustworthy stranger. Jamie turned to Kim for an explanation. But she'd disappeared. And when he looked back at William, he was gone too. Now he was alone at the funfair, holding a cone of pink cotton candy in a world of happy people.

He woke up to the scream of steel against concrete. Airbags crushed his chest. Streaking headlights slashed through darkness.

Spinning, spinning.

There was no pain. That would come later. Just a profound sense of relief as the car came to a stop with one almighty crash.

12 - Kim

<u>Venice, Los Angeles - September 18, 2013</u>

Reality, it seemed, was nothing more than a story we all subscribed to, and on that fateful night in Nassau, I'd bought a lifetime subscription to my own personal edition. I hadn't meant to lie. It had just happened. I'd washed up half-dead on the beach. That—and the pills, the booze, the phantom intruder, the empty bedroom and the bang stick— had all played a part. But the trigger was Jamie's face inches from mine screaming, *where is William*?
Guilt?
That I had aplenty. It churned in my belly. Instead of taking care of my son, I'd been negligent, indulging my demons. So I lied. I said I'd cut my foot on a broken glass and gone down to wash it in the sea because I couldn't make it back up the terrace steps. That was my story, my suicide attempt conveniently forgotten. I didn't plan the lie. I didn't even believe it was a lie. Strange that. But what I'd discovered was that the line between what I believed and *what I wanted to believe* was paper thin and scored with holes. So stuff leaked through. All I had to do was *want to believe* something hard enough, and pretty soon the *wanting* disappeared and all I had left was the *believe*.

I'd been a suspect at first. Make that—the suspect. But I'd dealt with that. And in the end, we were all on the same page. William had been abducted by a person or persons unknown. That was the official verdict. Even so, I ended up in the dock. Not in a court of law, but the far more savage court of public opinion. I was put on trial by the media and they promptly returned a guilty verdict. I'd been derelict in my duty as a mother. I'd gotten drunk and left the house wide open. Rumors swirled. I'd snuck off with a boy toy lover was the one that gained the most traction until Jamie threatened to sue. Whatever had happened to William, I was to blame for it and I deserved everything I got.

I didn't fight it. I accepted my punishment with stoic indifference. The savaging in the tabloids and the tide of venom that rose to greet me online and off was nothing compared to the pain I carried inside me. Theoretically, I could have told my side of it and begged for sympathy. I wasn't a bad mother. I'd gotten lost in the swamp that night. But that was no excuse. Swamp folk didn't deserve sympathy, especially not rich ones like me. My choice was either to take the blame for negligence, or the shame for the truth. I have always done blame better than shame. Better to be hated as a negligent, rich bitch than pitied as an unstable, barren woman who birthed a child after years of medical intervention only to lose him when she malfunctioned like a machine with a defective part. My pride couldn't take that. Our relationship had been the inevitable casualty of the aftershock. I still loved Jamie, but I couldn't live with him. Not with three of us in the marriage—him, me, and the lie. One of us had to go and in the end, it was him. Jamie believed my lie. But what if he'd known the truth? Getting distracted by an injury when you're high on pills and booze was one thing. He'd known the state I was in. But how long had I wallowed in the waves out by the reef, wanting to kill myself and then not? Forgiveness has boundaries, and his were no more limitless than anyone else's. Besides, what would telling him the truth achieve? Pity? Anger? Some toxic mix of the two? Not telling him was an act of kindness, the last vestige of our love.

Five years had passed since I'd first told that lie and now I lived apart from Jamie, taking my life one day at a time. I missed him. He'd call me and leave messages to tell me about his recovery after the accident and his continuing search for William. I was still searching for William too, in my own way. But my efforts were not in this world but the next. It was ironic that because when all this had been playing out in the daily news, we'd been inundated with psychics who'd said that they knew something about William. We'd ignored them. But I'd always wondered. Was it possible to communicate with the dead? I'd always believed that the world was stranger than any of us could ever imagine. *So* why not? Grief was like a terminal cancer to me and I was ready to try anything. So I hung out in psychic chatrooms, trying to pick up on someone selling something other than snake oil. That was how I got to be sitting here waiting for this psychic. But things were not looking good already, and he hadn't even shown up yet. His studio was festooned with phony psychic paraphernalia. I felt like a fool sitting in a fairground booth waiting to get my pocket picked. To make it all worse, his name was Eric, a more unlikely name for a psychic I could not imagine. He might at least have lived up to the decor and called himself *Amazing Eric*. It was late morning and sunlight streamed through lace curtains, picking out the crystal ball and the tarot pack on the plastic tablecloth in front of me. A crystal ball. I kid you not. I was so disappointed. I was reaching for my purse and about to go when he finally appeared.

"I'm so sorry to have kept you."

He sounded Irish. Much younger than I'd imagined. Early twenties. And he was wearing a suit and tie of all things. In California.

"You've certainly got all the works." I waved around at the paraphernalia. I don't know if he picked up on the sarcasm—I'd laid it on thick—but if he did, he didn't show it.

"This ..."—he spread his hands, thin fingers and manicured nails—"is like wallpaper. Decoration. It's not mine anyway. I'm renting the studio." He had lanky brown hair falling like a frame around his face. It was a strange thought, but I wondered if he was a virgin. He had this oddly asexual vibe. "All I need is something metal. Something you've owned for a long time. Something you always have with you. Any metal. Except gold."

"Why not gold?" I was thinking of my wedding ring. Yes, I still wear it. Call me sentimental.

He shrugged like it was a dumb question. "It just doesn't work."

I didn't wear a watch. *So what else comes in metal*? I opened my purse. Cigarette lighter? I didn't smoke. Pens? Mine was plastic. "How about this?" I offered him my dainty multitool. Jamie bought it for me when we were dating. What does that tell you about my ex? What guy buys his new girlfriend a multitool?

Eric took it—stainless steel, a couple of inches long—and held it in his left hand, his eyes dropping to the table.

"I see a man."

Here we go again. I could have saved myself the trouble and bought a box of fortune cookies. "What man?" No point in making his life easy.

He glanced up. No emotion. No irritation.

I waited.

I should have left earlier.

"Your man." He said it like I was an idiot not to know. "The man who builds castles in the sand." Now it was his turn to wait, his eyes gobbling up the look on my face as my arrogance drained away. "The Sandman."

One word.

I'd always thought there were only two camps in the school of second sight. Either you believed, or you didn't. Just like God. But at that moment, I learned that there was a third and I was its new recruit. In a single stroke, believing or not was reduced to mere sophistry. From here on out, I *knew* it worked. I went from scornful to fearful so fast it made me giddy. I felt naked, nausea uncurling in my belly like a venomous snake.

Be careful what you wish for, Kim Steiger.

He was talking about my father now, describing his whimsical sense of humor and our life together. Details he could not possibly know and I had long forgotten were bringing tears to my eyes. I wanted to stop him. But I stayed motionless, paralyzed with fear, like a rape victim from another dimension pretending to be somewhere else. But then, he said the words that were bound to find me wherever I hid.

"I see a child with fair hair."

"William." I'd promised myself to say nothing, to give nothing away. But that was before he'd opened me up like a can of tuna. "Is he dead?"

"I see the Sandman's child alive."

"Alive." I grabbed his collar and dragged him across the table. The crystal ball crashed on the floor. He glanced down at its shattered remains before looking back at me, his face inches from mine. I came to my senses and let go of him. He eased back into his chair and adjusted his jacket. Then he looked down at his tightly clenched left fist and back at me.

"The Sandman saves his child. The sea gives him up." He opened his hand and offered me the multitool. But I was too frightened to take it. "You must pray to the God of your father." That sounded less like a vision and more like friendly advice. My father's Catholic piety hit me like a wave, soaking me with guilt. How long was it since I'd been to Mass or Confession? I wasn't lapsed. I was lost. He pushed the multitool across the table and I picked it up reluctantly. He slipped his hands around mine as I did so, and for the first time I read emotion on his face, a tenderness in his eyes. "You must pray," he said, a supplicant tone in his voice, his hands tightening around mine. He was sparing me something, editing the tape. I knew it.

I left the studio and ran down to the beach. I sat in the wet sand at the water's edge, watching the waves rolling in and out. I burrowed into my purse, found the multitool and tossed it into the sea. Then I scooped up handfuls of wet sand and caked it all over my face. No idea why.

Hours later, wet and cold, I wandered back past the boardwalk vendors and street performers looking for my car. Nobody gave a second look at the scary witch of a woman hiding behind a mask of sand.

13 - Jamie

Miami Beach, Florida - September 18, 2013 (the same day)

The phone was ringing.

I woke up with a jolt, stumbling off the couch and cracking my thigh on the table. The ringing stopped. I cursed, my eyes skimming around the cabin.

Where is that damn thing?

I went to the refrigerator, popped open a carton of orange juice and gulped it, steadying myself with one hand on the wall as my neighbor's yacht rumbled out of its slip, its wake giving my sailboat a gentle nudge. My phone was peeking at me from between cushions on the couch. I'd been sitting at the table, checking the boat's wiring plans, and it must've slid out of my pocket when I'd fallen asleep. Impromptu naps like that were a part of my lifestyle now, a side effect of the post-surgical medications I was taking. I dumped the empty OJ carton into the recycle bin, went back to the couch and checked the phone. No caller ID.

Maybe it was Kim.

It wasn't much of a bet. We hadn't spoken in two years, not since the day of the accident. But lately, I'd been looking on the bright side of life, digging up the old Jamie, the cup-half-full guy. I was out of physio and my bones were healing. So if I could get my health back, then why not my son, and why not my wife? Yes, we were still married. With me facing multiple surgeries, my guess was that she hadn't had the heart to file the papers. And by the time I was into physio, she must have moved on.

But moved on to what?

And to whom?

I was wondering about that when the phone rang again.

"Dr. Steiger?"

I knew that voice. The Bahamian lilt was subtle, but it was still there, a hint of the islands with the sun squeezed out by the gray skies of England and a daily diet of serious crime.

"Inspector Rolle."

There was a pause. Was he surprised I'd recognized his voice? It'd been a long time after all.

"How are you doing, sir? Out of hospital. Pulling through okay?"

"I'm good, Inspector. Thank you." My pulse was hammering. "Is there some news?"

"I'm here in Miami." He ducked the question. "I'm attending a seminar put on by US law enforcement colleagues, and something came up before I left. So I thought it would make more sense to handle it personally."

I took a deep breath. But it turned out not to be deep enough. "With all due respect, a trip down memory lane with you is not much of a day out for me. Do you have anything new on William or not?" My abruptness took me aback. Our relationship with the Bahamas police had hit rock bottom more than once, but he didn't deserve that. The issue that would never go away was Kim. She'd been a suspect from the getgo. When kids go missing, parents always are. I'd been at the preview, so I was in the clear. But Kim was in the firing line because William had been in her care when it had happened. That made her either negligent or responsible. Their theory was that she'd taken William down to the beach and left him unsupervised while she'd gone swimming. But something had gone wrong. Something along the lines of him drowning. They hadn't laid it all out like that. Not at first. But things came to a head when I saw their boats trolling the waters out by the reef day after day, wasting their time looking for his body instead of finding the monster who'd taken him. Kim had been negligent. We accepted that. She'd left the house wide open and an intruder had taken our son. The situation with the police had gotten so bad that I'd had to get a lawyer. Finally, after endless combing of the shoreline and surrounding seas had yielded nothing but frustration, they'd changed course, treating it as an abduction. But the experience had soured our relationship with Bahamas Finest, and it had never recovered.

I was still waiting for Rolle's answer and wondering if he was going to hang up.

"Inspector?"

"This call doesn't concern the investigation into William's disappearance. It's about the incident at the hotel earlier that day."

"The psycho?"

"I assure you, Dr. Steiger, I wouldn't disturb you if it wasn't important. I was hoping we could meet."

I slumped into the seat at the navigator's station, my elbows on the charts. The police had seen the two events that day as potentially linked at one point, but then they'd ruled out any connection. I'd always seen that as a mistake.

"Inspector, I didn't mean to be rude. The truth is, I'm not okay, and your call hit me out of the blue. Stuff comes flooding back."

"No offense taken, sir. I look forward to seeing you. How about lunch? My hotel."

14 - Kim

I drove over the sidewalk ramp and down into the dimly lit underbuild. It was hardly secure parking, and that had almost killed the deal when I'd first viewed the apartment. But the building had appealed to me. I liked the center courtyard with the communal pool. It gave the place warmth, and not just because it caught the sun, but because of the human warmth inherent in the design. Every apartment opened onto the courtyard and in each corner, there was a table with a sunshade and chairs and stunted palms squeezing life out of a meager patch of soil. In some buildings, you never see your neighbors. But here, that would be impossible. There would always be people nearby, even if it was just to say hello. An instant community, close, but not too familiar. I liked the neighborhood too. I'd read that Palms had a high headcount of professional singles. That sounded perfect for a recently separated single in her late thirties, a place where I could be alone, but not lonely.

My new life was simple, my days following a strict routine. Mornings were the worst. They always started the same way. With a jolt! Asleep, I lived my old life, my dreams fully cast with the husband and son I no longer had. But every morning, the ogre of wakefulness would shoo them away and toss the suffocating blanket of reality over my face. Discipline was the lifeline that kept me breathing. I'd haul myself out of bed and click through the numbers of my preprogrammed day as though my life depended on it, which it certainly did. I'd spend hours at the gym, or doing laps in the pool. Then I'd pass by the health food store, head back home and work on my thesis, *After the Absurd: Albert Camus in the 21st Century*. I had no interest in getting a PhD. It was just a coping mechanism, an energy drain to exhaust me so I could tumble into bed at night and tick off another day successfully survived.

My eyes flicked around defensively, looking for lurkers in the shadows before I stepped out of the car and locked it. I needed a drink. I didn't drink much anymore. But I was still shaken up from the séance, still raking it over as I walked up the steps to the entrance. I checked my mailbox. Nothing. Why would there be? No one knew where I lived. Jamie had my phone number. But no address. Withholding it was mean but necessary. If I didn't, he was sure to turn up at the door sooner or later and I couldn't handle that. I passed through the lobby into the courtyard. The pool lights were on and the jets were running, making waves that flicked wisps of light in tremulous patterns around the walls. The courtyard was empty and I was grateful for it. I'd struck up a close friendship with one of my neighbors, another lonely thirty-something woman called Barbara. Everyone else was just a passing acquaintance. But they all knew me well enough to wonder why my face was caked in sand, and that was not a conversation that I was interested in having. I made my way up the steps, glancing down at Barbara's first-floor apartment. I felt like company, someone to talk away my psychic shakes and split a bottle of wine with, but her place was in darkness. My cell phone rang as I reached the door and Jamie's face lit up the screen, the old Jamie, tanned, strong, handsome. Mine. I stared at his face until the call went to voicemail and the screen went dark. Then I stood at the rail, looking down over the empty courtyard with its pool-lit shimmer, tears sliding down my cheeks.

As soon as I had locked the door behind me, I took a hot shower, wrapped up in a fleecy bathrobe, stepped into fake fur-lined slippers and made myself a cup of Earl Grey tea with lemon, honey and a shot of gold rum.

Medicine.

The call light on my phone was flashing. But it wasn't Jamie with his usual follow-up call. It was Barbara. She'd called me while I was in the shower. I slid over to the window and checked her apartment. The light was on, but I didn't call back. I needed some quiet time alone first. I sipped my brew, my eyes staring at the blank screen of the TV.

The Sandman.

Eric had slayed the skeptic in me at a stroke. But I was still listening to a cynical voice heckling from somewhere. Eric had staged a terrifying demonstration of psychic power. He'd hacked into my head as surely as if he'd drilled holes through my skull and run a set of wires. But he hadn't actually told me my fortune—my future—just snatches of this and that, soundbites describing his visions and most of them were from the past. That part of his act was utterly convincing. It was all true. Every word. But my past exists already. It's in my mind, even if I can't remember it. But what about the future?

The Sandman saves his child.

The future doesn't yet exist.

Or does it?

We think of time as a straight line, careening off into an unknown future. But according to no less an authority than the celebrated Dr. Jamie Steiger, the Aztecs saw time as a twisted rope, coiled and knotted, with every thread in touch with all the others. So maybe mind-hackers like Eric could cut into the stack and reach any thread. That old collegiate debate came to mind. Fate vs free-will. All the world's religions—not to mention umpteen *Terminator* movies—all say the same thing. There is no predetermination. Our choices determine our fate.

But what if they're wrong?

I glanced down at my phone. I sometimes listened to Jamie's messages, but usually I deleted them— some as soon as they arrived. Others I would keep for weeks, letting them pile up in a backlog, our relationship reduced to a communications savings account. It was odd behavior. But comforting. My marriage was on ice, but with a digital catalog of Jamie's life on my phone, it still felt alive. At least, until I had one of those spendthrift days and blew the whole account, systematically deleting one message after the next in a vindictive expression of what exactly I couldn't bring myself to say.

The sea gives him up.

I nurtured my toddy, my eyes transfixed on the blank TV. Everything Eric had said about the past was true. And as for the rest, I so wanted to believe it. But how could the sea give him up? The police theory that William had tried to swim in the sea and been swept away was possible. How long had I been in the water and lying unconscious on the beach? Enough time for our inquisitive son to wake up and wander down there. But years later, how could the sea give him up? Could someone have rescued William that night? It made no sense. We'd offered a million-dollar ransom, and all that got us was a wave of creeps claiming either to have seen William or to physically have him. But not one genuine lead.

I gulped down the last of my tea, picked up the phone, and hit the voicemail key to hear Jamie's message.

Hello, Kim, listen, it happened. I met with Rolle. Did you get that last message? So like I told you. I'm in Miami working on that old sailboat I bought, and he called me out of the blue. This is really important, babe. Please. Call me. We don't have to meet if you don't want. I'm cool with that. But we've got to talk. There's been a breakthrough. So please, PLEASE, call me. I love you and I miss you. I really do. Let's meet up somewhere and I'll catch you up on all this. I don't know what—

The timer clipped his sentence.

Jamie had always been convinced that his attacker and William's abductor were connected despite the police pouring cold water on the idea. But what if he was right?

Don't you dare hope?

That naysaying voice was getting fainter and fainter, and in the end, I ignored it and listened to Jamie's message again, sweeping tears from my face as I stretched out on the couch. I didn't delete the voicemails this time. I nestled my phone—my love bank, my hope nest—between my breasts and closed my eyes.

15 - Jamie

Detective Inspector Stewart Rolle of the Royal Bahamas Police Force was fingering a smartphone, his large frame eased back in an armchair. That droopy mustache was new, but otherwise, he'd hardly changed in the years since I'd last seen him. So how would I look to him? Barely recognizable, most likely, a shadow of the man I'd been back then. He thumbed some more, then looked up and caught sight of me. It took him a moment, confirming my fears that I looked like shit. Then he lit me up with a sunbeam smile—bizarrely at odds with his new whiskers—and leaped up, his hand outstretched.

We exchanged greetings, and he led me beyond the fish tank wall that separated the hotel lobby from the coffee shop. It was just before noon and the place was empty. We took a table close to the tank, and I picked the seat with the best view of the fish. We ordered club sandwiches and iced tea and made small talk. I hadn't been back to the islands for years, and Rolle brought it all back to me, the island vibe, the unhurried pace, and the circumspect approach in conversation. He'd been trained at a cop college in England, and he meshed that softly-softly British policing style with the sunny disposition of an out-island good old boy. Here was a guy you'd have to work hard not to like, the perfect *good cop* in that celebrated old routine, squeezing out confessions with empathy rather than a nightstick. A great cop on the face of it. Too bad he hadn't found my son.

When our iced tea came, I figured the small talk

was over. "You mentioned this meeting is not related to our son's investigation."

"It's about the murder of Jim Benson and the assault on you in the hotel. As you recall, Mr. Benson's murderer was confirmed by DNA-matching to be the same man who assaulted you. Now we have found him, his body at least. He was found dead on a skiff. We believe he'd been living rough, sleeping on the boat."

"Who was he?"

"We don't know. Not for sure. We haven't been able to establish his identity based on any of our usual forensic or social protocols."

"When did you find the body?"

"A few weeks ago. And as I was coming to Miami, I thought it was better I bring you the news personally and give you this."

He opened his notebook satchel and fussed around inside while I waited, questions piling up on my tongue. But they all disappeared when his hand emerged from his bag.

The *Mendoza Crucifix*.

He held it in front of me and let it swing from side to side on its chain. The tide of emotions welling up in my chest took me aback, and for a moment, I just stared at it, motionless.

"He still had it?" I took it from him.

"The boat was washed up on a reef. We believe it had been looted for whatever might have been on board. But two objects remained. They were on his person. Maybe the looters didn't want to get too close to the body in view of its decomposed condition."

"What was the other object?"

He fetched two sheets of paper from his satchel and handed them to me. They showed the front and back of a metal cross with a ribbon, a military medal. The back of the cross was stamped 1940.

"It's a Distinguished Flying Cross. A British one. Presented by the RAF. The Royal Air Force."

"1940?"

"Yes, it's very special. You see the clasp on the ribbon. Battle of Britain. Fighter Ace. Not many of these out there. Family treasures."

"He stole it, I guess, like my cross."

"That's what we thought at first, but maybe not. We believe this cross was awarded to Charles Bliss, an officer in the Royal Canadian Air Force. He was the heir to a mining fortune. Old British money in Canada. He had a property in the islands, on a cay down in the Jumentos. Was quite a character as I understand it. A member of what they'd call the Jet Set a decade or two later. When they got jets, I mean, and before everyone was flying in them."

"He died in the war?"

"No, he died later. Domestic accident."

"So how did the psycho get it?"

"Charles Bliss had a wife and a son. She was American, a movie starlet. The son, Raymond, studied abroad. Ended up with a British passport. Here's the photo." He passed me another photocopy, a black and white headshot of a man in his early twenties. His shoulder-length hair was like a time stamp from another age.

"Sixties?"

"73."

I studied the image. There was something about his chisel-sharp features and his eyes. Not the usual bright star of youth. Something dark, haunted.

"Can you see it?" Rolle passed me another photocopy as the waiter served up our sandwiches. I shifted my seat back and held out the images side by side for comparison. The second image was a close-up of my attacker on the day of the preview.

"It's him. The son. Raymond Bliss."

"It looks like him, except for one thing. Raymond Bliss died in 1979."

"How?" I checked the resemblance in the photos one more time with growing certainty.

"He inherited the island when his mother died. He started a hippy commune. Some sort of religious cult. That sort of thing was all over the place back then, a hangover from the sixties. But then, they all committed suicide. Or that's what they thought. Eighteen of them. But who's to know what really happened? Not much in the way of CSI back then."

"Raymond too?"

"According to the records. It was after Hurricane David. Some locals checked on the island after the storm and found all the hippies dead. Of course, by that time, with the decomposition and all, it's hard to say exactly what happened. That storm wrecked the big house there too. Nobody's ever lived there since."

"Who owns it now?"

"Some real estate firm in Chicago. Fat chance of selling it. Ragamoffyn Island. Who'd buy a place with that kind of history? Even the local fisherman stay away."

I'd heard of Ragged Island and I thought I'd misheard him.

"Raga?"

"R-a-g-a-m-o-f-f-y-n. It's an old-fashioned spelling. All these cays have one story or another. The locals still call it Key Bliss, though. Spelt with a *K*. Like you Americans do it. The late Mrs. Bliss called it that. Wouldn't hear of it called any other way. Do you know the area?"

"Not really."

"Me, neither. The Jumentos are pretty much off the grid even today, and back in the 70s ..." He trailed off as he picked up his sandwich and examined its contents.

I joined him, chomping into my sandwich. I was building a map of the Jumentos in my head, deserted cays strung out like a necklace hanging down towards Cuba. We ate in silence, one mystery solved. Jim Benson's killer, my attacker, was finally accounted for, and the *Mendoza Crucifix* was back in my pocket. They were mighty small steps in putting right the wrongs of that day, but they were satisfying nonetheless. The police had ruled out any connection between my attack and William's abduction. But I'd built a career out of mistrusting coincidences, and the idea that Bliss had killed Benson, laid a curse on me, and then my son had been abducted on the same day was a hell of a big one.

"Do you still believe he had nothing to do with William's abduction?"

Rolle looked up from his sandwich and finished off his mouthful.

"Anything is possible. But threats are seldom acted on—especially not when they're made on camera. He ran out of that hotel dripping blood with handcuffs trailing from his wrist. So minutes later, he turns up at your villa and abducts a child without leaving a trace of DNA. It doesn't make sense."

"He could have had an accomplice, one of his followers. Didn't that happen back in the sixties with some Hollywood actress?"

"Sharon Tate. Charles Manson did it." Rolle squeezed out his staccato account between mouthfuls.

"But Manson didn't do it, did he? It was his followers."

"But how would he know where you were living?" There had to be a smart answer to that, but my mind was blank. "Dr. Steiger, I'm a police detective. I sniff around weasel words all day long—maybe, could have, would have. But to move forward, I need something tangible like your crucifix."

"How do you mean?" I took it out of my pocket.

He stopped eating and wiped his mouth on his napkin. "Could you have found the *Capitana* without that crucifix?"

"Of course not."

"So where is my *Mendoza Crucifix*? There's always something—DNA, a fingerprint, a witness, a snitch. But your son might as well have been sucked up into a spaceship for all the clues they left us. That's what bugs me about this case. I keep telling myself it's there somewhere, maybe something that we know already that we're not seeing right."

"Maybe you should look again at my accomplice theory. Didn't you say there was a paddleboard missing?"

"So we believe."

"What if William was sedated and spirited off on that? They could have paddled over to that resort on the headland."

"It's full of CCTV."

"Or the beach on the other side."

"Or what if there was a mistake with the inventory and the missing paddleboard never existed? Or maybe a neighbor borrowed it and was too ashamed to return it after what happened."

"Are you going to go down there?"

"Down where?"

"Key Bliss."

"With all respect, sir, I can't justify that. We have nothing connecting Raymond Bliss with the abduction of your son. We're not even sure about the ID of this man."

"I'm sure, and if you won't go down there, I will."

He sat back in his chair, the hint of a smile under his gray whiskers. I had the craziest notion I'd swallowed his bait instead of the last of my club sandwich. Either way, I was hooked.

"Why not? It's a free country. I read your book. You're quite the detective." He paused, measuring me. "I tell you what. I'll dig out whatever I can about Raymond Bliss and that cult. But I don't expect there'll be much. People used to come and go in those communes. They didn't even use real names. They'd call themselves Dharma or Krishna or some such."

I fingered the crucifix, holding it up between us.

"Maybe that's why he was so fixated on me, on this, something to do with his crazy cult. They were calling me a blasphemer, a herctic. It must have hit a nerve."

"No doubt. But don't get your hopes up. Crimes like this are often opportunity based. The wrong place and the wrong time, that's all it takes. Your wife was alone on the beach. She'd been drinking. She had narcotics in her system."

"Painkillers. She had a headache. We went through all that."

"I'm not blaming her, sir."

"You already did, if I remember right."

He gave me a sharp look.

"I'm pointing it out because it affects her judgment."

"Okay, okay."

"Let me tell you one thing, Dr. Steiger. I'm never

going to give up on this case. I'm going to solve it, or take it to my grave. Now I could tell you that's because I have a son about the same age as William. And maybe that's part of it. Or I could tell you it's because I still remember your face on the night you lost him. And maybe that's part of it too. But the real reason is that it sticks in my craw. So I'll work with you if you make that trip. As I said, I'm on the line for this one."

"Thank you, Inspector."

We shook hands across the empty dishes. Then he wiped some salsa from his horseshoe with the back of his hand and lit me up with his beamer.

"More than welcome, sir."

16 - Kim

"Candles?" Barbara said as I closed the door behind her. She stood at the table, leaned in to catch their fragrance and gave it an appreciative sigh. "Table set for two. What's this all about? Expecting someone special?"

"Very funny," I said. "Egyptian jasmine. Just for you."

I poured her a glass of white wine and she sat at the table, shifting her tanned legs to the side.

"So,"—she flicked her long fingers at the table—"what's up?"

I sat opposite her. This was not going to be an easy conversation. But the fact that it was happening at all was good. Honesty. Frankness. I was getting there. I used to look at responsibility like a snake looks at his skin, something to be dumped by the road when it doesn't fit anymore. Those days were gone, but I was still at a loss for words. In the end, I didn't need any. Barbara read it all off my face.

"You're joking!" She banged her glass down on the table. "You're going back to him? You cannot be serious." She waited, but I still couldn't get it out. No confirmations. No denials. I could hardly explain it to myself, let alone someone else. "You promised me you wouldn't pick up when he called."

"He leaves messages every day."

"So ignore him. Change your number."

"He met with Rolle, the detective. There's been a breakthrough."

"William?"

"Not William. Not exactly. The guy who attacked Jamie and put a curse on him. He turned up dead. Jamie thinks it's all linked."

"That's bullshit and you know it. Think about yourself now. You're doing good, getting over it. How's this going to help?"

"He's going back there."

"The Bahamas? That's all you need to trip right off the edge."

"This will never get closed if I don't do something."

"Don't tell me you're actually thinking of going?"

I drank some wine. I knew it wasn't going to be easy. But now I could see it was impossible.

"I ordered us Italian for later."

"Fuck Italian. Don't do it. You're better now. Why go back? Why risk it? He'll only mess you up again."

"I'm not going back. It's not like that. There's unfinished business, and it's not going away by itself."

"So what then?"

"I have to finish it."

"Divorce?"

"Maybe. If that's what it takes."

"You don't have to go there to do that. Get a lawyer."

I poured more wine for us both.

"Stop looking at me like that. I'm not planning to go back to him. For sure, I'm not. But I have to see him. I have to close this out one way or another."

"One way or another? So what does that make me? *Another*? Thanks a bunch."

"We never made promises. I never said—"

"Promises are not what you make. They're how you feel."

That shut me up, but I'd already said too much.

Her face slid down to her wineglass and tears streamed down her cheeks.

I leaped up, but she was already halfway to the door. I grabbed her and spun her around.

"I'm not going back to him. But we can't go anywhere with all this sitting out there." She made for the door again, but I pulled her close. "Don't go. Please." She eased back. I cupped her head in my hand and ran my fingers through the waves of her blond hair, my best intentions wilting on the vine. It wasn't meant to be like this. It was meant to be a clean break. But I didn't have the heart to do it. Is lying always a weakness? Sometimes it feels a lot more like a kindness to me. Either way, I ducked it. "I'll only be gone for a few weeks." She looked up, her big blue eyes all over me, searching for the truth. "Can you wait that long?" I slid my hand down to her wet cheek and pulled her closer.

She tucked up her sniffles as she leaned into me and rested her head on my breasts. She didn't say *yes*. But that was okay.

17 - Jamie

I sailed alone from Miami to Nassau, but I wasn't lonely. I talked to my dad, planning the route and second-guessing the weather. My father was deceased. So our conversations were brief, but rewarding for all that. We'd learned to sail together when I was a kid, cruising the Channel Islands and the California coast. He'd always dreamed of owning his own sailboat, and he'd gotten his dream. More or less. He was an LA cop, and it was delivered by a crack dealer who punched a knife through his bulletproof vest. He survived the attack for a while, and his disability compensation check paid for his dream boat. My dad was a man of modest dreams, and so it was a modest boat, but it had been plenty big enough for father and son to learn on together and enjoy each other's company, and I still felt his warmth and wise counsel every time I hoisted a sail.

When I arrived in Nassau, I looked up Rolle and we had a few beers together. He'd been as good as his word, digging into the background on Raymond Bliss and the killings on Ragamoffyn Island, and he shared his findings with me. I continued the research the following day, sitting in the shade of the cockpit canopy on my sailboat, *Kiss the Sky,* hiding from the sun and pumping Google. But it was hard to concentrate. The distraction was my phone. I couldn't stop checking it.

Still no word from Kim.

I forced myself to ignore it, busying myself online, burrowing deep into ages past. Charles, the patriarch of the Bliss family, had lived a life that read like a Hollywood movie. I even found myself casting Leo DiCaprio in the lead role as I browsed story after story about this larger-than-life character. He was heir to the Bliss mining fortune, a world-class sportsman and Olympic equestrian. In the thirties, he married a B-movie queen, Virginia "Ginny" Roy. He loved planes and invented various gizmos for pilots. Then along came WWII and this rich kid didn't hesitate, no hiding behind family money in Canada. He headed off to Britain to fight the Nazis. He flew Hurricanes and was credited with sixteen confirmed kills. After the war, he bought Ragamoffyn Island as a present for his wife and built an airstrip there and a palatial residence. Unofficially renamed Key Bliss, it became a major hangout for celebrities. Hemingway, visiting from his home in nearby Cuba, went fishing there, and Bogart and Bacall partied there. This golden age ended abruptly in the fifties when Charles Bliss died following a fall on his island. He left behind his widow and his son, Raymond.

The Google trail ran thin after that, although Rolle's local knowledge helped me fill in the gaps. Virginia Bliss spent the summers at their home in Switzerland and the winters on her island. But with the charismatic Charles gone, the celebrity visitors found other haunts. A sad image of an aging dowager emerged, propping up her youth in the company of younger men, one of whom disappeared mysteriously in a scandal that ripped through the tabloid press. There were rumors of drink and drugs surrounding her death in the sixties. But people had moved on. The Beatles had replaced Bogart and Bacall in the headlines, and the controversial Vietnam war had called into question the concept of war heroes. As for Raymond, he'd been shipped off to a school in England after his mother's vanishing lover scandal. Then he faded off the grid, reappearing after his mother's death and setting up a community on his island. What kind of community was not clear. In an age rife with lifestyle experiments, another bunch of freaks holed up somewhere was not news. But that changed when they all turned up dead. That was a story worth writing, but not for long. Weeks later, it was buried in the headlines by Jonestown, the mother of all cult massacres with nine hundred and eighteen bodies to count.

My phone rang.

For all the times I'd checked it, when Kim finally called, my mind was elsewhere.

"Kim." I got that much out. Then my mouth fell silent, shaping words I couldn't find the courage to say.

"How's the physio going?" She bailed me out.

"Good. I'm walking OK. No sticks or crutches."

"What about the pain? They told me that was going to be bad."

"The hospital?"

"Sure. I went there after the accident. You didn't think I was going to let you die on me without saying goodbye, did you?"

"Thanks. I think. Anyway, I'm out of the woods."

Shock was wearing off. I was finally talking to Kim. But oddly, the weight of missing her was not lifted from my shoulders, but bearing down on me all the more. "How have you been?" It was all so awkward. I hoped the fact of the call was the real message and not these wooden words we were exchanging.

"Good. I play tennis now. I joined a club."

"Keeping in shape, eh?" That's what I said. But what came to mind was the social scene. Plenty of guys to hit on you at a tennis club. "So what about that news? About Bliss?"

"Do you really think it could be him? They said he died in the seventies."

"Only a couple of the bodies were identified positively and Bliss wasn't one of them. He was just assumed to be one of the dead."

"And you plan to go down there?"

"I've got a gut feeling about this. There's something down there for us." I rolled the *us* word off my tongue like it was still an everyday part of my vocabulary. "Why don't you come with me?"

The silence droned on and on.

I blinked first.

"Or we could just talk about it? I'm in Nassau. Why don't you fly over?" I waited some more. But then I couldn't wait any longer. "Kim. Say something."

"Let's have dinner."

"What?"

"I'm already in Nassau."

"Where?"

"You choose. But Jamie, I'm not promising anything. I just want to see you." I slumped back in the cockpit, choked up. "I miss you, Jamie. I really do."

18 - Kim

I found him on the terrace, sitting at a table with his back to the tropical garden, a palm frond riding a gentle breeze above his head. He was looking down, preoccupied with something on the ground. He reached out his foot—he was wearing an off-white linen suit that looked really sharp—and stomped on something. And as he dragged his foot back under the table, he looked up and saw me. From crushed bug to estranged wife, he didn't skip a beat. He leaped up, catching his chair as it fell backward and smiling an awkward smile. I was grateful for the whole performance, a goofy slapstick moment that sucked the nerves right out of me.

That's my Jamie.

He strode towards me, his face breaking up, a cascade of emotions squashed up behind that awkward smile. He hugged me. A big hug. I got the feeling that he wanted to hide his face so I wouldn't see the hurt written on it. "Thanks for coming." The crack in his voice told me he'd been sitting there wondering if I was even going to show up. That made me feel like a bitch. I hugged him back and said, "It's good to see you." It sounded perfunctory. But it wasn't. I didn't know why I was there, but I did know it wasn't to be a bitch.

The setting couldn't have been more perfect, the romantic table—discreetly distant from others, but close enough to feel that we weren't alone—the night, its warm air like a caress, and the man I'd loved, and probably still loved, sitting opposite me, his adoring eyes full of hurt. It was like a first date, but one that came with baggage, his eyes gobbling at me in pieces, working on the courage to look me in the eye. He lifted his cocktail, some green concoction in a highball glass.

"Mojito?" I said.

"You got it. Green painkillers."

"Hey." I reached across the table and squeezed his hand. "You're not going to need painkillers on my account."

"That's good to hear." The waiter appeared. "Yellow Bird?" Jamie suggested my favorite island cocktail and for once it felt good to be so predictable.

I nodded my confirmation.

"What do you think?" I flipped out my hands, framing my makeover and running them down my body to flaunt the new me.

"Fantastic. Better than ever. I always loved your hair long like that too. And those blond bits. Great."

"Highlights."

"Suits you. You look in great shape too. Really. Better as you get older. More gravitas. Shame about me, though." He spread his arms to the side. "I messed myself up pretty good on that freeway."

I didn't take the easy way out by telling him he looked the same. He didn't. You don't get to live through an accident like that and end up the same. Besides, there was no reason to lie. He still looked every inch the man I'd fallen for, even with a few dented bits and pieces.

"Don't sweat it. You're still a hunk." He nodded a gracious acceptance of my compliment. "You son-of-a-bitch."

"That's my girl."

We laughed in sync, like we'd been rehearsing it all day long. It was all so easy. No problem with eye contact now. I guess chemistry was something we'd always had and it was already brewing up something. My drink appeared and we toasted each other. Then we ordered linguine and lobster. And as we worked our way through it, washing it down liberally with cocktails, we chatted away, roaming around the horizons of our lives. I told him about my tennis lessons, about my killer backhand, and he told me about his physiotherapy and his damaged C7 nerve. It was all so much easier than I'd feared.

Our happy feasting and pleasant conversation continued unabated as we picked our desserts, but it was starting to feel like a shield protecting us from the business at hand. Sooner or later, that shield would have to be lowered and the enemy engaged. I'm kidding, of course. Jamie was not my enemy. He was my husband. But he was also a stranger, a charming, sexy stranger, the oddest of novelties, a man both intimate and fresh. It was a cocktail that put the Yellow Bird I was drinking in the shade. But I couldn't let myself get carried away. We had an agenda.

"What about Bliss?" I said.

"His connection to William?"

"The cops never believed there was one."

"No, and they still don't. Rolle took me through all the forensic stuff, and it's pretty convincing."

"So, what do you think now?"

"I wonder why someone would steal this." He held up the *Mendoza Crucifix* hanging around his neck. "And lay a curse on me like some biblical prophet hoping it would come to pass by chance? I don't believe in coincidences or curses."

"Surely you don't expect to find William down there?"

"No. If I thought that, I'd be on my way with a

SWAT team. Anyway, I'm all out of expectations. This is not going to be like some Hollywood movie where we snatch William from the jaws of death in the last scene. This is real life. No black and white solutions. But if we could just…" He leaned back and looked around the restaurant like the words he was after might be hiding somewhere close by.

"Closure? The last time we brought that up, it nearly killed us."

This conversation was hurting now, but I had to push it. Closure was what we needed. Our marriage was on life support. Most likely, William was dead. That was what the stats told us, and how many years can you zig-zag between hope and despair? Eric's vision, fired into life by desperate longing, had gotten me on that plane, and I wasn't regretting that. I was happy to be sitting opposite my husband, enjoying a gourmet dinner instead of another toxic encounter. But where was I going with this?

Jamie reached across the table and took hold of my hand. "I want you back, Kim." He let out a blast of air like the words had been stuck in his throat and he was glad to have finally coughed them up. "Will you come?"

The waiter arrived with our desserts and I was grateful for the interruption. I took my hand back and used it to finish my drink as he served us. I was ducking the question, but I wasn't playing games. I needed a smooth slope and plenty of time to amble up it. Jamie was offering me a steep cliff and a deadline. We were silent after that, spooning our desserts, although I was more preoccupied with my thoughts than my soy milk panna cotta with hibiscus sauce and fresh raspberries. That kind of dessert washed down with a few cocktails puts me in a good mood and seriously open-minded about romance.

But I knew that tonight would not be the night. If it was going to happen, then it would come in its own sweet time. But before then, we had a lot of luggage to unpack. I'd already tried living with Jamie in the aftermath of that day. It hadn't worked. And if we made love now, we'd be headed down the exact same path.

"So, when would we go?" That's what a few cocktails will do for you. I had accidentally dropped the *we* word into my sentence. Jamie's eyes popped open, his dessert forgotten, almond cake crumbs and tangerine sauce still wet on his lips. "I mean, if I decide to come."

"That's up to us." He tried to look casual about it, clearing his throat and licking up the errant sauce. He was such a hopeless actor, all that money they'd spent on acting coaches totally wasted. "The hurricane season's about over. There's a tide on Thursday. That would be good. Unless you want to hang around this place."

Now that was a good move. What mother would want to hang out in a town with such woeful memories? He left me with it and went back to his dessert. Maybe those acting lessons were paying off after all.

"Why don't I come by the boat tomorrow?"

It wasn't a *yes*, but it was getting closer.

"Sure, I'll give you the tour."

So that was it. We had done it. We had survived our first encounter in years and we had a plan. No commitments. No promises. But we had hitched a lifeline—an umbilicus—to a new day waiting to be born. But much as I liked to be optimistic, I was to birthing what Jamie was to acting. So when we closed the evening with a toast to better days, I hoped it wouldn't come back to haunt us.

19 - Jamie

When I was a kid, I could never sleep the night before a big day. And here I was again, on the eve of Kim Day, snatching bits of sleep strung together with dreams. I couldn't remember any of the dreams, just the characters who were in them. It was like sleeping through a movie, then waking up at the end and reading the cast list. My mother was in one dream. I can't imagine why. She'd walked out on us when I was a kid. I'd only seen her once since, years later, when I graduated college. She was living in Chicago with the guy she'd run off with. I don't know what I was expecting, a pat on the back perhaps, a rekindling of maternal affection. But what I got was amused disinterest. The woman who'd grown me inside her looked at me like I was a fish in a bowl she'd left behind on a doorstep when moving house. I'm not one of those modern guys who tears up at the end of a rom-com. But sitting in the airport heading back to LA, that cut me open.

At first light, I gave up on sleep, took a shower, then gobbled down a bowl of muesli as I planned my day. Kim hadn't yet agreed to come on the trip. But as far as I was concerned, that was a formality. There was no way she would fly to Nassau and spend four hours guzzling cocktails with me unless she had made up her mind at some level. But first impressions count and the boat was a mess, so I set to work cleaning it up. When it was shipshape, I headed down to the store and bought supplies, fresh food, gourmet cans and prepared meals, and of course, a treasure chest of liquid booty, alcoholic and *non*. I piled it all on the deck and I was ferrying it down below when Kim appeared on the dock.

"Sloop rig. Nice."

"Still got your sailor's eye." I offered her my arm as she hopped on board. We air-kissed, our cheeks grazing. It was only a touch, but it was enough to fire up my synapses and set my heart pounding.

"Stocking up for the trip?" She nodded at the bags and boxes on the deck.

"Yeah, just got back. So how's your head?"

"Good." She paused as though that might need some qualification, but evidently not. "Yeah ... good. We put a few back last night, didn't we? How about you?"

"I'm good." It was all a bit clumsy.

"Okay. Let me help you get that stuff out of the sun."

And so it began. The trip of promise. We ferried the goods below and set to work, packing them away.

"What's this?" Kim was looking at an open panel in the woodwork near the galley, where she was packing cans in a locker.

"A little electrical problem. I can finish it later."

"Why don't you do it now? I'll stow the rest of the stuff. Then I'll make us a sandwich."

"Okay. Good."

That was perfect. I wanted her to have time for herself, to feel comfortable on board. On board with me. I pulled out my tools, sat on the floor by the open panel and went to work. I won't say it was like old times. But it was getting there. And as I worked, the sound of her moving behind me, the feel of her in the same space, triggered a contentment I'd forgotten I'd ever known. When she was finished stowing the goods, she started on the sandwich, working in the galley a few steps away from me.

"Why didn't you buy a new boat?"

I pulled my head out of the paneling.

"I wanted a project and I wanted to work with my hands. A sort of natural physio. She's in pretty good shape now, don't you think?"

"Sure."

"I bought it from an aging Dutch hippie. Henk. Nice guy."

"Hendrix fan?"

"*Kiss the Sky*, yeah … he told me about that, his life story. He drove a camper full of hash from Morocco to Holland back in the sixties. Just winged it. Then he sold the dope, bought the boat and dropped out. Been sailing the planet ever since. *Kiss the Sky* was his time capsule, his fortress, protecting him from a changing world he didn't much care to be a part of. His plan worked too. At least, until he got cancer. That's why he was selling the boat. But he even laughed about that. He told me the great thing about chemotherapy is *your doctor finally tells you to smoke pot*."

"Sounds like you bought his story, not the boat."

"I guess so. I gave him the asking price. Way over the top."

"Maybe it was all bullshit."

"What?"

"About the cancer. It's tough haggling with a guy who's dying."

"Henk? No way. He cried when we did the paperwork."

"She's all yours now anyway."

"Yep, and she's a boat with character, real old-fashioned karma."

"Can't even smell the pot, eh?"

I winked. "Not unless you sniff real hard."

I went back to work, and when the job was done, I tucked the wires back in place and looked up at her. She was slicing a tomato. She looked glorious, her figure trimmed back to how it had been in our early days. Even better. Stronger, more athletic. She was wearing white sneakers and denim shorts. I've always been a leg man and hers were perfect, contoured calves and muscled thighs framing her loins to perfection. Her weight was parked jauntily on one leg with the other bent at the knee, the heel raised off the floor, her ass in profile.

"What about the hair of the dog?" She nodded at the pile of six-packs. "I'm nearly done here."

"That'll work. There's some cold ones in the fridge." I rubbed my hands together like I'd just finished working instead of sitting there checking out her ass. "I'm about done here too."

She gave me a beer, and I winked at her as we touched the cans together. She smiled in return and went back to the sandwich board as I supped my beer.

The day's agenda was simple. Above all, we had to avoid any type of disagreement or confrontation. Beyond that, I had to get her to commit to the trip. She was halfway signed up. I was sure of that. Otherwise, she wouldn't have been on board making me a sandwich. But I had to hear the words, and so did she. Linked to that was something else—let's call it an *implication*—part and parcel of what it means to be husband and wife. *How do we get from strangers back to lovers?* The question had been on my mind since the moment I saw her walking towards me in the restaurant. I set the beer can aside and replaced the panel, my thoughts far from electrical connections, at least the type that needed wires. Sex had always been important to us both.

Whatever problems we'd had, we could always resolve them in bed. But now we were strangers and there was a palpable tension between us, our interactions riddled with fumbling. It was all so unnatural. Sex had been the start button on our love. Now I needed to find the restart. In the old days, we used to initiate sex in a couple of different ways. The first was scheduled, although that makes it sound boring, which it certainly wasn't. Everybody needs structure in their lives, and Kim and I were no exceptions. So we'd fix a time that worked for us both. Kim used to call it a *cinq à sept,* which was French for *five to seven*. It was a reference to the happy hour, a traditional time in France for sloping off with your lover before heading home to your spouse. Our second method was pouncing. My word, of course. That was more of a random event. We'd enjoyed it either way. The familiarity of a *cinq à sept* was like having your favorite dinner in your favorite restaurant. You knew what was coming, but it still tasted great. On the other hand, the drama and impact of a good *pounce* could make your whole week.

I considered briefly proposing a *cinq à sept*, tossing it casually into our conversation halfway through lunch.

What about a fuck this afternoon?

Only kidding. One misstep and my fucking days with Kim were over. Strictly speaking, they already were. But there was a lifeline floating around, and all I had to do was grab it on the first attempt. There would be no second chance. That was for sure. So a *cinq à sept* was out of the question. That was for lovers, not strangers. That left pouncing—an appealing prospect, but risky. Back in the day, this was the sort of moment I would have chosen—when she was preoccupied, absorbed in some activity, her mind a million miles away from sex. I ran my eyes up and down her body as she spread low-fat mayo on whole wheat. I was sitting on the floor, virtually at her feet. I could see it all playing out in my mind.

I flip her around, jamming her against the galley. I make short work of her pants. No belt. Just a stud and a zipper. She yelps a protest. She always does. But in seconds, her pants are down her thighs and I'm working on her with my tongue. Her protests stop. They always do. I slide up onto my feet as she kicks her pants aside, my nimble fingers relishing the wet warmth of her. It's all so sudden. She's dripping. Now I'm inside her and she's begging me to come, our loving so fierce it echoes through the boat, rippling in waves like a halo in the waters beyond Kiss the Sky.

"Are you going to eat this?" The plate was right under my nose. "Or are you going to sit there all day looking at my ass?" I stared at the tuna sandwich, my fantasy fuck in tatters. She had made it with tomatoes, cress and avocado, and soaked it with mayo, the way I like it. Evidently, it was time for lunch, but the chef's special was off the menu.

20 - Kim

The tuna sandwich went down well with Jamie lavishing compliments, and I must admit to getting a furtive buzz out of his enthusiasm for my rudimentary culinary skills. He was trying so hard to make me happy. After lunch, we stayed in the cabin and talked. Jamie was washing down the sandwich with another beer and I was helping myself to it, slugging it back from the same can. Evidently, sharing spit with my stranger-husband was not an issue. But as far as exchanging body fluids was concerned, that was about as far as I was planning to go. I'd rebuffed his visual groping in the galley on purpose. That was a policy decision. He was way ahead of himself. All we needed to do right now was talk. That was enough. We needed to build a new bridge between us and *talk* was the perfect construction material.

Jamie had already walked me through the practicalities of the trip. That was all clear enough. But now he was talking about the why of the trip and things were getting fuzzy. Jamie was still flying a flag for Mr. and Mrs. Steiger, and so was I. Even though mine was still folded in my back pocket. But if this trip was about us, then why the Bahamas? Anywhere else on the planet would be better. I wanted to tell him about my séance with *Amazing Eric*, but that was unthinkable. Jamie was a skeptic. He'd be dismissive at best, and at worst, all this newfound amity between us would be lost in a pointless row about psychics. Besides, there was no way I could convey the power of that séance and the effect it'd had on me. I didn't buy Eric's account. Not wholesale. But it was still part of the tally in my ledger. So, skipping that, I moved the conversation onto the Bahamas police instead. Jamie had been buddying up with Rolle. That was new. And given the bumpy road we'd traveled with those guys, I was curious about it.

"Did you get anything from Rolle?"

"Locker room talk ... unofficial stuff."

"About William?"

"Bliss."

His eyes were furtive, casing me out.

"Jamie ... what? Tell me."

He tossed up his hands in surrender.

"Raymond Bliss cut out Jim Benson's heart."

"Jesus."

"They didn't mention any of this at the time, of course. Cops always hold back details like that. And get this ... the cutting was expert."

"Like a surgeon?"

"More like a *Papahua*, an Aztec priest. Rolle asked me about their techniques. The autopsy found cuts on the inside of his thoracic vertebrae. No broken ribs. That meant the heart was cut out from under the rib cage."

"While he was alive?"

Jamie nodded. "And those freaks back in the seventies on Key Bliss, their cadavers had no hearts either. They'd been dead for weeks. So the cops put that down to decomposition and predators. But now they think Bliss killed them all in some sort of sacrificial ceremony, then escaped in the mess after *Hurricane David*."

"Are they reopening the case?"

"No. This is all off the record. No one's interested

in a bunch of hippies who died forty years ago. Even if it was Bliss, he's dead now. So what's the point? Case closed."

"And what about William's case?"

"That's open. No change."

The sweet taste of hope I'd nurtured on and off since the séance with Eric was turning sour in my mouth. The thought that Bliss, a macabre serial killer, had been involved with William's disappearance was too sickening to even contemplate, and I could only pray that the police were right to rule it out. Jamie slid around to my side of the table and put his arm around me.

"No connection. The cops are right. No one threatens the father of a child they're about to abduct on camera in front of a room full of journalists. I was wrong about that. But we've come this far. So let's go down there anyway. Let's put our hearts at rest. Let's do it for our little boy … and for us. There's an early tide tomorrow. We can still catch it if you want."

My head was burrowing into his chest, my tears soaking his shirt. I couldn't bear to look at him. That was when I knew. I had to tell him the truth. How I'd left William alone with the doors open. How I'd spent hours trying to kill myself while someone was stealing our child. I had to tell him. Not now. But soon. On the trip. There'd be a time and a place. We could search Key Bliss from top to bottom, and when we found nothing, I'd tell him everything. He'd be angry. But Jamie had never been a violent man. He'd never laid a finger on me.

"Okay."

So that was how it started, a whisper washed out in a rinse of tears. We sat in silence, my head riding on the rise and fall of his chest, the rhythm of his breath calming my fears.

"Do you remember eyeball navigation?" Jamie was changing the subject, steering my mind away from black thoughts. And for once, I was happy to be led.

"I remember that ditty you taught me." In the Bahamas, many islands are fenced with reefs, sandbars, and wrecks, and skill at picking your way through them is called eyeball navigation. Knowing my love of poetry, Jamie had taught me the rules with a rhyming mnemonic. I pulled myself off his chest and wiped up my sniffles.

"*Water that's blue is deep and true; As it shades to green, the water gets lean; White or yellow will ground a fellow; If the water is brown, you'll run hard aground; If the water is black, you'd better tack.*"

"Sounds like I've got my first mate."

"Aye-aye, Captain." I leaned up and kissed his lips. Brief but heartfelt.

"Did I get that wrong, or did that *kiss* answer the *us* question as well?"

"Maybe. But I'm not sure it was meant to. Let's stick to crew for the time being. Us is a very deep and murky ocean."

His laugh was just as I remembered it from the last time I'd heard it when he was in the pool with William at *Paradise Found*.

"That's my kind of sea." He pulled my hands up to his face and kissed them, his eyes never leaving mine.

21 - Jamie

Our route through the Exumas was leisurely by design, easy days with short hops weaving in and out of its three-hundred plus islands. Pirates ruled these waters in the seventeenth century, and more recently, drug kingpins ascended to their thrones. The Exumas ooze Bahamas, bijou cays so perfect they made not just one, but two James Bond movies here.

Kim and I spent beautiful days together. They were marred, but still beautiful. We were sharing a boat, but not a bed. And as the days passed, my concern about that was growing. Life is a habit. What we do is what we become. And at the rate we were going, we were two strangers heading for friendship. I'd expected the *bon moment* to arrive all by itself. There would be a spark, a look between us, a naughty smile on her cheeks after a couple of drinks. Something less romantic would have worked too, something straightforward, like her crawling under the sheet next to me in the middle of the night. Of course I could have done that too. But if I did, and it failed—and it would fail—then *us* would crash and burn. We might be strangers. But we were strangers who knew each other inside out, and I knew this had to be Kim's play. I'd made my intentions clear in Nassau and she had done the same thing. We were a crew, not yet a couple. A gear change was pending. But she was holding the stick, and I was holding my breath. *Kiss the Sky* was the stage. The scene was set by sunbaked days and warm nights candlelit by stars, and the cays, laid out like white jewels in an ebb and flow of tropical sea and sky, made the perfect Hollywood backdrop. All we had to do was follow the script, that eternal man-woman script called love. But somewhere, we had lost our place. We were amateur actors fumbling our lines. Heading out of Nassau, I'd been relaxed about it, sure it would happen sooner or later. But five days into the trip, we were way into *later* and closing in fast on *too late*. Pretty soon, being just friends would be the status quo, a bad habit it would be too late to break.

Why is it taking so long?

There was only one answer that made sense. She had a new man. Desperate measures were called for. I had to bust this logjam even if it took a stick of dynamite. I had to find out the truth.

Our first day out of Georgetown, we anchored off Little Exuma Island north of Hog Cay Cut. The following morning, we got an early start and passed through the cut on the rising tide. By noon, we had reached our waypoint northwest of Water Cay, and by the time the sun was ready to set, we were anchored inside a cove at the north end of the island and well protected from the prevailing southeast winds.

Kim prepared some food while I checked the weather, tuning in to the sideband service that gives cruisers local forecasts. There were some thunderstorms south of Jamaica, but nothing to concern us. I also checked the hourglass in my head. It was all out of sand. Key Bliss was a day's sail away.

So what comes after that?

Assuming no surprises on the island, we would turn around and head home—she to hers and me to mine.

After we were done with our food and our chores,

I sat on deck under the cockpit enclosure with my back to the sun, my eyes lazily scanning the island. Kim soon joined me, sitting next to me, sharing my view of limestone cliffs and a blue sky with slashes of cloud floodlit pink by the setting sun at our backs.

"Looks like we escaped the crowd … the armada," I said.

"Isn't it glorious? Not a boat in sight all day. It's like another world already. So what's on this island?"

"Same as the rest of the Jumentos. Nothing. Nobody. The only settlement is Duncan Town down at the other end. There's about eighty people there, I heard."

She wriggled around, kneeling on the seat to look behind us. "Look at that sunset." I turned around to catch the fireworks in the west. The sun was exploding in streaks of gray cloud, turning them purple and shooting them through with spikes of gold. I put my hand on Kim's waist as if to steady myself. But it was a ruse, and that magnificent sunset held my interest for only a moment. Her face was inches from my lips, glowing in the softening tones of the setting sun. I went to kiss her. But she flipped back onto the seat, brushing me off, her eyes never catching mine.

"I was looking at the charts," she said, papering over my clumsiness. "Key Bliss looks real inhospitable, miles from any other island, ringed with reefs, nowhere to anchor. So why did Charles Bliss buy it? He was a party animal, and this is the most isolated, off-the-beaten-track island in the entire Bahamas."

I took a deep breath, funding a sigh that was loud enough for her to get the message.

"He was an aviator. He never came to the island by boat. He used to fly in. And this was before the

Cold War. Before Castro. Cuba was a US ally in WWII, and right after the war it was party town USA. Cuba is just a spit away from Key Bliss by plane. It's the Cuban embargo that makes this place a backwater, not geography."

"Even so, it's odd." She stood up. "Ready for a beer?"

"Sure."

She slipped below and came back with a cold pack. She gave me one, but this time she sat opposite me. We drank in silence awhile. Then she said, "I wanted to tell you something." The tone in her voice made it sound like a confessional. Dark clouds of doom loomed on the horizon and I'm not talking about that sunset which continued to dazzle in the background unattended. "Promise you won't go ape on me." Eliciting such a declaration was hardly encouraging.

Here it comes. The other guy.

I shrugged my acquiescence and steeled myself.

"Okay. I wasn't going to tell you this. But as we're a day out from Key Bliss, I think I should. This is going to sound weird. But I found a *real* psychic."

I couldn't believe my ears. This big build-up for some drivel about a psychic. My thoughts must have been written large on my face because she was suddenly defensive. "I know this is crazy. I just want you to listen because, in fact, it's not crazy. I know we had all those assholes coming on to us after William and I know they were all conmen. I agree. But that only makes this even weirder."

"Okay." I squeaked it out again, my irritation surely obvious. With all the issues between us, her top pick for a conversation was *my trip to the psychic.* If anything was going to light that stick of dynamite, this was it.

"He could see things. Like the Sandman. Who knows I call you that? Did I ever call you that in front of anyone?" I kept my mouth shut, knowing full well that nothing good was going to come out of it. "How did he know that? And what about my dad? Detailed things. Private conversations. Things about me not even you know. Minute details. How is that possible?"

I struggled for composure. Kim was obviously sincere about this. I had to hear her out.

"I honestly don't know. I believe you, but—"

"What?"

"Mind reading. Telepathy. Maybe it works. But they've never been able to prove it."

"That's because it's random. It's not like a computer."

"Even if it does work, it's not divination. Reading someone's mind is not the same as seeing their future."

"I know that. But he never said *such-and-such will happen* like those phonies did. He described visions. He didn't interpret anything. Past, present, and future. He left all that to me."

"Did you ask him about William?"

"No. I didn't want to give him any clues. But he didn't need any. *The Sandman saves his child.* That's what he said. I swear it. *The sea gives him up.* I wish I'd recorded it. Now it's all broken up in my head. But I remember that."

"Kim, you're killing us with this garbage."

"I swear to it. He had second sight. His visions were like metaphors—"

"Very convenient."

"Don't be a cynic. Add it up. I've got this amazing guy who can describe true stuff he couldn't possibly know, and he's telling me you save the child. Of course, I didn't believe it literally. Not really. But how could I not check it out? Meantime, I've got you telling me about this breakthrough."

I almost choked on my beer. I wiped my mouth with the back of my hand and looked at her long and hard, so she'd well know what was coming.

"That's why you're here? That's why we're together? Because some crazy psychic told you to come. Son-of-a-bitch. For a moment there, I thought it was because you wanted to be with me."

"Don't be like that. I wanted to spend time with you. It all came together at the same time is all. I didn't mean it to sound like that."

"While we're on the subject of *us*, I've got something pretty big I want to ask you too."

"Here we go."

"No. Here we *don't* go, baby, and that's the problem. You said you wanted to spend time with me, but what as ... brother and sister, or husband and wife?"

She stood up. "I need a proper drink."

22 - Kim

I was locked in the head. That's what they call a bathroom on a sailboat. No idea why. I was composing myself. Although how to get ready for a train wreck I wasn't sure. According to Jamie, we were brother and sister instead of husband and wife. That was true. It wasn't what I wanted. It was what I needed.

Making love had once been the core of our life together, the forum where our two souls had melded into one, and I think it had always stayed like that for Jamie. For him, sex was like a magic train, and whatever station he jumped on board, it always took him to the same destination. But for me, it was more like a door in a wall with the world beyond it hidden until I turned the handle and stepped through. When we first met, the door opened onto a magical landscape, a place of wonder and oneness. But as the years passed and I failed to conceive, it led to a factory where I worked on a production line, repeating the same movements endlessly, engaged in the manufacture of something. I didn't know what exactly, as I never got to see what rolled off at the end of the line. William's arrival changed all that, and we recovered much of what time had stolen. But that ended abruptly when we lost him. Our lovemaking stopped, and although it started up again, it was different, a comfort blanket, sex as life support drip-feeding us solace. On bad days, it wasn't even that. It got to where I didn't know if I was making love or making hate, the line between them blurring in an emotional fog of guilt and pain. So we drifted apart. I abandoned my husband emotionally and sexually, effectively shipping him gift-wrapped to Sydney Kingston. So that was where we were on the third anniversary of William's abduction, the day of Jamie's accident. We argued of course. That wasn't unusual. But then, it all went wrong. I hit him with my fist. It was so sudden that I didn't know anything about it until it was all over. Jamie was sprawled in the chair he'd fallen back into. He was holding his jaw and looking up at me like a hurt little boy. Then shame hit me and I went running out the door. Later that night, I got a call from the cops. I thought they were going to arrest me for spousal abuse. But it was about the accident. Jamie was in hospital, severely injured.

Commitment has consequences.

Every relationship has a thermostat, and you have to know how to control the heat. I was planning to tell Jamie the truth. I'd committed to that, and this time I was not going to back out. Our making love would pump up the heat. I'd lose conviction. I'd be back where I was, living a lie. I couldn't let that happen. I had to be strong. Sex was the red line on our thermostat and with the heat turned up, anything could happen.

Knock, knock.

"You okay?" Jamie was calling through the door.

I took a deep breath. It was time to turn the handle and step through the door.

On the table in the salon was a tub of ice, glasses, a bottle of rum and a plate with limes cut into quarters. Sitting behind it was Jamie, smiling and making our drinks. I joined him on the couch and we touched glasses and drank. Then we drank some more. Evidently, this topic was as tricky for him to navigate as it was for me.

"What was it you wanted to ask me?" I said.

He shrugged like it was of no importance.

"If there was anyone else? That's all."

"Nobody special. What about you?"

"Who? The nurse changing my bed pan?"

"You weren't in hospital the whole time."

"No, but you were prancing around Europe."

"I went to Florence to learn Italian."

"Sounds romantic."

"If you're in the mood. But I can't say that I was."

"What about LA? No suitors at the tennis club admiring your *killer backhand*?"

"Is that what you think? That the reason we're not having sex is because of someone else."

"I don't think anything. I'm just asking. You've been alone in LA for a long time. You must have some social life."

"Not really. I made friends with a woman in the building where I live. I spend time with her when I'm lonely."

"That's not what I mean. You know what I'm talking about."

"Yes, I do. I do know what you're talking about. And that's what I'm talking about too."

It was like I'd sprayed him with liquid nitrogen and he was flash-frozen. He said nothing for a while. Then his eyes opened ever wider, and they roamed around the room as though he'd just woken up somewhere strange and couldn't remember how he'd gotten there.

"You mean ... a woman!"

23 - Jamie

It was incomprehensible. Kim had never shown any interest in other women, at least not like that. She'd always checked them out, commenting on their looks, but not with desire, more like an appraisal, like an athlete checking out the competition. Other women were rivals, not potential lovers. Or so I'd thought. I washed down my shock with a slug of rum as she filled in the blanks.

"I thought about trying it at college like you might some recreational drug to see what all the fuss is about, although I didn't have any genuine desire to. But where I live in LA, my apartment looks down on a communal pool. And there was this woman, Barbara, who was always there. She never swam. She'd just lie by the pool and soak up rays. Long blond hair, in her mid-thirties. Old-fashioned looking. She seemed lonely. No friends. We'd said hello once or twice as neighbors do. Then one night, when I came home late, who should come stumbling down the steps as I was walking up them but Barbara—more than a little drunk—arm in arm with a butch amiga, a chunky Hispanic chick. Her face flushed like a stoplight when she saw me."

This was taking forever.

"What are you trying to tell me? You're gay? You're bi?"

"I'm just telling you what happened. Anyway, I wondered why it was an issue for her. That blush I mean. In this day and age. In LA? Unless, of course, she had a crush on me. So then, one day—"

"How about you cut to the chase? You're an item now. Is that what you're telling me?"

"I wouldn't say that. We're friends. Sometimes a fantasy is best lived in the mind where it belongs and reality turns out to be a letdown."

"So in the end you didn't...?"

"Oh sure we did. It never felt quite right for me. But it didn't feel wrong either."

"So just the once, like an experiment?" I was pushing my luck and I knew it.

"I didn't keep a scorecard. But definitely no more than fifty or sixty times." She giggled, smothering her mouth with her hand. "Your face is priceless. Relax, Jamie. I don't know how we ended up having this conversation. But you asked the question. It was just a way for two lonely women to be friends. I needed someone to trust, someone to hide behind."

"Hide from me?"

"Maybe I was hiding from all men."

I tried to look worldly, but I probably just looked confused. On the inside, I was a vortex of swirling thoughts and emotions. I waited a beat until something recognizable made it to the surface. Relief. That was the big one and I grabbed it at first sight. The way she'd laid it out, this was a dalliance and no threat to our relationship, nothing on the scale of Sydney. An overreaction on my part would be fatal. I had to play it down, and Kim was making that easy. She was still snickering—I must've put on quite a show—enjoying the tease. But two can play at that game.

"I don't suppose you took a video by any chance?"

Her snickering stopped dead.

"You fucker." She punched me on the shoulder. Now I was laughing, and she followed suit. We were laughing together.

"So, there's no one special. We took a bit of a detour but we got there. "

"I lost William, then you. There wasn't much left of me to lose after that, but I found a way." She shrugged. "That's it. I'm lost, plain and simple." Her face puckered up, suddenly serious, as though she was about to cry.

"Hey, none of that." I lifted my glass. "You are now officially found."

She went to speak. I could see the words framing behind her eyes, but they never made it to her lips. She swallowed them and went for a curt nod instead. We cracked glasses and downed our drinks. "Shit..." It looked like the rum had helped her find those words. "Why don't we kill that bottle, talk trash—anything you like—then sneak off and fuck like we used to before we knew what a bitch life was?"

"Deal."

I squeezed the limes for another round.

"This is like one of those sleazy daytime talk shows where they hash over an affair. Then some old lover pops out from backstage." She put down her glass, her eyes measuring me. "What about your shenanigans? And don't worry, I don't have Sydney Kingston stashed in back there somewhere." If that was a joke, I didn't like the sound of it. But I ignored the dig, determined to stay upbeat.

"Well, there was that gay Filipino nurse." I sidestepped the bait with a joke, and she took it in good spirit, aiming a fake shot at me. "Okay. I'm kidding. I'm still straight. Actually, I'm a monk. There's nothing like spinal surgery to take your mind off sex."

"Just Sydney? But that's okay. I know all about that. So what went wrong?"

"You. I guess. I never stopped loving you."

"I thought you two were perfect together. Dr. Seacrets and Supergirl. You never stopped talking about her."

"I'm sorry. I never meant to rub it in your face."

"Is she still around?"

"No. She's with some Wall Street guy. They've got a kid now."

"Of course they have. I'm sure Supergirl can pop out kids like a farmer's prize sow."

"Hey." I pulled her close and kissed her forehead before slipping my mouth down to hers. It was our first real kiss in years. She joined in. But she was still holding back something. Too bad Sydney had joined the conversation. She broke it off, sliding her face off mine. Not abruptly, not a rejection.

"Who ended it? You or her?"

Evidently, we were going to have to squeeze this topic to death before we could move on.

"I guess it was mutual. I was no fun to be with. I was still in love with you. And I was still cut to pieces about Will. Maybe that was a big part of what soured it too. Her part in that night."

"That night?" The sharpness in her voice was like a pointy pencil, highlighting my mistake. I hadn't actually said it—just half of it—but half was enough for Kim. "William's night? Her part in what?"

"I just mean it was all connected."

"No, you didn't." Her eyes flicked around the cabin before zooming in on mine. "You fucked her that night, didn't you? That's where you were." I opened my mouth to protest, but something stopped me. "I was sure of it that night. But when I heard about the attack, I thought ... *no way*. But it was that night. You lied about it."

"No, I didn't." It was a pathetic Bill Clinton defense, but it was true. I'd never actually lied because the question had never come up. With everything that had happened that day, it had fallen between the cracks. That made it easy to live with. The lie that never touched your lips was always the best one. But unspoken or not, it had stayed a lie. And now, I'd blundered my lines, and Kim had read between them.

"You fucked her that night, didn't you?"

The answer was *yes*, but the word sounded so wrong. *Yes* didn't explain the madness of that day, the attack, the murder, and Sydney as I'd never seen her, raw and vulnerable, her eyes full of longing. But now, in the fierce glare of Kim's anger, I could see *yes* stripped naked. I'd tried to say *no* that night, but not hard enough. I'd wanted Sydney for so long, and when the door of opportunity opened I'd slid through it on a mat slicked with easy excuses and convenient justifications.

"I can't explain."

"Try."

"Sydney broke down. I was comforting her. And it turned into a clinch. But I broke away. I said *no*."

"And?"

"She made some remark about me being the perfect gentleman like Jim Benson. Then she kept weeping and weeping. It was unbearable."

"So you did the gentlemanly thing to comfort her. To stop her pain, I mean. You fucked her. Instead of giving her an aspirin."

"Don't be an ass. I didn't plan it. Everything was unreal that day. She broke down and so did I. What the hell difference does it make when it first happened?"

"Because if you had come home to your wife and son, maybe, just maybe..." She leaped up, then stopped as if she was trying to figure out what to say in some foreign language. "I've blamed myself all these years for what happened that night. But I was right about one thing. You were killing our family. I knew it. I'm your wife, goddamn it. I feel what you think." She snatched up the rum bottle and gulped it so fast it left her gasping. "You're such a dumb bastard too. That's the worst of it. You fell for the oldest trick in the book. I'm sure she put on a performance worthy of an Oscar. Desperate, feeble sniffles like an injured dog lying by the side of the road. Well, fuck you, Steiger." She marched off into her cabin, swinging the rum bottle at her side like a baton. A few seconds later, the door burst open. "And another thing. First light. This boat heads back to Georgetown. I'll get a plane from there. Do you get that, Captain?"

The door slammed behind her.

I leaned forward on the table and buried my face in my hands. I stayed like that for an age, no thoughts, my mind numbed into emptiness. Well into darkness, I eased myself up on my feet and made my way to the nav station where I clicked on the light and plotted the route. When I was done, I clicked off the lamp, pondering my options in the dark as my eyelids drooped and I slumped over the table, my face pillowed on charts of the islands.

24 - Kim

The boat was moving. I steadied myself, sitting on the edge of the berth, the night before drifting back into focus. I had lost my cool, but not my control. That was progress. Too bad I had to bring up Sydney, but that was a sore I couldn't let alone. Like some old boil crusted over by time, but still itching deep inside, I had to dig my nails into it and tear it open. Blessedly, the collateral damage was minimal, and I had even moved one step closer to telling Jamie my truth. I don't know what stopped me. It was the perfect opportunity, but I couldn't get the words out. There was something wrong about the moment. The truth about my aborted suicide that night would never come out like that. Never in rage. It was too hurtful. The truth would have to be squeezed out of me in pain like a newborn child. Jamie's revelations had finally put that night's events into focus. My fears about losing my family had been justified. But now I could see it all through his eyes too. Hyped up and emotional after the fight with Bliss and reeling from the news about the murder, he'd been easy pickings for a predatory bitch like Sydney. After that, he'd come home soaked in guilt, his tail hanging hot and wet between his legs, to find me in tatters and his son missing. Later, when I'd come under suspicion, Jamie had defended me aggressively. He'd never blamed me for negligence. Now I knew why. He'd been too preoccupied with his own guilty conscience.

I struggled into the head and splashed water over

my face. Then I stripped off and stood under a cold shower. My head was clear. Good island rum. Just a fuzzy feeling around the eyes and a furry tongue. I brushed my teeth and sipped some mineral water. Then I stretched out on the berth. I wanted some time to organize my thoughts, but I dozed off instead and when I woke up, the boat was tossing around on the open sea. I finished off the water bottle and tried to figure out how best to handle Jamie. It wasn't so much the affair that had set me off. I'd already known about that. It was the timing of events on that night, the way our worlds had turned like spokes on the opposite sides of a wheel, Jamie seduced by the tears of another woman at the exact moment that his own woman was literally drowning in hers. I have always liked that word *synchronicity* and its undertone of kinship. But this was something else, something sinister and frightening. I stood up, gathering myself together. At least we were equal now. We were both at fault that night. That had to make it easier to tell him the truth, if nothing else. I could hear him up on deck. I went through to the galley and got myself some cereal and milk. The sailing was smoother now. I checked out the porthole as I ate my muesli. Then I busied myself with housekeeping chores until I noticed we had stopped sailing. I checked through a porthole again. We were anchored offshore from some cay. I went up the companionway. Jamie was in the dinghy halfway to shore. The water was shallow and *Kiss the Sky* was anchored amid reefs.

"Jamie," I hollered, my voice carrying easily across the sheltered waters. He stopped rowing and waved.

"You okay?" he said.

"Sure. I'm okay." There was not much of a

conversation we could have at this distance and perhaps that was for the best. "What's up?"

"I need to check something. I'll be back in an hour." He gave me a thumbs up, which I returned.

All this was good. We had said *hi*, and now we had an hour to cool off. It couldn't have worked out better. I watched him tie the dinghy up to a broken-down jetty. I could see huts beyond the beach half-hidden in trees. We exchanged another wave. Then he disappeared into the trees. Those huts got me thinking. I headed down into the cabin to check the GPS.

Son-of-a-bitch.

He had flat-out ignored me. This was Ragamoffyn Island. I double-checked. There was no mistake. We had arrived. He had ignored my instructions. I chuckled. My husband may have broken his back and a few ribs, but he obviously hadn't lost his balls in that accident. I was oddly relieved. He'd read me right and that wasn't easy. I was still hungry. Anger burns up calories like crazy. So I boiled an egg and ate it with toast. Then I had a yogurt. I looked around, wondering if Jamie had gotten himself breakfast. Probably not. He gets excited and forgets to eat, or else he snacks on those infernal energy bars he takes everywhere. I checked the freezer and took out some steaks to defrost and a bottle of Cabernet from the wine cabinet. Then I went to my cabin, planning to move my stuff into Jamie's, but I got waylaid by my reflection in the washbasin mirror. My face had picked up some color and I looked healthy. But my eyes looked like shit. I opened my cosmetics bag and set to work, stopping when an eyeliner pencil rolled off the shelf and into the washbasin. I stared at it. Like everything else on board, the shelf was designed so that objects would stay put. But the pencil had hopped over the raised edge designed to stop it from falling. And now I was grabbing a rail to steady myself as the boat tossed awkwardly.

Where did that come from?

I was no sailor, but I'd spent enough time on sailboats to realize that something was going on. I hurried up on deck. The sky in the south was kaleidoscopic with an inky black cloud, edged with bands of gold, blotting out the sun and flaming the sea beneath it with streaks of orange fire. I looked towards the shore. Jamie was on his way back, oars looping rapidly in and out of the water. He had obviously seen it too. I checked back with the sky. The seas beneath the cloud were chopping up white like nervous prey smelling a predator close by. I went down to the nav station to check the weather report. But after fiddling with the radio for a few minutes, I left it to help Jamie with the dinghy. If this was what I thought it was, we had to get away from these reefs, and fast.

"What is it?" I said as he tossed me the painter and clambered onto the swimming platform at the stern.

"It's probably a squall. But it looks mean. It's coming from the southwest, so we'll scoot around the island and weather it from the other side." He jerked his thumb at the island. "Key Bliss."

"I know." I waved his confession aside and turned back towards the cloud that was burgeoning ever closer, blanketing the light of the sun. "What was the forecast?"

Jamie was fixing the winch davit to haul up the dinghy. He stopped and looked up at me.

"I'm sorry."

"You didn't check it?"

He went back to the winch.

"I was rushing. I forgot." He groaned. "The one damn time in my life."

"It's OK." I helped him at the winch. "Good old Murphy's law."

Even shielded by the reefs, the boat was getting difficult and securing the dinghy took valuable time. I could see the frustration on Jamie's face. He was mad at himself. He had survived countless dangerous encounters with the sea because he always planned for safety. But now he had made the biggest blunder of the lot. He had set out in a sailboat without checking the weather. But I could hardly blame him. I was fifty percent the cause. That explosive row had left us both raw and distracted.

Down below, Jamie went to the nav station. "I'll check the forecasts. We'll use the engine to get us beyond the reefs. We've got plenty of fuel. We'll cut north till we clear the island, then head east. We'll tuck in somewhere on the other side and weather it."

"What should I do?"

"Make sure everything is stowed, all the lockers fastened, nothing to fly around or fall on us if it gets rough. Zap some cans of stew and soup in the microwave and put it all in Thermos flasks. Coffee too. And check the safety locker, so you know where the medical and other survival stuff is." He stopped. Maybe the look on my face stopped him. "Hey...." He stepped over and hugged me. "It's going to take more than this blow to kick the stuffing out of us." He kissed me on the forehead, then turned back to the nav station.

"Jamie." I blurted it out so loud he turned in wonder.

"What?"

I said it silently, big lips mouthing every syllable.

He grabbed my face with both hands and kissed me hard. "I love you too, babe."

LOVERS

Nestor

<u>*Crooked Island Passage - November 2013*</u>

Jamie was in the open cockpit as a glimmer of dawn broke. Rain was lashing horizontally like a spiked whip, cutting through his heavy weather gear, its rhythm timed to a shrieking wind that built to a pitch at the top of each wave before fading to a growl in the lull of each trough. There was something merciful about those valleys, a moment of respite from the worst of wind and rain. But the tops were reality. They delivered the view. No land, no ships, just huge waves raging in a fury of white.

Except ... he strained his eyes, peering through a fog of rain and spray at the black wall rolling towards him. It was a monster, dwarfing the other waves. He wiped his eyes with the back of his hand, but it was no mirage. He swallowed, gulping on empty, mouth parched dry with fear.

A rogue wave, a freak.

Jamie lost sight of the rogue as Kiss the Sky slewed into a trough. He groped his way back to the cabin, unlatched the hatch and stumbled through it, battening it behind him. Kim was where he'd left her, tied to a bunk, her stomach retched dry, her strength gutted with dehydration and seasickness. Three days had passed since they'd scooted around the island to shelter from the squall. But a squall it wasn't. Overnight it had turned into a tropical storm, and with no safe harbor available, open waters had looked like a better bet than sheltering on a coast fringed with reefs. Besides, according to the radio, it was going to break up, and even if it didn't, it would most likely follow the usual track of Caribbean storms and head west before veering north.

Most likely.

But this was the unlikely storm, and it was soon ugly enough to have a name, Nestor, from the Greek for "traveler," a noted character in Homer's Iliad who longed to return to his homeland. For seventy-two hours, they'd worked through the A to Z of sailboat hurricane survival, fighting a losing battle against the storm and physical and mental exhaustion. But their playbook was no match for Nestor's, and the weather reports soon confirmed what the wind and seas had already told them. There was no outrunning this storm. Those forecast tracks were probabilities, not rails in the sea. Nestor was now officially a wrong-way hurricane, and they were trapped in its north wall with west winds driving them back towards the reefs of the Jumentos. Out of options, they'd lain ahull, sailorspeak for letting the boat drift at the mercy of the storm. They had not yet given up the ghost. Not quite. Not yet. But they had long ago exhausted their survival options. Nestor was a Category 5 hurricane with sustained winds over 160 miles per hour. Coastguard planes and helicopters had been grounded, and while Hurricane Hunters were flying ten thousand feet above them, even they would be wary in a storm of this magnitude. They'd considered the life raft. But the rule is—never get into it until you have to step up to it. In other words, stay in your boat until you are sure it is going under. But the life raft, and escape itself, was a vanity.

Escape to where?

Jamie stripped off his wet gear and lay next to Kim, tying their bodies together with lee cloths and ropes. He snuggled in close, her warmth charging his batteries, the feel of her feeding his spirit. Huddled like that, out of the rain, the wind and the crashing waves, it was almost possible to believe in survival.

Almost.

No need to tell her about the rogue.

At times like this, it was best not to know.

Too bad he knew, and too bad he knew too much. That monster wave was readying itself to die. It was way too high and too close to the rock shelf beneath them where shallows measured in meters fell away into an ocean a mile deep. It was hitting the edge of a fluid dynamics equation best left scribbled on a college chalkboard and surely never witnessed from a sailboat bobbing like a matchbox toy in the black pit at its feet. He held Kim tighter. Fighting Nestor had welded them back together. They were a couple again, a single, living entity. It was what he'd hoped for and here it was.

The howling wind died abruptly.

A moment of peace.

Only one explanation.

They were nestled in the lee of the rogue. Jamie braced his body, locking his arms around Kim and stiffening his sinews.

Here it comes....

The monster had to be right outside, looming above their plastic cocoon, a hundred-foot wall of water curling around them, tighter and tighter until—

The wave broke with the sound of a Bullet Train hitting the buffers. They flew off the bunk, ropes snatching them back, jerking them like puppets.

They cried out, a single voice, as the bunk slewed from under them and a groan echoed from the belly of the boat, then faded into a whoosh of air. They hit the ceiling with a thump and a gasp, taught ropes cutting into their bodies.

Darkness.

Emergency lights flickered and storm sounds faded. No commentary was needed. Gravity worked even under water. Kiss the Sky had capsized. She had rolled 180 degrees. It was time to give up the ghost. No more good calls or bad. Now it was all down to luck. Or to God. If you believed in God. And if you didn't, now was a good time to start. There was only one thing left. The end. Their prayers were all through.

No one was listening.

25 - Jamie

My arms were wrapped around her, one hand pressing her tight against me, the other holding a rope and a handful of lee cloth. Her face was buried in my chest, her steady sobs a rhythmic pulse, a counterpoint to my raging heart. I had run out of options. That was official, but as yet unannounced. All my life, in a tight spot, I had always found a way out. There had always been a tool, a weapon, a technique, a key to an escape hatch. But not here, not buried in the breast of nature's fury by a monstrous wave. This was disaster on a biblical scale, and I was neither Moses nor Noah. I had never in my life called on God. I'd talked about Him often enough, but never *to* Him. So with those blots on my copybook, there was no reason to expect Him to be waiting for my call, or to pick up on the first ring. Kim's tears were wet on my chest, her sobs begging my soul to find a way out. She'd always counted on me in a crunch and I'd always come through for her.

But not this time.

The hull creaked and moaned. There was a long ratcheting noise, sharp at first, then fading into muffled silence. Under this pressure, bolts would shear. The deck would give way and get ripped from the hull. It was only a matter of time. Water was streaming all around us. I held her tighter. Soon it would be a deluge. We would drown and had only moments to live. *Kiss the Sky* was about to join the thousands of vessels wrecked in these waters. Our names would be written in that lengthy catalog of adventurers whose ghosts constituted the human fabric of these seas every bit as much as the living souls who frequented them. I'd always believed the sea was my friend. I loved the sea and it loved me. But here I was in a wet coffin with just enough air left in my lungs to say farewell. So long as it was short. *Never turn your back on the ocean.* That old Hawaiian proverb could be my epitaph. But I had done so. I had sailed without checking the weather beyond the horizon. And I had inveigled Kim to get her on this boat with me, steering her like a master mariner, delivering her to a miserable death by drowning.

A jagged, creaking sound crept through the hull and the spring flow of water was suddenly a tide. There was a jolt, and we were thrown to the side of the cabin before falling back on the berth. The wind roared again, tearing at our faces. *Kiss the Sky* had righted herself. The concrete ballast in the keel had held and done its job. But this was no reprieve, just a stay of execution. Kim must have known that too. She wrapped her arms tighter around my neck, her face squeezed against mine.

"Forgive me," she said.

"Don't say that." My mouth was an inch from her ear, but I had to shout over the screeching wind.

"We're going to die."

"No, we're not. She's righted. We're okay."

"Forgive me. God won't. I beg you."

"Forgive you for what?" She sobbed harder, her body racked with tears. I had to get her out of this. We couldn't end our lives wallowing in regret like losers. Something crashed against the smashed porthole and blocked the storm beyond it. The decibels dropped, the wind reduced to a spine-tingling howl. "It doesn't matter now. None of it matters."

"It does." She jerked herself off me and seized my face in her hands. "It matters more now. I killed William. God will never forgive me. But you must—"

"No, you didn't. Don't do this. You're not responsible. You had a headache. You hurt yourself. You—"

"The suicide. I wanted to die. I couldn't abandon my son. So I went back for him."

"What suicide?" In the faint glow of emergency lights, her face was ash white, gray eyes buried in black pits. "What are you talking about?"

"I was afraid you'd take him away. You and Sydney. She'd have her own kid and torment William because he was mine. I had to protect him. I swam back. I got a board and paddled us both out past the reef. But I couldn't do it. I came to my senses and tried to get back to the beach. But it was too rough. I must've slipped and hit my head—"

"William?" Surely I'd misunderstood her. *She backed out of a suicide attempt to go back for our son and include him in her madness?* "You killed him?"

"I woke up on the beach. My head was all messed up."

"You lied all this time?"

"I didn't lie. I saw a man and William was gone. I didn't remember any of it. But now I can't NOT see it—*me on the paddleboard with William.*" She pulled at her hair and punched her head. "I'm going crazy." I grabbed her wrists. "This storm is God's punishment. I'm going to hell. I killed my son."

I pinned her hands to her sides and wrapped my arms around her, nausea churning my guts. *She drowned William? His own mother?* Hate coursed through me, the urge to kill her overwhelming, to hug her so tight her ribs cracked and cut into her evil heart. I squeezed tighter, locking my hands behind her back and crushing her until her wailing was cut to a desperate gasp. I was sobbing, trembling. But suddenly, I let her go, horror draining my strength. Not the horror of what she had done, but of what I was doing. *Yes, I could squeeze the last breath out of her, and it might even feel good for a moment. But what would that make me?* Death was stalking us both. In moments, we would be reunited with our son, a family again, and this prospect gifted me with the philosopher's stone. Regret, hate, guilt. That was the baggage of the living we no longer needed. She was sobbing in my arms, sniffling out the word *please* every few beats.

"Do it." She lifted her head off my chest, her face inches from mine, her eyes imploring. "Kill me. Please. You must want to. Make me suffer. Then God will forgive me. Do it."

I hooked one arm around the lee cloth to keep us steady and held her face in my hands. If my pain was unbearable, how bad was hers? Kim had once been a loving mother. Now she was soaked in the blood of her son and living in the shadow of madness. Imminent death had cracked open her fragile reality and truth had emerged. There had to be a word for that, a terrifying memory buried so deep by trauma that it ceased to exist until a new trauma brought it flooding back in Technicolor. It'd be a word from Greek or Latin, a word some doctors would know. But not this one.

"I forgive you," I said.

Her eyes widened, searching mine—

Something broke. Something big. And an almighty roar ripped into us. Kim cried out and buried her face in my neck as *Kiss the Sky* rolled on its side and we were thrown against the wall, the lee cloth and rope still tying us together. The world was closing in on me—Kim's body against mine, the water sluicing around us, our death screaming its way through the hull. It was time. Words were done. I couldn't save us. But I could redeem us. We could hold our death in contempt by relishing our life to the end, by exalting our love above it. *Kiss the Sky* lurched like a crazed hobby horse and water flooded all around us. *Seconds left, maybe not even.* I whipped her underneath me, chaining us together with one arm entangled in the ropes. I ripped at Kim's pants and our mouths locked together, her body limp with need. We had made love a thousand times. But this was the first and the last, the alpha and omega. The emergency lights flickered and dimmed. We were in total darkness now. No matter. My hand was between her thighs, my fingers spreading her wide. I drove in deep and held my belly tight against her. She gasped. Our lips fell apart and we lived one last moment of stillness, of perfect conjugal union in the midst of chaos. There was a jolt and a searing rip as fiberglass and metal were torn asunder and wind and water raged around us. My hips were thrusting, our bodies slamming together. I felt immortal, certain that death could not touch us as long as my cock blazed in her heat. Sheets of lightning traced patterns all around us, strobe-lighting her face. There was a blinding light. Kim arched her back and screamed, and her fingers ripped into the flesh on my back. I drove into her, my life resolved to a single stroke, and I let go as with an almighty roar, *Kiss the Sky* exploded and scattered in winds and waves.

26 - Kim

The day started as a dream and ended as a nightmare. I was on a lake in a rowboat with my father. I was sitting in the back of the boat, arms like two straight rods anchoring me to the seat, my hands clasped tight to its coarse-grained wood worn smooth by decades of use. I was looking up at my father, my hero, as he rowed the boat. The lake was near our home in Switzerland. I must have been six or seven years old. Switzerland has many famous lakes. But this was not one of those. Our lake was a modest affair tucked between hills in a forest. It was just big enough for the wind to break its surface, coaxing from it the gentle waves that bobbed our boat whenever my father stopped rowing to catch his breath or elaborate on one of his points. He worked for an agency in Geneva and traveled around the world training doctors in tropical medicine. He was talking about Africa that day, the land and its people, and what it was like to be a doctor there. He talked about ethics, responsibility and the preservation and protection of life. I listened with avid attention, my father looming in stature with every stroke, becoming little short of a god in my eyes. That afternoon, my life had been perfect. I'd had everything I'd wanted in that boat. I'd been complete, maybe for the first and last time in my life. I sometimes think that if I had to spend my whole life as a single afternoon, that is where I would be. With my father alone in that rowboat on the lake.

I opened my eyes and the dream ended and the

nightmare began, reality clicking into focus bit by bit—the grinding beneath me, the dark sky above, a sun somewhere, but filtered through layers of black, the lulling motion of waves. My hands explored around me and my memory raced back.

The storm. The confession. The forgiveness.

God had saved me.

Why?

Jamie was close by. Face down. Motionless.

Dead?

"Jamie." I tried to reach him, but ropes cut into the flesh of my arms. I panicked, my heart slamming my ribcage like an alien birthing.

Where are we?

Some beach, a sandbar, a reef?

It had to be a reef. The grinding below was too hard to be sand. It had to be rock. I wriggled until I could slip from under the ropes. I was still on the berth. The lee cloth and ropes had tangled with our half-on-half-off clothes and anchored us to the remains of *Kiss the Sky*. My flesh was scored with rope burns and there were bruises and scuffs all over me, but I was in surprisingly good shape. I crawled over to Jamie and felt for life at his throat.

A pulse.

But faint.

He'd taken the worst of it. He'd been on top of me when the boat had blown apart and that had saved me. I looked around, figuring out how much of a mess we were in. The storm was done. *Kiss the Sky* had broken to pieces. But we were still tied to a good-sized chunk of it, part of the hull, the berth, and some lockers. There had to be something buoyant in those lockers that had kept us afloat. We were perched on a reef and I could see land some way off. Distance across water is deceptive, but it looked to be about a thousand yards. I could swim that. I could raise the alert.

But what if it's uninhabited?

Besides, how could I leave Jamie? I had to save him. God was showing me a path of redemption. He was giving me the chance to do the right thing. Jamie was naked except for his chinos. They were still hanging off his ankles, caught on his sneakers. He had made love to me like that, with his pants around his ankles and his shoes on, like in a porno movie. His belt was still threaded through the belt loops of his pants and his jackknife was clipped to it. I pulled it out and flicked it open using the thumbhole in the blade. The edge was serrated and it sawed through the ropes around Jamie in seconds. I rolled him over and blew air into his lungs. I took a course on CPR once, but I'd forgotten all that. So I winged it, based on the recovery scene in *The Abyss,* Jamie's favorite movie. It worked and he was soon coughing up water, although he didn't regain consciousness. I stowed his private parts in his briefs and pulled up his chinos. At least I still had my husband. He had a heartbeat and his sex kit was intact. Things could have been worse. We could have both died. Or worse yet, I could have been washed up on this reef alone. My chance of survival in that case would have been zero. I would have spiraled down into the swamp and consigned my body to the waves. But now I had Jamie to take care of. Jamie needed me and his dependence was my lifeline. I couldn't let him down. I was going to have to swim it with him in tow.

But how?

I hadn't eaten for days. I was dehydrated and weak. My T-shirt had survived, but I was otherwise butt-naked. I ran my hands over my body. No serious damage. But I was wasted from the fast of seasickness. Most likely, I couldn't swim more than a few hundred yards, especially with Jamie in tow. I fastened his belt around my waist and clipped his knife to it, improvising a belt for him out of rope. Then I checked the lockers, hoping to find some food and a survival kit. But all I found was trash. Jamie was big on recycling. So he set aside empty plastic bottles and crushed them periodically to save space. I found two lockers jam packed with uncrushed empties, inadvertently turning them into improvised flotation devices. But there was no survival kit and crucially no life vests. That was a blow. Life vests have signaling devices that broadcast your location. So that was our chance of a quick rescue gone. In the third locker, I found a six-pack of water. I drank a bottle in a series of thirsty gulps.

Now Jamie.

I dribbled water into his mouth, then massaged his throat and he swallowed reflexively. Plenty of water was wasted. But that hardly mattered. I couldn't swim to shore carrying bottles of water anyway. Another locker contained canned food. I could hardly swim with that either. But there was also an unopened and still dry packet of muesli. I ate handfuls of it as I figured out what to do. Then I tied two trash bags bulging with empty plastic bottles to Jamie's rope belt, so they ballooned out on either side like black wings. I also attached the muesli in a plastic bag and stuffed a bottle of water in his pants. All I needed now was a swimmable route off the reef. With no shoes or wetsuit, I had to avoid stepping on the rocks or scraping against them at all costs. I considered borrowing Jamie's sneakers. But his size elevens were not going to cut it on my feet.

Blood.

That was on my mind too. We had cuts all over us.

Listening to Jamie over the years, I'd learned a lot about many things. Sharks was one of them. If there is a molecule of blood in the water, sharks can smell it from miles away. And storms bring sharks into coastal shallows where they scavenge dead animals that get flushed into the sea by water running off the land.

Two facts I wished I'd never learned.

I kneeled on the swaying berth and prayed. I prayed for forgiveness and I prayed for Jamie. I might not deserve to live, but surely he did. My prayer was interrupted with a jolt. Waves surged against the reef head. I looked up at a black wall of clouds stretching above a bed of white foam. I'd made a mistake. The storm wasn't done or even in recess. We were in the calm of its eye. Nestor had not yet finished his business with us. Light was fading too. I checked on Jamie one last time. He was sleeping peacefully in his swaddling of trash bags. A wave of loneliness swept over me, skin tight as a body glove.

Tears ... so let 'em come.

I smiled right through them as I took Jamie's face in my hands. This man had forgiven me for the greatest sin a woman could commit. I kissed him, grinding my lips into his.

When I broke away, waves were riding up around us, easing our fiberglass tub free of the reef. I swallowed the taste of his lips along with my fears and slid into the ocean, tears and all.

27 - Jamie

I remember sounds and sensations.
Water. Motion. Woman.
I felt her body against mine, her breasts against my back, her thighs scraping mine in rhythmic motion, her long hair flailing about my face. I heard water, close and comforting, like a splash on your face as you wash in it, and distant and dangerous, like the rumbling thunder of enormous waves detonating against gravel and rocks. In close encounters with death like this, many people claim to have had a mystical experience. But I'd already piled a Porsche into a concrete wall with no such transcendental vision, and now my sailboat had been cracked open on a reef like a farm fresh egg on the rim of some cook's frying pan. But there was still no blinding white light, and my life did not pass before me in a spiritual slideshow. My near-death experience was far simpler, yet more profound. A woman and water. More like a birth than a death.

Another chance?

I opened my eyes. I was lying on wet sand. I was in a cave with a rock wall framing Kim's face in half-light. I went to speak above the muffled roar of the wind, but I was silent, neural pathways for speaking not yet ready. Kim dribbled water on my lips. It was acrid and foul. It brought me around. I lifted my head, but a stab of pain cut that move short. I fell back limp against the sand and tumbled into darkness. Kim was sitting beside me when I came around the next time. I felt better, at least in a relative sense. The pain in my head was still there, but it was no longer a sharp axe splitting it in two. As I tried to move, Kim calmed me with a hand on my chest.

"Rest. Here..." She slipped a drop of water from a bottle into my mouth. "Not too much." I pulled myself up on my elbows and licked the wetness off my cracked lips. My tongue was swollen and furred. "Sorry about the taste." She nodded at the bottle. "The water in the rock pools is salty and I couldn't make it up the cliffs. So this is recycled the old-fashioned way." I looked at the bottle doubtfully, still stumbling my way to reality. "Actually, this is the gourmet one. I saved it for you, being as you're the patient. I only pissed it once. You should check what I'm drinking." She pointed to a bottle propped up behind her against the cave wall. "It's pure poison."

Slowly, I lifted one arm and waved toward the bottle. I didn't know how long I'd been out. But death from dehydration couldn't be far down the road. She lifted it to my lips and I gulped it down.

"Where?" My first word, my voice a rasp.

"Some cay."

"How long?"

She picked up my arm and checked my dive watch.

"We were wrecked on a reef, still tied to a bit of the boat. I'll show you. Can you move?"

I didn't know. I looked around like a helpless child.

"Here..." She helped me shunt along the floor to the mouth of the cave. Beyond patches of sand and rock, a dark sea raged, the skies above it brooding bundles of gray and black.

"You see those waves?" I followed her finger to where white tops were breaking over a reef head a mile or two offshore. "That's where we ended up. I filled some trash bags with empty plastic bottles and tied them to you. Then I swam us here." She was so matter-of-fact about it. "It was 11:30 by your watch when I kicked off. It took me six hours. That was three days ago." She tapped the watch. "Three days."

"You swam? With me?"

She nodded, looking back towards the reef as if she could hardly believe it herself. "We were washed up there in the eye. And as I swam, the other wall hit us." She kissed my forehead and peered into my eyes. "You gave me the courage. I kept asking myself. *What would Jamie do?* And I swam and I swam. And when my legs gave out, I just held onto you. I never let you go once. When the wall hit us, we lucked out. It was blowing onshore and those big old trash bags were like sails. We windsurfed the last half mile or so. But I had to carry you over the rocks at the shoreline." She pulled her feet around. They were covered in denim swaddling tied on with rope. She untied her makeshift shoes and unwound the cloth. The soles of her feet were shredded with deep wounds. "It's why I couldn't look for water. There are cliffs right along this beach and I couldn't climb them with feet like this." I looked back out to the reef, grappling with it all. My tragically flawed wife had moved heaven and earth to save us, fueled with nothing but courage and love. Tears dribbled down my cheeks. She looked at me oddly.

"Hey." She pulled my head closer. "Don't waste that water." She licked the tears from my face. "Or you'll have to drink more of my piss."

28 - Kim

In the days since we'd arrived on that beach, I'd had plenty of time to think, and at night even more time to dream. Out of kindness, I will spare you the blow-by-blow account of those. Suffice to say, with the glitch in my recall circuits fixed by Hurricane Nestor, William's night flooded my dreams with horrifying details. I'd wake from a feverish, fitful sleep, shaking and delirious, grateful that a primordial survival instinct was still censoring any image guaranteed to trigger a total meltdown. But enough gaps were filled in for me to know with certainty that I'd set out to kill myself and my son, and when I'd come to my senses, my attempt to save us both had gone wrong. That's the nice way to put it. More bluntly, I'd killed my son. I'd never recover from that. There'd be no moving on, and that reduced my life to a single question.

Can I live with what I've done?

Jamie had forgiven me, or so he'd said.

But how long does forgiveness last?

Given my track record as a failed suicide, my odds of long-term survival were not good. But for the time being, I was safe. Hunger and thirst are compelling drivers. Besides, Jamie was counting on me. I couldn't let him down.

His first day back with the living was a short one. He kept shuffling down to the mouth of the cave on his butt to peer out towards the reef and then back at me, his expression shifting through shades of awe. I stayed quietly proud, soaking up his unspoken kudos. After so much in my life had gone so wrong, I had done something right. It was a straw I could clutch at, an emblem of hope that I wasn't rotten to the core. He fell asleep around two in the afternoon. I made him comfortable and stepped outside. I wanted him to sleep as much as possible. He had to recover for us to survive. We were out of food and water. Food we could live without. But unless we found drinkable water, we'd be dead in days. I was already showing signs of dehydration, dizziness, nausea, and I was having trouble walking with an odd tingling sensation in my legs. Peeing was painful too and pitifully sparse, and what came out was the color of mud. We had to get water. But my feet were in no condition to face the rock climb up off the beach. Jamie had sneakers. He could make it up the cliff if he could only stand up and think straight. I hobbled along the beach, my clothbound feet taking careful mincing steps like some latter-day geisha. The going was hard, rocks of different shapes and sizes strewn haphazardly making progress painful and slow. My goal was the tide line, or whatever they call that part of the beach where the stuff gets washed up. We had come ashore in a cove, bound at either end by cliffs about twenty to thirty feet in height. We were on the east side of the cay, the Atlantic side, the side with the big waves. Theoretically, this was the side that should get the flotsam and jetsam. But there was precious little. Junk wood. Plastic bags and empty bottles. But then I found a tire, a truck tire by the looks of it. I pulled it upright, catching sight of water slopping around inside. I crouched and sampled it.

Fresh.

Rubbery, but fresh.

I held the tire steady with both hands, stuck my

face into its innards and lapped it up like a cat. It was my first fresh water in days and it hit me like a double espresso with a shot. After I'd licked the rubber dry, I had an idea. I flipped the tire on its side and hacked away at it with Jamie's knife. After a few false starts, I was holding two sheets of rubber the same size and shape as my feet. I unwound my foot bandages and tied the rubber under each foot. Now I had makeshift shoes. I couldn't wait to show them to Jamie. He was a master of improvisation and he'd love these. Refreshed, I resumed the search, snug in my new shoes and giddy with optimism. The storm. The shipwreck. Maybe we would survive it after all. Insurance companies call hurricanes acts of God. So maybe this was divine surgery, a heart transplant on a love affair on its last legs. We were now post-op. There were wounds to nurse, and the staples were still ripe in our chests. But those rotten old hearts were gone and the new ones were beating just fine. I strode onward, comforted by the stiff rubber between my feet and the rocks. I headed towards the bluff at the end of the beach where I could see a pile of jumble washed up in the storm. It was the strangest of things. But I started to laugh.

29 - Jamie

Force of habit.

Like most of us, moments after a new day trickles into view, scrubbing the senses clean of the tail end of a dream, I take stock. My organizing brain takes over and builds a checklist.

What day is it? Where am I? What's on?

But when you've been shipwrecked in a hurricane, rescued by your wife who'd recently confessed to drowning your son, and you are dying of dehydration, and your body aches like it was a single tormented sore, then *taking stock* can be seriously overwhelming. So I skipped it.

Water, food.

I struggled up onto my elbows, ignoring the pain scything through my head. I'd been tapering off painkillers prior to the trip, but I'd still been popping a few right up to the last. So now I was cold-turkey on pain pills with some juicy new wounds to add to the mix. But none of that mattered.

Water, food.

Kim was crouched in the half light near the cave entrance.

"Hey, Sandman. Ready for breakfast?"

She hadn't called me that in years. Her face was bright and animated. That was new too.

"What's up?"

"We're done with the Island Buffet. No more stale muesli and organic homebrew for us." She reached behind her. "Tan-ta-ta-ta." Her hands appeared in front of me, holding two cans and a bottle.

"What?"

I flicked my head at the bottle of brown liquid with its ragged, washed-out red label. I knew damn well what it looked like. But I didn't dare believe.

"Co-Ca-Co-La."

"For real?"

"It was in the locker of a smashed up skiff on the rocks at the end of the beach. And look." She showed me the cans. "Spam, baby. And pineapple." She passed me the Coke bottle. "Take it easy. I had a mouthful. It's amazing."

I swigged it, swilling it around my mouth like a vintage Bordeaux.

Coca-Cola.

The elixir of life.

Effervescence, sweetness, fruitiness, an entire laboratory of designer flavors exploding in my mouth and bubbling down my throat. I could never remember anything tasting so good. Back in the real world—or was this the real world?—I'd never have touched this stuff. I was a low-fat, low-sugar, organic type of guy. But here in our new real world, this was ambrosia. Evidently, there was nothing like a diet of piss and muesli to recalibrate your health-geek yardstick big time. One swig and I was in heaven even before those calorie-laden sugars had gotten anywhere near my bloodstream. I took another mouthful, my taste buds milking every nuance of flavor, sensation pumping through my body and my heart racing.

"One more, a little one," I begged before taking one last sip and returning the bottle. She had a long, lingering mouthful, then put it aside. I picked up the Spam, gloating in anticipation, my organic food credo a distant memory. They love Spam in Hawaii. They have it for breakfast. They even make Spam sushi. Musubi, they call it, a proud local tradition. I'd always thought that was wacko.

How wrong can a man be?

Spam made the perfect breakfast. I'd been wondering if we might catch some crabs or something. But fuck the crabs. All shell and tiny bits of stringy meat. This was what we needed. Gobs of fat. A massive jolt of calories. And protein too, although that wasn't too helpful when you were dehydrated and trying to avoid pissing. Ditto for all that salt and preservatives. I checked the pineapple. Canned in sugar syrup. More calories. And Vitamin-C as well, something to feed the dying health geek inside.

I held the cans steady as Kim hacked them open with my knife. Then we feasted, in silence mostly, taking our time, our bellies rejoicing in a symphony of sounds that had us both laughing despite all our misfortunes. We finished the Spam and pineapple completely. My reasoning was that we had to recover enough strength to get off the beach and find water and food. We had to use the calories and hydration from this feast to get us to the next place. My starving wife did not argue with my logic. She had to be even more ravenous than me. I'd slept much of the time, but she'd been awake, and her vigorous efforts to save me and keep us both alive must have taken every reserve of her strength. Despite that, she made me eat the lion's share, she, the lioness, who had bagged the game. After breakfast, we were both unexpectedly sleepy, the food hitting our stomachs like a sleeping pill and the effort of digestion taking its toll on our depleted energy stores. But we fought the temptation to rest. We had a narrow window of time now. We were fed and somewhat hydrated. We had to make a move or die on this beach. Kim stood up. "Tan-ta-ta-ta." Her trumpet call heralded more good news. She danced on the spot and pointed at her feet.

Sandals.

With all my attention on the food, I hadn't even noticed. She'd made sandals from tire rubber and strips of cloth.

"Great. We can get over the rocks."

"Sure can."

"Was there an inner tube in the tire?"

"No, just a little water. I drank that. Why?"

"Just wondering."

"There might have been one nearby. I didn't notice. I was looking for food and water."

"What other stuff did you see down there?"

"Plastic. Bits of wood. Nothing useful."

"Plastic bags?"

"Trash bags. But none of them had anything useful inside."

"What about containers?"

"Maybe. Some Tupperware. But no lids. And nothing in them. A few empty cans."

"Okay, let's go." I got to my feet—it was easier than expected—and gave Kim a hug. "My Amazon Queen." I led her out of the cave and down to the sea.

That breakfast of champions had saved our lives, but it wouldn't last forever. Our spirits were up and so was our strength, and we would need both to survive. The island was almost certainly uninhabited, and it might be days or even weeks before we were picked up.

We collected trash bags to use as carryalls, then separated to comb the beach at different levels. Within an hour, we had cherry-picked the best of what there was, and I'd even found that inner tube. By now, the storm was just a memory and the sky was clear with whiffs of white cloud. The sun was up too, marching briskly to its noon station and conspiring with the trade winds to leech our bodies dry. Kim was wearing a T-shirt and a skirt made of cloth she'd cut from my chinos. So that left me in ragged shorts and shoes. Dressed like this, we were set to fry by lunch, assuming we would have lunch. We had to find water and stay out of the heat as much as possible.

Considering the Bahamas has no mountains or hills, we had managed to get washed up on a beach cut off by substantial cliffs. In one sense, that had been a blessing. The islands are made of a limestone readily eroded by the elements and the cliffs of Lucky Beach, as we had named it, were studded with caves. Kim had picked the biggest as our sanctuary. But the cliff that had protected us was now holding us prisoner. Our best shot at getting off the beach was a place where overhanging rocks had collapsed into a scree of boulders and stones. It was steep but climbable. At least I thought so, but Kim was in trouble from the start. Her sandals were a masterpiece of improvisation and they'd worked well on the flat beach. But on wobbly rocks, their stiff rubber soles kept slipping, and halfway up, she stumbled and gouged a chunk of flesh from her foot. I helped her back on her feet and gave her a broken paddle I'd found earlier to use as a staff. I could see the pain on her face. But she never said a word of complaint. She never did. She never whined or complained once on that island. I admired her for that.

30 - Kim

After I fell, every step up that cliff was brutal. When I finally hobbled up to the top, I wanted to collapse on my knees and thank God. But instead I leaned on Jamie, draping an arm across his shoulders and easing the injured foot off the ground for temporary relief, while he stood stock still, eyes sweeping back and forth.

"You know something?" Jamie brought me out of my pain trance. "We're back where we started." I looked around. We were on a narrow spit of land that cut off to the south and tapered wider as it fed off to the north. "Ragamoffyn Island. This is Key Bliss. I'm sure of it. That afternoon, we were moored up there." He pointed up the coast on the west side. I remembered him tying the dinghy to a broken-down jetty, but I couldn't see it from where we were standing.

"Did you get to that big house?"

"I was heading there when I saw the weather turn, so I raced back to the boat. But I checked out the settlement around the jetty. There are sheds, workshops, simple homes. It was a village for the staff, housekeepers, gardeners, maintenance guys."

"Can we find shelter there?"

"Sure." Jamie was looking out over the Atlantic Ocean. "Nestor took us in a big circle." He pointed east over the waters of the Crooked Island Passage, their uniform deep blue contrasting with the kaleidoscopic blues and greens to the west, where the reef-laden shallows of the Bahama Banks stretched for miles. "Let's go." Jamie slipped his arm around my waist. But I shrugged it off.

"I'm okay."

"Sure?"

"Totally."

So we set off, two bag people, homeless and unwashed, making our way along an overgrown and broken trail that hadn't been walked in years. Jamie led the way with me tracking him step by step as the path weaved its way through straggly trees and scrub, all of it sinewy and tough, inured to storms.

"You think we can eat any of this stuff?" I was thinking out loud.

"Not really. The native flora is real bush tucker. But I saw fruit trees in the village. Planted stuff. Bananas. Coconuts. Maybe there's some more up by the house. And we can get seafood and fish. We just need to improvise some kit. I saw some bits and pieces in the village. Stuff we can use. Don't forget, the last residents checked out in a hurry." He stopped and turned back to me. "And they didn't need to pack."

Jamie's shot at humor hit me with a jolt. I'd all but forgotten about the hippie cult. Murder, suicide, human sacrifice. I looked around, the sunlit scrub shading darker.

"Is that where they did it, the village?"

"No idea. Rolle never told me."

The spit was widening and the trail hit a high point, rocky and exposed with sparse vegetation. We stopped to take in the view. The land swept out on both sides ahead of us, wooded for the most part. But it wasn't uniform. In places, there were low bushes with scraps of parched rock showing through, in others, stands of trees. Jamie pointed towards the west side of the island.

"You can see the jetty and those rundown huts."

Rundown or not, having a roof over our heads while playing *Robinson Crusoe* would be a major upgrade from the cave, and the prospect took my mind off the nagging ache in my foot.

We named the village Salvation.

What else?

It had been cultivated with a variety of imported trees. They were all taller and more luxuriant than the local bush, but a lot less hurricane proof, and Nestor had inflicted severe damage with most of them broken or bowed. The shacks had taken a pounding too, although I couldn't say what damage was new.

Jamie stopped to survey it. "What a mess. But at least we won't have to climb trees to pick fruit."

Nor did we.

All we had to do was forage and in minutes we were eating bananas picked straight off the ground. The coconuts were just as easily found too, and after shaking a few and finding one full of water, Jamie went to work on it with his jackknife. It took forever, but the sweet juice was worth the wait. We sat in the shade of a broken tree and drank it.

When we were cool and rested, I said, "So what's our plan?"

"We need to separate. So let's make this spot our meet and greet."

"Agreed."

"You've got two jobs. The first is gathering. Number one is coconuts. Look out for brown ones. Bananas, of course, and other fruits too, limes, mangoes. Check for vegetables. Some of the stuff they planted probably died out without irrigation. But others will have adapted. Sweet potato and cassava. Peppers, tomatoes. Garlic and onions. Keep your eyes open. It's been a Darwinian laboratory for forty-odd years. Who knows what survived?"

"And the second job?"

"Find us a house and make it habitable. Look in all of them, then make your choice. They're all in a state. So you'll have to clean one up. Look for a broom. Or make one."

"Make one?"

"Hey, Sandals Girl, you can figure something out. And if you can't get a broom together, at least get a stick."

"What for?"

"Poking." He waited a beat, his eyes checking me out. "And whacking."

"Oh, great. There're no snakes, are there?"

"I wouldn't think so. Nothing to worry about. But these buildings have been empty for decades. Nature always fills a vacuum. Spiders. Scorpions. Just be careful. Don't stick your hand into anything. Poke it first with a stick."

"Can't I use this?" I held up the staff he'd given me.

"Sorry, I'm going to need that. I picked it especially. And I'm going to need the knife too. But you can keep the belt. It looks better on you anyway."

"What are you going to do?"

"I'm going to make a solar still to get us some drinking water."

"Isn't there a pond on this island?"

"It'll be salty. After all this heavy rain, maybe it's drinkable, but we'd need to boil it even then. We might be the only humans on the island, but we sure as hell are not the only mammals. There could be goats here, maybe pigs, and certainly rats. They all shit. Then the rain washes it into the pond. You're talking about parasites and bacteria. If the water is fresh enough to drink, those guys survive. If it's salty enough to kill them, then we can't drink it. In our condition, a gut infection could kill us. So forget about the pond."

"What about a well?"

"First, we'd have to find it, and then we'd have to see if it was working and not contaminated. A solar still is guaranteed pure water and I can get it together in a few hours. Then I'm going to figure out how to catch us some fish. That's why I need this stick." He held up the broken paddle handle and surveyed it. "I'm going to make a polespear."

So that was it.

The who-does-what debate was done and dusted. It was democratic in its way. We were each doing what we could do. Even though Jamie had made all the decisions like an imperial monarch. But I had no complaints. We were up against it. And when civilization was whipped from under your feet, and you realized how helpless you were, with fewer survival skills than a bug, then you were mighty glad you had an overgrown boy scout like Dr. Jamie Steiger on the team. Nonetheless, I couldn't help but notice that I, the woman, ended up with the shit jobs. Jamie got to build the solar still. He loved building things. He would have done that for fun. Then he'd go fishing. *What a pleasant way to spend the afternoon.* In contrast, I got to poke around dark holes infested with bugs and clean out decades of shit.

"Great." I swallowed my pride with blithe indifference, wondering where I might find a big stick. We hugged each other ritually, and I headed off towards a likely-looking clump of broken palms.

"Say, Jamie." I turned back towards him. He stopped rummaging through his trash-bag and looked up. "Are you sure they cleaned it all up? The bones and stuff. The dead hippies. Do you think they could have missed anything?"

"I'm sure they did. I didn't see any traces of them at all. I thought there'd be something—weird symbols, graffiti. But I didn't see anything. It's like the hippies were never here. I guess the Realtors cleaned that stuff up. They're trying to sell the place after all. So don't worry about the dead. Just watch out for those spiders. They're sons of bitches."

I nodded, comforted. I'd forgotten Jamie had already made the tour. If there'd been anything, he would surely have seen it. He turned his attention back to his work and I looked beyond him through the broken trees. The beach was pink in the late morning sun and the shallow seas were alive with shifting patterns of blue and green. It was a scene screaming for a camera, picture postcard perfect, and soundtracked by lush, silky waves. "How could they do something like that"—my thoughts came bubbling out—"in a place like this?"

Jamie stood up and looked around.

"Drugs, I guess. Some psychological..." He trailed off, shrugging his shoulders. "I don't know." He dropped his eyes back to his trash bag, but not before I saw a dark, sour look strip the life from his face.

"Crazy, you mean?" I nearly added *like your wife*. But thank God, I kept my mouth shut.

"I guess so." He looked back at me, pulling himself together behind a forlorn smile. "But if you see any demonic images scrawled on a building, then pick another one for us. Let sleeping ghosts lie, eh?"

"You got it."

I headed towards the broken cluster of trees.

Sleeping ghosts.

It was funny he'd said that. Jamie was the last

person to believe in ghosts. He was the world's most famous tomb raider, unafraid of anything, living or dead. At least, that was the old Jamie. So this was the new one. Not so bold, more wary. It was only to be expected. He'd gotten a news update concerning his wife—*she killed your son.*

Sleeping ghosts. I'm an expert on those and Jamie is right.

Better let them lie.

31 - Jamie

I watched Kim as she set about her tasks, taking timorous steps on her injured foot as if scanning for land mines. Her comment about the killings was unnerving me. But I had no time for negative thinking and no energy either. On a desert island, survival is a full-time job, and I had to get to work. Theoretically, we could live off bananas and coconuts, but I had no intention of doing so. These waters were as bountiful as they were beautiful. All I had to do was harvest their protein and oil-rich fish and seafood and we would be on the road to recovery. I walked down the jetty. It was concrete over the sand, giving way to rickety planks on wobbly wooden piles as it stretched out over the sea. I stayed on the concrete, crouching on my heels and getting to work. I didn't sit down because the concrete was egg-fry hot. That was the point of the location. A solar still is all about simple physics, evaporation and condensation, processes fueled by heat. I filled a plastic container with seawater and put it in an old wash bowl. Then I covered the bowl with a tent made from a trash bag. In direct sunlight on blistering concrete, the temperature inside the tent would soar. The seawater in the container would evaporate and saturate the limited air in the tent. Then fresh water would condense on the inside of the trash bag and trickle down into the washbowl.

Job done, I walked off the jetty, sat in the shade of a tree and prepared the inner tube and staff to make a polespear. That's basically a spear with a big rubber band attached to it. I whittled the plastic staff into a jagged point, rigged it with rubber from the inner tube, and tested it on a patch of sand. It worked like a charm. So I made my way along the jetty and out over the sea. It was a few feet above the water, a perfect fishing platform. I was halfway to the end, my eyes scanning for fish on either side, when my foot disappeared through the wood. I pitched forward, tossing the polespear aside, my body hammering onto the deck. Pain shot through me and I cursed. Thank God I'd had the sense to throw the spear clear, avoiding a potential tragedy. I could just see Kim finding her husband sitting in a pool of blood with a spear up his ass. I dragged my leg out from between the splintered, rotten planks. My shinbone was stripped of skin and humming with pain, but there was no serious damage. I splashed water onto the wound, then stood up, wincing and moaning, and continued along the jetty, testing every step with exaggerated care.

I was at the end of the jetty when a stingray cruised out from underneath my feet. I jerked up the spear. But the ray was gone before I could even load it. Stingray was not ideal eating and not what I had in mind. But stranded and starving, it looked like a great catch to me. I watched it disappear, dissolving into the seascape in a blur of chiaroscuro, its wings beating as gracefully as a ballerina's arms. I had an idea that inshore rays like that fed at night, so I'd probably disturbed this one when I fell. The noise of me crashing through the jetty had no doubt shooed away other likely targets for my crude spear too. So I tied a sack around my waist and swam out over the reef, where I soon learned that this fishing business was going to be a lot tougher than I'd imagined. In my mind, the guy fishing was the athlete I'd been five years before. But that guy was long gone. Back in the day, I could hold my breath for three to five minutes of diving. Now I could barely make it to one and even then my lungs were bursting. I tried to relax more, running a program in my head to slow down my heart underwater. I was still working on the technique, swimming down by a ledge in the coral when a lobster walked out right under my spear. It was a clumsy mess from start to finish, but lobster versus starving man was only ever going to end up one way, and after a battle fit for a Jules Verne novel, I had him bundled in the sack. Exhausted, I swam back to the beach and heaved my catch up onto the jetty. I checked my watch. It was time to siphon off the fresh water and recharge the solar still while there was enough sunlight left to get another load. We would soon be drinking pure water and dining on fresh seafood. I looked back towards the shore. No sign of Kim. Hopefully, she'd found us a place.

I rested like that, looking around, catching my breath. I thought about how beautiful it all was—innocent enough as thoughts go—but it hooked me into something else. And moments later, I was back at *Paradise Found,* playing in the pool with William. I hadn't meant to go there. But it was such a short hop I'd made it inadvertently. The stepping stone had been Kim's comment—*how could anyone kill somebody in a place like this?* My legs buckled as the replay hit me in 3D, William abandoned by his mother in a dark, empty ocean. I slewed against the jetty and retched up the breakfast of champions. Then I stood motionless, watching the cola-colored cloud of Spam, pineapple and bananas wash back and forth in the pristine waters. I'd forgiven Kim. But that had been in the belly of a doomed sailboat when I'd been convinced that we were going to die.

How much harder is this going to get?

I pulled myself together. Kim wasn't a murderer. She'd had a breakdown. It wasn't a murder-suicide. It was a double-suicide. But why take William? That was the part I couldn't figure. *Her fears about Sydney and me*? I dismissed all that. There had to be more. Something must have gone wrong in her head, and not for the first time. I wasn't a doctor—at least, not that kind of doctor—but I didn't need a medical degree to figure that out. She needed help. But how workable was that? Where did US law stand on a mother-child, double suicide? I wasn't a lawyer either, but my guess was on the side of the child. Could she be arrested? I had no idea. But she'd never survive if she was—I knew that—and neither would *we.*

Switzerland.

It popped into my head. The perfect solution. She'd been born there. They had great doctors too. A plan emerged. I had to convince her. It was not going to be easy. We hadn't mentioned William since her confession on *Kiss the Sky*. I'd need to be patient and bide my time. I headed towards the beach, hope building step by step. I'd found a way out of this. If only we could survive Key Bliss.

32 - Kim

I stood in the middle of Salvation, turning around on the spot, taking it all in—stonewall shacks in billowing green, white walls, red roofs riddled with holes, boarded-up windows, and doors hanging off or lying on the ground bedded in grass and weeds.

Emptiness.

The sound of wind and waves brought it home to me, natural sounds stretching a canvas where the absence of human sounds was so obvious. Children playing, old men laughing as they mended nets, women gossiping as they went about their work. It felt as real as if I was seeing and hearing it. People had lived here. Everyday people. Before Raymond and his freaks. Normal people who had built these huts and lived and loved in them. The Bliss family must have had a legion of staff to take care of them and their visitors. Marlene Dietrich, David Niven, Ernest Hemingway. This village must have buzzed with rumors and gossip as the celebrities flew in and out. I wondered if any of them had come down here to the village. Papa Hemingway was a famous fisherman, so surely he had. He would have set out in his boat from that jetty, then puffed a cigar with the locals before heading back to the big house to party. Then all that changed. The good life ended. Innocence fled.

Human sacrifice.

Beating hearts and blood-soaked bellies, living victims, their eyes blank with horror, I had to forget all that. *Keep busy.* I had to work. I was the forager, the gatherer, as well as the bug killer of course. Jamie was the hunter and builder. I could see him in snatches as the wind rustled through the foliage down by the beach. He was crouched on the jetty, fiddling with bits of plastic. I left him to his work and got on with mine.

In the battle between Nestor and the coconut palms, Nestor had won handily and the village was strewn with their fruit. I gathered up nine ripe coconuts. I was desperate with thirst already and the slosh of refreshing water inside was driving me crazy. But since Jamie had the knife, there was no way I could get into the darn things. So I continued foraging, clambering over broken banana trees and finding a bunch so huge I could barely lift it. I was struggling to pick it up when a spider the size of a rat dropped out onto my foot, its hairy legs brushing my ankles as it scurried off. I dropped the bananas and screeched, Jamie's advice echoing back to me.

Get a stick!

A row of workshops ran parallel to the beach. Behind them were two larger buildings and between them was a shed. The first hut I explored had double doors like a garage or a warehouse. The windows were shuttered, but there was enough light coming through the doorway for me to make out the wreck of a truck parked in the corner, although *parked* is rather a fancy word for a truck with only two wheels. The back was fine, but the front end was wrecked, jacked up for a repair still pending after decades. It was such a bizarre find on a desert island that I stared at it in disbelief.

A truck?

That meant tools.

I searched the cab first, but no luck. No potential whacking sticks. I went down on my hands and knees and peered under its rusting chassis, finding a prybar and a dirty rag. I squeezed under the truck and grabbed the prybar, then shunted back out. It was a roughneck bar coated in black paint with a hook at one end. I hefted it. It was too short to make a good whacking stick. But it would simplify breaking and entering. And holding it, I felt a lot better. You need to be castaway naked on a desert island to realize how helpless we human beings are. We don't even have decent teeth or claws. I tested my new tool by flipping over a tarpaulin in back of the truck where I found a screwdriver. I reached over to grab it. But as I leaned against the truck, it crashed to the ground. I staggered back, nursing my bruised ribs. The jack had given way. The front of the truck was now on the floor. I stared at the spot where the engine block rested on the concrete.

That's exactly where I was.

How stupid was I?

I'd crawled under a truck that had been jacked up before I was born. I couldn't get the image out of my head, the squashed bug one, where my legs were poking out from under the engine and still wriggling. Even with the weight of the pry bar to steady them, my hands trembled. If that haunted truck was sending me a message, then I was reading it loud and clear. Call me superstitious, but maybe there was a reason this place got its name. Ragamoffyn was a character in *Piers the Plowman*. He was Satan in disguise. And let's face it, when it came to misfortune, this island rated it. Case in point. Poor old Charles. He'd had Nazi pilots shooting at him for years and he'd never picked up a scratch. But back on his own island, he'd slipped on one too many gin and tonics and kissed it all farewell, a tragedy followed by the disappearance of Ginny's paramour and Raymond's horror show.

I moved on to the next hut, where my trusty pry bar made short work of its locked doors. It turned out to be a boathouse. Unfortunately, there were no boats in it. At least none that were serviceable. There was a wooden dinghy hanging on the wall that got me excited until I noticed the yard-long gash in its hull. There was some fishing kit too. No rods or spear guns, just a bundle of knotted line with a few hooks in it and some broken lures. I moved on to a bigger building with double doors and shutters. It was the most house-like of all the buildings. The doors were closed and jammed in place by thick grass that I cleared away with my pry bar before peeking in gingerly.

No voodoo dolls. No incense jars hewed from human skulls. Just some sort of abandoned living accommodation. In fact, it was rather homely with built-in cupboards, a large table, and what looked like a propane grill or stove. There were a few rickety wooden chairs too, a couch and even a dart board hanging lopsidedly on the wall. It must have been a mess hall, a room for cooking, eating, drinking and hanging out. I explored further, finding a corridor with rooms partitioned off by head-height walls and hanging-bead doorways. Some rooms still had beds in, and one even had a threadbare mattress.

Our new home.

I went back to the mess hall to check the cupboards and drawers and I soon had a collection of damaged kitchenware. Essentially, it was trash, bent cutlery, cracked or chipped porcelain, pots and pans too old to ship out or too worthless to steal. But from the ground zero viewpoint, it was all useful stuff. Today, Jamie and I would take that first crucial step up the evolutionary ladder. Henceforth, we would be users of tools, not animals scratching our way with our fingernails. I continued my search, hitting pay dirt in a tall cupboard. A brush, several in fact. Beaten to death, their bristles worn to stubs, but functional. There was even a bin in the corner still piled with trash. I looked for a place to dump it. I checked a nearby shed, discovering that it was a toilet under construction with a disconnected toilet bowl filled with debris. I emptied the bin on top of it and there was a tinkle of breaking glass as a picture frame skittered off the pile and onto the floor. I picked it up and took out the photo. I was hungry, thirsty and tired, but also curious. It was a black-and-white shot faded through sepia, a man and a woman holding the hand of a young boy. They were standing by the pool of a splendid house. They were white, the man in shorts, a sports shirt and sandals, and the woman in a floral-print dress. Next to her was a black woman, shorter, older, heavier. Everyone was smiling. I checked the back. The inscription was written in an elegant script, redolent of the days when handwriting was still an art. *Charles, Virginia and Raymond Bliss with our beloved Charlene at Four Winds, Christmas 1952.*

I couldn't take my eyes off Raymond. He looked about the same age as William, a happy little boy. I walked back to the mess hall, forgetting the trash bin but remembering the photo. I sat at the table, studying its faces. Then I flipped it over and read the inscription again, my eyes watering up, watching as my silent tears transformed it into a billowing black cloud of smudged ink.

33 - Jamie

Survival—it turned out—was the biggest high of all. And exhausted and edgy as we were, that first night in Salvation, we laughed like clowns as we organized our feast. We dined on lobster and conch sashimi drizzled with fresh lime juice, followed by a banana and coconut compote. We washed it down with a 2013 coconut juice, finding it well-rounded with a pleasing after taste, and accompanied it with freshly distilled desert-island water. Or at least, that was how we billed it.

Kim had cleaned up some cutlery and kitchenware and we had chairs to sit on and a table to eat off. I had squeezed two full pints of water out of my makeshift still and Kim had laid on a pile of coconuts, so we had plenty to drink. Our battered and beaten bodies were finally nourished and rehydrated. This was the tipping point and we both knew it. We had food, drink, and shelter. Our survival was assured. All we needed now was rescue and that was surely only days away.

When we got to eating, we toned it down. That was serious business, and we conducted it in a silence interrupted only by grunts of satisfaction. When we were done, we cleared up and settled down in the bedroom I'd made ready, sitting on the bed with our backs against the wall, looking at the bare wall opposite in fading light. It was decorated with rectangular stains, marking the picture frames that had once hung there.

"How long will it be before they find us?" Kim was

echoing a question that had been running through my mind all day.

"Anywhere from a day to three or four weeks."

"Four weeks? This is not the seventeenth century. America's just up the road."

"Think about it. Who's going to find us? A cruiser? In the usual way of things, there might be a dozen or more sailboats down here around this time. One or two might check out Key Bliss. But the problem is—"

"Nestor kissed off the usual way of things."

"Exactly. The islands must be wrecked. No one is going to be sailing down here anytime soon."

"So that leaves the locals."

"Fishermen have to fish."

"Didn't Rolle tell you they avoided this island?"

"Yeah, the *cursed island* syndrome. But I don't believe that crap and I don't expect they do either."

"What about that MAYDAY you sent?"

"Coastguard planes were grounded by then. They will have flown around after the storm to survey the damage and look for survivors. But that'll all be called off by now. And why would anyone expect us to be washed up here? Let's face it. The ink's dry on our obituaries already. We're risen from the dead. People don't plan on resurrections."

"So it's down to chance."

"A boat might turn up tomorrow. Or it may be a few weeks. But we might miss it when it comes. We have to take care of ourselves. We can't sit by a signaling fire all day like they do in the castaway books."

"It's like that reality TV show where they get stranded on a tropical island."

"Except we don't have medics available."

"And we can't holler *get me out of here* when

we're fed-up with it."

"Reality TV is not a bad idea, though. We could re-enact this after we're rescued. Some of it anyway. Without the fights. A redacted version."

"With or without the death fuck in the hurricane?" She poked her elbow in my ribs. "Serious ratings there, pal."

"You bet. We could buy a new boat with the proceeds."

"You're pulling my leg. I never want to see another sailboat as long as I live, unless it's a rescue boat turning up to get us out of here." There was silence for a bit. I had no trouble seeing myself in a new sailboat. But now was obviously not the time to get into that. "What was it you called it—*a boat with real karma?*" She laughed. "*Kiss the Sky ... Kiss my Ass*, more likely."

That had me laughing too. I squeezed close and whispered in her ear. "I'd love to oblige you, darling. But I've got this terrible headache."

She chuckled and we held hands in silence, enjoying the moment.

"Hey." Kim hopped off the bed. "I forgot." She disappeared, returning with a bundle of paper in her hands.

"I found this." She pulled out a photo faded with age and gave it to me. "*Four Winds*. The Bliss house. I guess Charlene was their housekeeper."

I studied the photo and the smudged inscription on the back.

"She was Raymond's nanny."

"How do you know that?"

"Rolle looked up some locals who'd worked here back then. The ones that were still around. He talked to this woman's daughter. But all he got was background stuff. What a smart kid Raymond was.

He used to draw stuff, and he could play anything by ear on the piano after hearing it just once.”

She unfolded some crumpled sheets of paper.

“These, I guess. I found them dumped in that half-built John next-door.” They were pencil drawings, beautifully done. Island scenes. Landscapes. People. “They must have been up on the walls here.” She nodded at the stains on the wall.

“He was gifted, but weird. He used to talk to imaginary friends.”

“Lots of kids do that.”

“Not all day. He was like that kid in *The Shining*. Anyway, Charlene and the rest of them, they all quit when Raymond was still a kid.”

“Why did they quit?”

“I don’t know. Charles was dead. Ginny was an alcoholic, shacked up with some sleazy boyfriend. One day, he just disappeared. Then she shipped Raymond off to school in England, and the rest is”— I waved both hands—“the living history we’re sitting in.”

I gave her back her treasure trove of Bliss memorabilia and stretched out on the bed. She tucked the papers under the mattress and stretched out next to me as the last of the light faded.

The next morning we started early, as early as the sun, whose rhythm we were bound to follow like all primitive people must. I set up my still while Kim prepared some fruit. Then we gathered around our table. It was a simple breakfast and assembling at the table was a simple act. But it was profoundly satisfying as it blessed the start of our first day in Salvation with an orderliness that buoyed us both. *Routine* is a word with a bad reputation, laden with the baggage of humdrum. But now, here it was, sitting with us at the table wearing a new set of clothes, enticing and desirable. We had survived weeks of chaos, of terror. And to us, the distant beat of humdrum was the melody of a life we had taken for granted, that we had lost and now dearly missed. We ached for refuge, for the peace and comfort of routine. We needed no new plans, promises, or goals. We needed the succor of same. We needed to wake in the morning in the same bed under the same roof, in anticipation of the same breakfast at the same time. Our new god was orderliness, and this first morning in Salvation, he made himself known to us in the silence of daybreak as we sat at the crude wooden table and munched our bananas and coconuts.

We set to work afterwards, our agenda succinct.

Recover.

That meant drink, eat, sleep. Rescue would have to wait its turn, or else drop from that clear blue sky. Our waking hours were fully booked. My battle with the lobster had ended in victory, but that had been more by luck than judgment. So I was planning to try hooks and lines. With that in mind, Kim worked on the tangled ball of fishing line she'd found in the boatshed while I did the groundwork on starting a fire. In the Bahamas, a fire was hardly an essential. But I was damned if I was going to eat raw fish forever. I might be fond of sashimi, but not on a mandatory basis. We also needed the option of boiling water to purify it and to cook certain vegetables and fruits to make them edible. Beyond that, fire was civilization, controlling it was mankind's first badge of rank as master of all he surveyed, and if anyone ever needed a hearth to comfort them, it was the bruised and battered Steigers.

I foraged in the brush, gathering up my fire-starter kit. Then I built the barbecue outside our new home using bricks from damaged huts and abandoned building projects. By the time I was done, Kim had untangled an impressive length of fishing line and sorted through a collection of broken rods, hooks, lures and sinkers. I assembled these into a makeshift fishing rig. Then I left her to forage for food and made my way down to the beach, tiptoeing along the jetty with inordinate respect for the rotten wood at my feet.

As a fisherman, I was an amateur. So what was out there and what it would take to catch it were mysteries I could only solve by trial and error. But after plenty of both had yielded nothing, I was wondering if the polespear might not be the better option after all when I pulled out a small crab. Not much to eat. Not for me, at least. But maybe a tasty snack for a fish. So I threaded the hook through the corner of the shell, cast it out on the reef and caught a fish within minutes. It was big, eighteen inches at least. I think it was a permit. But whatever it was, it was unceremoniously whacked on the head, then dumped in a bucket of salt water and hurried out of the sun. I gave Kim my catch and left her bug-eyed at the kitchen table while I set to work on the fire. I hear tell that you can start a fire by rubbing two sticks together.

Good luck with that.

My approach was more technical, using objects found around the village. I bent a branch and made a bow by stringing it with a length of twine. Then I scraped the start of a hole in a plank and cut a notch next to it. I jammed the plank under my foot, stuck the end of a dowel rod into the hole and looped the bow string around it. I checked back through the doorway. Kim was busy cleaning the fish. Too bad. A show like this deserved an audience. But off I went without one, sawing the bow back and forth and spinning the rod in the starter hole. After a minute or two, smoke spiraled as the hardwood drill burned its way into the softwood plank. I snatched it up and blew on it, then tapped out a glowing sliver of wood between the notch and the hole.

That was my tiny coal.

I grabbed a bundle of dry grass, dropped the coal into it and blew on it gently. Smoke billowed. And as it burst into flames, I tossed it under the grill and reached for the kindling, catching sight of Kim in the doorway. She was watching me, slouched against the doorpost, arms crossed, nodding slowly, a smile curling her lips.

34 - Kim

We pigged out on Jamie's fish, our first hot food in weeks. We were so full afterwards that we had to walk it off, wending our way along the beach, hand in hand, with murmuring waves brushing our feet before fading into a lush backwash. A half moon lit the darkening sky and a cooling onshore breeze allayed the day's heat. Salvation Beach was not the typical eye candy showcased on travel web sites. No uniform pink sand stretching for miles here. This beach was the garden variety, bits of this and bits of that. Sand interspersed with sheets of rock, and here and there, the dark hues of coral. When we had walked enough, we picked a patch of sand and settled down to watch the day give way to the night in rippling patterns of moonlight on the water.

"Galician beef." The silence was over. Jamie's thinking had finally found his tongue, and it was still preoccupied with food despite our feast. "Like those ribs we had one time in Madrid—*à la plancha*."

"I can live with that." This was a running conversation we dipped into from time to time, tweaking the menu on each visit. *Our dream dinner when we get out of jail.* "With a sturdy Ribera del Duero, perhaps."

"That'll work. But we'll skip the seafood tapas. Okay?"

"Deal. I think we're done with the seafood and fish menu for a while."

"And then the red fruit *pasteleria*, the one with that fluffy cheesecake layer between the chocolate and the red fruits."

"And we'll eat it until we're sick."

"Amen."

He shuffled his hand around in the sand, pulled out a stone and flung it out to sea. The day was almost gone now, with early stars faint in the light of the moon. I rocked back onto the sand and looked up at the sky.

"That house in the photo. *Four Winds*. It looked incredible back then," I said.

"Sure. But did I show you the shots I got from the Realtor? How it looks now?"

"Yeah, spooky, and totally wrecked."

"And that was before *Nestor*."

"But we should still go up there and take a look."

"Sure. When we're rested."

"Do you think it could be haunted?"

"The house?"

"The whole island."

"I think people are haunted. Not places. This is just a beautiful island where bad things happened."

"But one happened to me yesterday too. I was nearly killed."

"How?"

"In the garage. That truck crashed off the jack, right where I was under it seconds before."

"I told you to be careful." I accepted the rebuke. It was merited. Crawling under a jacked-up truck had been reckless and stupid. Nonetheless, getting a ticking-off from Mr. All-Thumbs was hardly appropriate. Jamie was the maestro of maladroit, and I couldn't help but notice he was wearing a lot less skin on his shin than he had been when we'd walked into the village. But I let it go.

"What about Charles Bliss? And Raymond's freaks? And Ginny's boyfriend?"

"Charles just ran out of luck. He'd always pushed it his whole life. As for her lover, he probably got tired of shacking up with an old lady and lit out on some passing fishing boat."

"I think places can be haunted. They absorb bad stuff, then feed it back to new arrivals. Didn't the Aztecs believe that? That's what you told me."

"That's college textbook stuff. Nobody knows. I was trying to impress you ... let you know I wasn't just a pretty face and a big dick." He nudged me with his elbow, but I ducked his blundering pass.

"What did they believe exactly?"

It took him a beat to drag his mind out of his pants and get back into the conversation.

"That time and space shape each other. Time is the mirror in which objects appear. Objects are clocks. They record time and store it like batteries."

"Like Amazing Eric and my multitool."

"Who?"

"Nobody. Nothing."

We were quiet for a while. There was something else I wanted to talk about too, something that was troubling me a lot more than the island's ghosts.

"Where are we going to go when we get off this island?" I'd been wondering about it all day. It hadn't occurred to me when we were fighting to survive. But now our survival was no longer moot, the question of *after this* loomed large and ominous. Our existence as castaways was fragile. But our Robinson Crusoe status was no threat to our relationship. On the contrary, it sustained it. The new Steigers, the reborn Steigers, had been birthed in a shipwreck. Nestor was our midwife, our marriage counselor and therapist. He had worked us through our differences, laundered our dirty linen and minted our love fresh.

Or had he?

I was flipping between two schools of thought, one romantic, one cynical. The romantic view was that what had happened to us on *Kiss the Sky* was cathartic. Face to face with our death, a thousand veils had fallen aside to reveal multiple truths. That we loved each other, despite everything, had been one of them. The cynical view was that Jamie was a man biding his time. Key Bliss was a penitentiary and so long as he was locked up here, he needed me to survive. Our love was safe here. But what would become of it back in the other world?

"I have an idea about that." There was something strange about the way he said it, the casual tone and circumspect phrasing. Jamie didn't normally do circumspect. "How about we try a new place and get a fresh start?"

"Like where?"

"How about Switzerland?"

"Seriously? Have you looked at a map lately? Switzerland? You'd get a nosebleed that far from the sea."

"Not necessarily. I'm out of the business now. I thought I might teach."

I tucked my hands under my head like a pillow and gazed at the stars, tracing their patterns and shapes. Maybe it wasn't such a bad idea. But it was odd to think of Jamie in the land of mountains and lakes.

"Is that the Southern Cross?" I pointed to a likely-looking cluster of bright stars.

"Wrong sky. That was Mauritius."

"Remember the song, the Crosby, Stills one? It's been going through my head lately. But I can't remember the lyrics—"

"You're not expecting a serenade. I hope."

"… just a few words."

"Why did you think about that? It's really sad. All that stuff about *dreams dying*."

"All these stars, I guess. The imagery seemed to fit … the metaphors … like love being an anchor tied with a silver chain."

"Hold on. I'll whip out my phone and Google the lyrics for you."

I groaned. "Don't you miss that?"

"Fifty times a day—"

"*Can you eat plant x? How do you blankety-blank*? I take back all the bad things I ever said about Google." We were quiet for a while after that, and some of me wanted it to stay that way. But I couldn't let the moment pass without hearing him say it. "*Coming day,* yeah, that was the line in the song. That's what made me think of it. So what about our coming day?" I propped myself up on one elbow and I turned his head towards me. I needed to see his eyes when I heard his mouth. They had to be in sync. "When we get off this island, you won't leave me, will you?"

"Of course not."

"Because of what I told you in the storm. Not after everything we've been through."

He pulled me into his arms and kissed me. But that wasn't the answer I wanted. I slid my lips off his and pressed them against his ear.

"Say it. You'll never leave me. Say it."

"I'll never leave you. I swear it."

So that was it. Commitment. The wrong constellation of stars and a half-forgotten love song had wrung it out of him. My lullaby on the beach. I held him tight, his warmth oozing through my body and floating me off to sleep.

I woke with the sun. Jamie was still asleep, in his medieval sepulcher pose, his hands folded on his tummy. I stripped off and walked into the sea, its ebb and flow swirling around my thighs. The ocean that had threatened us, beaten us to death and resurrected us was now pure seductress, fondling me like a lover. I cupped handfuls of water and cascaded it against my face, sluicing more against my breasts and under my arms. Then I dived underwater and swam before rolling over and floating up on my back, hands trailing in the water. When I got back to the beach, Jamie was still sleeping. I'd read somewhere that women were blessed with a body that was in its entirety a sex organ, unlike poor men whose sex was trapped in an appendage between their legs. Standing over Jamie, my shadow a black ghost dwarfing his sleeping form, I couldn't help but notice his appendage was already awake. More or less. It was twisted up in his pants, crying out for freedom. I slid my hands from my thighs to my breasts, relishing the sea-wetness, something strange coming over me. I felt like a god. Not the goody-two-shoes type of god, but an impish one with a sense of humor and a healthy libido. I crouched and untied his rope belt, suppressing an artful giggle. Then I pulled his shorts down and tied his ankles together. No plan exactly, just feeling playful.

And why not?

This scene was cut-and-pasted from that red yoga book I'd read as a teenage suicide apprentice. Jamie was Shiva, the male god, lying in the sleep of death. I was Shakti, the main character, the female god. I was yearning to procreate and I needed the spark of life he kept in his loins. This must sound crazy, I know. But no internet, no TV, no social media. What would you do for entertainment on a desert island?

Really getting into it, I danced to bring him back to life with the lure of my vagina, weaving my arms and body to the beat of the waves, my shadow clinging to his sleeping corpse. I kneeled astride his legs, rocked forward onto my hands, and worked on his appendage with my mouth. *Gently.* I didn't want to wake him up, just get him ready. He said something. Not a word. He was still asleep. But only just. I shuffled up astride his hips and eased down on him, barely touching him, stroking back and forth.

No penetration. Not yet.

Jamie tossed his head, his eyes buzzing under their lids. It was time for my god's resurrection.

This is going to be one hell of a wake up call.

I fell on him, pinning his wrists in the sand, my greedy vagina swallowing his cock whole in a single gulp. His eyes popped open, lit with alarm, but that soon faded into an easy smile. His body went limp and a sigh rumbled up from somewhere deep inside him.

When I'd finished, I flopped on him like a wet blanket and buried my face in the sand by his head. The sun was hot on my back, my skin a thermometer measuring its heat against the coolness of the breeze. Jamie's chest was rising and falling underneath me, the rasp of his breath orchestrating the melody of wind and waves. My mind drifted, tracking Jamie's fingertips as he caressed me, his hands lingering in the small of my back, across my buttocks and down between my thighs.

Who needs the internet anyway?

ENEMIES

35 - Jamie

Days passed. Busy, but contented.

The Steigers had been reborn, transformed from victims of the storm at the mercy of the island into its masters. A husband and wife again. Survivors in every sense of the word. But our survival had come at a cost and written on the bill was a riddle that had to be solved for the account to be settled in full.

How can the same woman stage a double suicide with her own child, then go through hell to save her own life and that of her husband?

For the time being, I was content to ignore it, setting it aside as if charged on plastic. But sooner or later, I would run out of credit. That bill would have to be paid and the riddle solved. In the meantime, our days in Salvation were untroubled, albeit long and hard, our lives an endless stream of chores without the benefit of modern appliances. But we had plenty of blessings to count. We were alive, our wounds were healing, and Kim had more or less agreed to our making a new start in Switzerland. As for her getting therapy there, that was another can I'd kicked down the road. When we were snug in our Alpine chalet and laughing about our days as castaways, that would surely be an easy enough topic to bring up. I finally had our future all mapped out. It wasn't a detailed map like you get from Google. Mine was more like one of those antique maps with a few bits designated as known surrounded by unknown areas with intimidating subtexts like darkest jungle. But at least I had a map.

On the practical front, I had built two more solar stills. So we had plenty of water. We had also learned how to dry and smoke fish and seafood, so we were less dependent on getting a fresh catch daily. This gave us more freedom and we used it to explore. That was how we found Shoe Beach, an exposed strip of shoreline on the rugged eastern side. It was littered with junk—pure treasure to us—including what looked like every shoe ever lost in the Atlantic. Kim found sandals that actually fit and my bonanza was a diver's face mask. The strap was broken. But that was an easy fix. And I soon added a snorkel improvised out of plastic tubing. So with my diving kit upgraded, my fishing scorecard improved and with the larder full, we felt secure enough to take a day off and make the trip to *Four Winds,* the Bliss family home.

The roadway was two tire tracks baked as hard as concrete with a line of tufted grass running down the center between them. We were upbeat as we walked side by side in the parallel tracks. A day without chores. An adventure. The cultivated trees around Salvation soon thinned out, replaced by scruffy grassland speckled with bushes. We stopped when we reached the hut at the overgrown airstrip, but we didn't tarry there. We were too eager to get to the house and get some answers. Back in Nassau, the big question mark had been on the connection between Raymond Bliss and William's disappearance. But in the light of Kim's confession, all that was now moot. In its place was a new question keyed to our chance of getting rescued.

Should we move to Four Winds?

The problem with Salvation was visibility. We were tucked behind bushes and trees with a scant view of the beach and the sea beyond it. Unless a boat came right up to the shore and hailed us, we would probably miss it. I might catch sight of one while fishing, but I wasn't sitting on the pier all day with a fishing pole like Huck Finn. As for Kim, she was either working in the house or out foraging for food. The effort involved in maintaining our existence was taking up all of our time and energy. *Four Winds* was our best hope. Judging by the realtor's photos, it was built on a bluff overlooking the sea. If it wasn't too damaged and inhospitable, we could make it our home. I had my eye on another mystery too.

Why was Raymond Bliss obsessed with me?

Why had he stolen the *Mendoza Crucifix*, then returned it to me on his deathbed?

That second point was speculation. But why else would he have had it on him when he'd died? He had to have known that the crucifix would get back to me. And what about his father's military medal? That was a virtual identity card and the oddest thing imaginable for a character like Raymond Bliss to be carrying around in his pocket. It was as if he'd been sending me an invitation, constructing a mystery so inviting as to be irresistible.

I stopped and pointed at the big white house emerging from behind billowing palms at the end of a cape of craggy cliffs. "It's still standing anyway."

Kim scanned it, shielding her eyes from the sun with both hands. "I can see why they called it *Four Winds*."

"Yeah, it's really exposed, but perfect for us. If we build a signal fire, they'll see it for miles."

She lowered her sun-visor hands and turned to me.

"Did you ever find out why they called it

Ragamoffyn Island?"

"Rolle said there was some story to it. But he never told me what. Something from way back in the pirate days. I thought it meant a scruffy kid."

"No. Spelled like this, it's Lucifer's helper in *Piers Plowman*. Whoever named it really knew his Middle English poetry, and my guess is he knew this damn island pretty good too."

"Having second thoughts? We can always go back to Salvation."

"No way. Not with my bold knight to protect me. But I was thinking ... it must be why Ginny Bliss changed the name."

"No doubt. But that didn't turn out too good either, did it?" I set off towards the house before Kim could change her mind. Her imagination was running riot. "It's not the devil you need to worry about. It's rotting timbers. This place is sure to be a health and safety nightmare. It was falling apart anyway, and *Nestor* will have rattled more of it loose. So just watch your ass. Don't forget that haunted truck in Salvation."

"Aye-aye, Captain."

36 - Kim

As we approached the house, the track widened out, feeding into a courtyard. I guessed it had once been a garden laid out with grass and flowering shrubs. But now it was wild with one bush having won the survival battle and colonized all the space. The house was built in three wings with the west wing providing the living accommodation. So that was where we started, passing through French doors hanging from broken hinges, their windows smashed through. We entered a vast room with a high ceiling, and for the longest while we stood in silence, eyes roaming. This was the heart of the house with roof beams and a sweeping staircase up to a second-floor gallery that offered an eagle-eye view of the goings-on in the lounge. Who'd leaned on those railings and what had they seen? My imagination ran riot. Three fans hung from the beams, and one of them was catching the wind and spinning lazily, giving it the effect of being powered on. I didn't know what impressed me more the sight of its faded majesty or the feeling of it, the sense that it was a person grown old, diseased and dying, but still with life enough to remember when it had been a crucible for those who'd gorged on life. Noel Coward. Did he sing at that piano? Bogey and Bacall. Did they dance to vinyl spinning on that gramophone? Did they make love on that worn leather couch?

And then the other part.

Raymond Bliss grew up here, played here as a

boy. This was the house that grew the monster.

"Creepy, eh?" Jamie summed it up. I guessed he was having a special moment too. "Let's look around. We should split up to get it done quicker, but if it creeps you out..."

"I'm good."

"Then you check the terrace and the pool and the living accommodation. I'll do the east wing, the garages and utility rooms."

"Okay."

"And another thing." He pointed to the staircase. "Stay off those rickety steps. They're a deathtrap."

He dumped his pack and headed off, a claw hammer with a makeshift handle swinging from his hand. I headed towards the pool terrace, passing a grand piano propped up by a wooden crate and a wet bar stocked with empties. I stepped out onto the sunlit terrace. The pool was empty too, except for a wind-blown pile of rusty patio furniture and a shallow pond of green water with a TV half submerged in it. I walked around the pool, admiring the blue ceramic tiles like frescoes on the floor. At one end of the pool, a stone pedestal was ringed by stools finished with the same blue tiles. The pedestal was jagged where the tabletop had been broken off it. An odd thing to steal, I thought. I stood by the stone wall at the edge of the terrace, sweeping my eyes from the khaki and taupe tones of the island across the bay with its white crescent beach and blue-green seas through to the deep-blue waters of the interisland cut. I could see no ships. But our thinking had been correct. This was discovery terrace. This house had to be visible for miles, and in an ocean of empty islands who wouldn't look up at a notorious mansion high on a bluff.

The wind was kicking up, dragging its fingers

through my hair and flicking raggedy wisps about my face. I turned back to the pool, a snapshot coming to mind, a living artwork written in paradoxical objects, the abandoned villa with its derelict pool, the old TV, a technology relic, broken in the heart of a forgotten paradise. And me, of course, a feral woman bearing mute witness, sun-toasted, naked, save for a strip of cloth around her hips. I liked the image. No idea why. It just fit together. And I fitted too. The place was derelict alright, but its beauty was way more than skin deep, and its setting was breathtaking. Just a brush of imagination and it leaped into life. Beautiful women, stars of the silver screen. Rich men, fat with the money of the day, mining, oil, and new-fangled technologies like plastics and aviation. Days by the pool. Or maybe a spot of fishing or diving if you're up for it. Parties around the piano and the gramophone. Romantic nights under the stars.

This was our new home. I decided it there and then.

I explored the north wing next, passing through a dining room with panoramic views of the cut and finding a games room with a broken pool table and a gym with rusty equipment. Then I found the library, and if I'd had any doubts about making *Four Winds* our new home, they were gone the instant I stepped through its door. Books, their pages burnished brown and as stiff as boards, but still books. Loads of them. Some on shelves. But most strewn across the floor or piled against the wall. Instinctively, I began to gather them up and line the shelves. But then I stopped. That would be a labor of love for a later date. I stepped back, my eyes lingering on the covers and spines. Some were familiar, but most were unknown.

Virgin books.
What an unexpected treat.
I made my way back to the lounge. No sign of Jamie. But I could hear him banging somewhere with his hammer. I sat on the piano stool and plucked at a few keys. Out of tune, of course. I used to play the piano when I was a girl, but I'd given it up after my father died. I checked inside the piano stool and took out a sheaf of sheet music. The titles were vaguely familiar and I tried to tap out a few on the stiff keys.

"Okay?" I said, as Jamie came back into the room.

"Sure. But I'm hungry." He turned towards the cabinet housing the ancient sound system, pulled out a handful of vinyl records and rifled through them.

"Beatles?"

"These look earlier."

"Same as the sheet music here. I guess the monster didn't dance."

He looked up at me, his face not registering. Then he went back to thumbing through the vinyl.

"We got some Frank Sinatra. And Billie Holiday. Lots of him."

"Her. She was a Jazz singer."

"Oh." Jamie sounded impressed.

"*Four winds.* They got the name of the house from one of her songs." I pulled out the sheet music and gave it to him as he came over. "*Blues in the Night.*" I played the first few bars while Jamie read the lyrics.

"Not exactly upbeat, is it?" he said. "Men are not all two-faced."

"That line changes according to the singer. A male singer would badmouth the women in his life. That was the zeitgeist after WWII. The Atomic bomb. The

Iron Curtain. New words like *nuclear holocaust* doing the rounds. No internet. Not much TV. And Hollywood ruling the roost with mean hunks and dazzling femme-fatales. Some of whom may have practiced their deadly arts of seduction right here." I tapped the top of the piano.

"Is that an invitation?" Jamie tossed the sheet music on the piano and grabbed me for a smooch.

I love it when he does shit like that.

But then again, I pushed him off.

"I'm too hungry."

"Yeah, me too." He let me go. "Let's eat." And with that, he fetched his carry bag and unpacked our lunch.

37 - Jamie

I like to linger over waking up, stretching out that warm sudsy soak of half-sleep as the new day floats me back to consciousness. But this was the opposite—a jolt, abrupt, unfriendly. One moment, I was sound asleep, the next, wide awake. Not alert, but disturbed, my eyes hollowed out, mind and body aching for slumber.

Something woke me up.

A sound.

I sat up and listened.

But it was only the wind singing its shanty, playing in and out of the nooks and crannies of the vast house. It was dark, but darkness on the cusp of light. Kim was sleeping at my side. We were upstairs in the master bedroom, Kim having discovered that we could safely negotiate the stairs if we walked close to the wall and avoided certain steps. Five days had passed since our first foray to *Four Winds* and this had been our first night in the house. The moving days had been long. Cleaning up the house and transporting our meager tools and taking care of our daily feed had kept us going from dawn to dark. So I'd expected to sleep like a dead man. But I'd woken up early like a nervous insomniac. I slipped out of bed, irritated, knowing I had no chance of getting back to sleep, not with these pissy eyes and jangled nerves.

I went downstairs and out onto the terrace where I checked our signal fire, a pile of wood and rubber with two cans of flammables close by. Not much, just the dregs I'd drained out of various cans. It promised a real stinker of a blaze, and to kick it off, we had our *pièce de résistance*. Matches. I'd found a box in the kitchen, real old-fashioned unsafety matches that still lit like a charm. I sauntered over to the wall at the edge of the terrace and looked out over the sweeping bay beyond. We'd named it the *Bay of Plenty*, hoping to catch plenty of fish there, and also because its orientation was similar to its New Zealand namesake.

I wandered outside. The order of the day was food. After days spent moving house, our larder was empty. So I needed to check out the local fishing spots. I had a choice of trails from the house to the sea. The main path was well trodden, an easy incline heading down to the Bay of Plenty. But I took the less promising route, following rough-hewn steps down a steep path to the point of the cape where a scruffy beach was washed by vigorous seas. Not a swimmer's beach. And not much of a fishing beach either from the looks of it. I walked the length of it and tried to get to the Bay of Plenty without going back up to the house and down the other path, but a spur blocked my way. I sat on a rock, enjoying the transformation in colors as the morning light filled the sky. I was about to head back when I looked up at the house and saw Kim at the end of the terrace. She was standing at the wall. I went to call her, but I wasn't sure she would hear me over the wind and waves. There was something else stopping me too, something about her. She was bent over the wall as though she was looking intently at something below.

She's going to jump.

I bawled out her name as her body whipped up straight, then snapped down against the wall. But she didn't jump. She threw up. She was still holding the wall and gasping when her eyes eased up and she saw me. She didn't wave or make any sign of recognition. She just stared at me, motionless but for one arm that wiped the sick from her lips. I stared back. Nothing to say. An avalanche of fear was lying in wait. But at that moment I was so shot full of disbelief my thoughts and feelings had drained out empty. I sat down, my eyes sliding off the terrace and down to the rock pool at my feet.

She's pregnant.

I felt a glimmer of something. I won't call it joy. Hope more like. Something on the plus side, something befitting a father to be. But that glint of good was gone in an instant. I wanted another child. Of course I did. But that was back in Nassau. Back when I thought Kim was a mother broken by the loss of her child, not a broken mother who'd drowned him.

Pregnant?

I didn't think it was possible. It had taken half the doctors in America the last time. Now we had pulled it off without even trying. My head was spinning. My plan had been to ease her into therapy after we moved to Switzerland. If we had a child after that, it could be a carefully controlled event. But this changed all that. We were castaways. Now I was alone on a desert island with a pregnant wife whose dark trail of motherhood cast a frightening shadow over the child inside her. Pregnancy and birthing trigger profound changes. I'm no expert, but I was a father once and I know that at least. Most mothers handle the issues and challenges and some even relish it. But Kim was different. For her, pregnancy was a fuse and I'd just lit it.

38 - Kim

So that was how it happened. That was how we became enemies. Or at least, that was how it started. That was where the seed was sown. That was how the trust and love we had grown organically from our magical coupling in the storm was tossed aside. Every night since then, we had built our coupledom, lying loin to loin as lovers. Every day, we had cemented it, fighting to survive, standing shoulder to shoulder as man and wife. These experiences had welded us insolubly. Or so it had seemed. But now I felt it all draining away. Like a holed ship, we were doomed to founder. The prospect of our miracle child, its genesis sparked in the belly of a storm, did not bring him joy. No cigars. No congratulations. My husband's first reaction to the news that he was about to become a father was fear.

Fear of me.

And if I'd felt it watching him on the beach, I knew it for sure as soon as he walked into the room and opened his mouth. I was resting in the master bedroom, lying on the four-poster behind the torn strips of mosquito netting we had hastily improvised.

"Are you sick, honey?"

So casual. So contrived.

He snuck under the netting and pecked me on the forehead before stretching out beside me on his back. That was all contrived too, calculated so we wouldn't be talking face to face. So I wouldn't see his eyes. As if I needed his eyes to tell me he was lying.

"So are you okay?" He tried again.

"I'm okay." And with that, I duly signed in to the game. I pulled myself up and sat on the edge of the bed with my back to him. "I'm going to clean up. Get your own breakfast."

"Sure."

I could feel his eyes on my back as I left the room. I don't know what he was expecting. But evidently, stone-cold Kim was not it. I headed down to the beach in the bay where I took off my skirt and walked naked at the water's edge. I felt claustrophobic despite the open space, dirty despite the crystal-clean white sand at my feet. I ran, desperate to escape. Not running to, but running from. When my lungs burned and my blood pounded, I stopped, bent forward and gulped air. Straightening up slowly, I ran my hands up and down my body, scraping off the sweat and kneading my tender breasts. Then I walked into the sea, ducking under the water and washing away the dregs of my husband's mean spirit. I should have confronted him. Stooping to his level had been a mistake. I swam out further and floated on my back, my eyes soothed by the blue sky. I felt pure, despite all my sins. God had forgiven me. The child in my belly was Her message. I had killed my son through negligence and I had been punished for it, imprisoned in a hell of my own making. But now I was going to be a mother again. God had returned to me the keys to a woman's immortality. I swam lazily to the shore and headed back towards *Four Winds*, picking up my skirt and sandals on the way. I was calming down, seeing Jamie's side of it. He knew I wasn't a murderer. But there was no denying what had happened. He was bound to be concerned. It was just that this time there was no need. This time, everything was going to be perfect.

This baby was not a gift of doctors, but a gift of God. That made a difference. And nobody was going to harm him, least of all me.

I was at the trailhead back to *Four Winds*, but I was reluctant to return to the house. I needed more time to myself, and so did Jamie. And as I was standing there, wondering what to do, I caught sight of a shadow in the cliffs below the house. I couldn't make out if it was a cave or a trick of the morning light. I continued to the end of the beach, then clambered over the rocks towards it. The going was easy at first. But then I was on the cliff face, stepping from ledge to ledge. I checked below. It wasn't so high. Twenty feet or so. And the water below was deep enough to take the fall if I stumbled. So I pressed on, discovering a cave with steps hewn in the rock leading down to a mini-dock at the foot of the cliff, a slab of concrete set with an iron ring.

A cave with its own mooring.

Jamie would be psyched when I told him.

I sat on the top step to catch my breath, but a sudden sadness caught me by surprise. Why? I didn't know. I wiped away the tears it had triggered, irritable now. Spontaneous tears were a flashing red light, part and parcel of my path to motherhood, mood swings with no discernible driver. I'd been a rock since the day I'd set foot on this island. But now I was pregnant, a living rock, a volcano, and they need to vent.

And sometimes they *explode.*

I pulled myself together and cleaned up my face with my forearm. *Some days on this island, I could kill for cosmetics.* I stood up and cast my eyes beyond the shaded waters below and out across the sunlit bay. This was our paradise now. Charles and Ginny Bliss and their liquor-soaked parties and celebrity guests, all that was history. Raymond and his gobbledygook cult, his psychedelic drugs and insanity, all that was gone too. Now it was our island. We had shipwrecked here and made it our own. Some company in Chicago had a sheet of paper saying it was theirs. But that wasn't worth shit. The child in my belly was the only deed that counted. This island didn't give a damn about pieces of paper. This island was alive. It had its own will and it had claimed us as its own. I turned my back on the sunlit bay and crept into the darkness of the cave.

waist. He was crouched in the bow, steadying himself with one hand on the bowsprit, eyeballing the waters ahead. They were so close I could read the T-shirt slogan on the sumo's broad back.

FART DOWNLOADING

I was up to my knees in water, screaming over the din of the motor and cursing the onshore breeze that was fanning the outboard's fumes in my face and sending my hollering back to the beach. I grabbed a rock off the sea floor and hurled it at them, but it fell short. Shouting was hopeless. The cackle of the motor was deafening enough back on the beach, but sitting on top of it, they had to be deaf to everything. I dived in and swam after them. My only chance was that one of them would look back and see me swimming. In the weeks since Kim had dragged me half dead out of the water, I had recovered my strength. Swimming for hours every day and eating a diet of fruit, vegetables and fish, I'd gotten in great shape.

If I could only...

40 - Kim

The day was fading, the viscous light of dusk soothing, a welcome relief after the glare of tropical daylight. Everything was ready for dinner. The fire was built, the vegetables chopped, the seasoning prepared. All I needed was the fish. And of course, my husband.

We had ritualized our daily routines and our meals were no exception. Without electricity and with the minimal light of our fire and primitive lamps, sundown meant shutdown and dawn was the rooster summoning us to our chores. Our food routine was always the same. We ate fruit for breakfast with more fruit and dried fish or seafood for lunch. These were light meals. So by evening we were famished. That was when we sat down for our big meal with catch of the day on the menu. Jamie was a good provider and we either had one large fish or many smaller fish. Either way, as dedicated carnivores, we would stuff ourselves with the rich oils and proteins our bodies craved.

Where is he?

I was getting hungry. I lit the fire under the grill and added some kindling.

I'm pregnant, damn it.

The coals were ready for the fish and I was poking them to keep them alive when I finally heard him making his way into the lounge behind me.

"Kim, I'm sorry." He was apologizing even before he reached the terrace although I didn't give a damn about his excuses. I was just pleased to have him back. "I saw a boat. On Salvation Beach. I swam after it. But they gunned it outside the reef and I lost them. Then I was on the wrong side of the tide. I had a shitload of trouble getting back to shore."

"You swam after a boat?"

"I thought they would look back." He dropped his eyes from mine. For my husband, failure was always a personal event. I hugged him, his head lolling down and resting against mine. His chest gave a little heave, like there was a sob in there somewhere he'd manfully trapped inside.

"You're one dumbass son-of-a-bitch, Jamie Steiger."

His head nodded in agreement. He was still squeezed up against me, holding me tight. Too tight. That wasn't about the boat. It was about the morning news. I stroked his matted, damp hair.

"And now I've got no fish."

"It's okay. I didn't eat much lunch. We've still got some dried fish. I'll fry some plantains. We've got plenty of fruit and veg. You rest." He pulled himself off me and sat by the fire. His legs were peppered with cuts and scrapes. He must have hauled himself out over rocks. I fetched him a mug of coconut water to get him started, then set to work on a makeshift dinner.

My island cuisine had come a long way since my crude first efforts. Not only were we sourcing a greater variety of ingredients, but we were making basics from scratch. Coconut oil was a case in point. You have no idea how important oil is until you live without it. I'm not just talking about cooking, but medicine and cosmetics. Coconuts are loaded with oil and they were abundant on the island, and I'd figured out how to get the oil out. There was no science to it, just loads of hard work. I'd spend hours slicing and pounding coconuts, squeezing the pulp until my hands ached, then heating the resultant milk to skim off the cream, all the while thinking about my food processor back home and feeling humble. But thanks to all that hard work, we had oil for cooking, as a salve for cuts and as a balm for our scorched and desiccated skin.

Jamie rested while I made dinner, his eyes flicking over my way now and again, measuring my mood. We ate hungrily and in silence, and it was dark by the time we scraped our plates and tidied up. Jamie lent a hand as he always did, but I told him to rest and gave him some oil to put on his beat-up legs. Then I made us a hot drink of coconut milk flavored with bananas and nuts. It was our special treat drink.

"How's the legs?"

Jamie was finishing the last of the oil I'd given him, rubbing it into his torn skin.

"A thousand times better. It stings, then soothes."

We supped our drinks and stoked the fire back to life so we could watch the flames.

"I'm sorry about this morning." He looked up at me. "I was shocked. It's wonderful you're pregnant."

And with that, he grabbed me, crushing me in a bear hug and burying a sniffle in my shoulder.

"Jamie." I pushed him off me. "It's okay. It was a shock for me too. Look at the doctors we needed last time. But this time it's beautiful. A miracle. Our love in the storm was sacred." He pulled himself together and took a slug of his drink. "Need a shot of rum in that?"

"You bet." A smile creased one side of his weepy-looking face.

"It's been a weird day."

"We've got to get off this island."

"We will. I can feel it coming."

Our eyes drifted back to the fire, comforted by its flickering flames.

"I found a cave," I said, reaching for a new conversation.

"Where?"

"In the bluff right under the house. But it was so dark I couldn't explore it much."

"I guess there's lots of them around." And that was it. He dismissed my new discovery just like that and I hadn't even told him about the steps. "We need to talk about William."

"Don't worry. I'm never going to harm myself or my family ever again. This whole experience we've gone through—it's a rebirth—you said it yourself. I can't even understand that woman who tried to kill herself, who..." I couldn't say it. I'd said it once after finding it buried in the pit of my mind. Once was enough.

"So let's go to Switzerland. We can get you some help."

"Help? You think I'm crazy?"

"Don't be like that."

"It was a question."

"No, I don't think you're crazy. But you got depressed. You tried to commit suicide. And even before that, you freaked out when William was born."

"They took him away from me. They wouldn't let me touch him."

"He was premature. He needed help. You accused them of stealing him."

"That was just an expression. I was angry."

"And doing medical experiments on him."

"I was frightened."

"They were doctors, for Chrissake. They were trying to save his life."

"They had him wired up to machines with tubes sticking into him like a Frankenstein movie. I was confused. And you were ten-thousand miles away. This time you'll be there with me."

"We can't stick our heads in the sand. This is—"

"You cannot believe I am going to kill this baby."

"Of course not."

"Then why Switzerland?"

This conversation was hurting me, but I was desperate to jam up my tears and stay rational.

Jamie put his arm around me.

"All I'm saying is ... let's get some professional advice. I want to protect you *and* our baby. That patient-doctor confidentiality thing in the US is not going to hold up if a child—"

"I know that. I'll get locked up."

"So let's go to Switzerland. A doctor there will have a duty of care to you, not some foreign law."

"But why do we have to tell anybody? The entire world thinks that William was abducted. And there's nobody to say anything different except you and me. And I'm not going to tell anyone. What about you?"

"Don't even ask."

"We can't change what happened. Nothing like that could happen again. Everything will be okay. This child is God's gift. He's my redemption. You must trust me on this. It's the only way it can work."

"I trust you." Now both his arms were around me, his hands cradling my head. "Of course, I do."

41 - Jamie

Peace characterized the days immediately following the news of Kim's pregnancy. She was sick every morning, but otherwise well. And for the rest of the day, she busied herself with her duties in quiet preoccupation. As for me, I was getting that warm, fuzzy dad feeling every time I looked at her. My close encounter with Fart Downloading had convinced us that our rescue could come at any moment and that it was more likely to be a random event than the fruit of hours spent waiting by a signal fire with a box of matches. So five days later, with calm reigning between us and our larder well stocked, we took a day off, looking for adventure.

Kim's Cave Day.

Her discovery had been swept aside by the news of her pregnancy. But it was intriguing. There were plenty of caves on the island. But this one had steps leading down to the sea. So we kitted up and set off to explore it. I'd made a torch by soaking a dry stick in oil siphoned from the engine of the abandoned truck. It turned out to be a disaster, close to impossible to light, and when I did finally get it going, the fumes were so noxious I had trouble holding it and breathing at the same time. It was an inauspicious start. But we soldiered on, making our way deep into the cave and up yet more rock steps, ending up in a cavernous chamber. I swept the toxic torch around so we could take it all in.

"No bones," Kim said.

"And no jewel-encrusted skull on a chest

brimming with Aztec gold."

"Now that would have been nice."

"Not all treasure is silver and gold, mate," I said, doing my Captain Jack Sparrow impression. But my feeble attempt at humor was lost on her. She was pointing at the far wall, her jaws easing apart in wonder.

A door … a big old wooden door.

I gave Kim the torch and checked it out, thumping it with my fist. It was heavy and locked solid with a rusty iron ring in the middle like the entrance to a medieval monastery. I pulled on it, but it didn't budge.

"I bet the locks and hinges are rusted," I said. "Let's give it a good go together."

Kim leaned the torch against the wall, and we both grabbed the metal ring and threw our combined weight into an almighty pull. We ended up on the floor, rolling out of the way as the door fell on top of us with a rip of sheared metal. We sat there, dumbstruck. It was a door to nowhere, opening directly onto a concrete wall.

"It's been sealed off." Kim broke the silence. "What do you think?"

"I think we found the *Bat Cave*. Even money there's a secret passage up to the house."

"You're kidding. We searched the whole house."

"Obviously, not well enough. What else could it be? There must be something behind this wall. Otherwise, why brick it off?"

"Can we get through it?"

"No way. No proper tools."

"How then?"

"I'll map the cave and superimpose it onto a plan of the house. Then we'll zone in on it from the house side. It must be sealed off on that end too. But it'll be easier to work on there."

"I always wanted to live in a house with a secret passage like those old movies."

"Me too."

So that was it. Kim's cave day ended, and we made our way back into the sunlight and down the steps to the sea. We swam back to the beach and dried off as we speculated about what was behind the wall. We were animated, excited. The Steiger's had a new mystery.

What's behind that wall?

My morning schedule was always the same. As I opened my eyes, the good news would hit me.

I'm going to be a mother.

Then the dank smell of the master bedroom would wipe the smile off my face and send me scuttling out to my bucket on the veranda. Every day Jamie left a bowl of water and freshly crushed flowers on my nightstand to mask the smell of the room, and I would bury my head in the fragrance of its sweet oils whenever I felt queasy. Sometimes it worked, and even when it didn't, I cherished his thoughtfulness. Thankfully, my morning sickness was just that, worse on wakening and easing off as the day progressed, although the smell of cooking could set it off at any moment. So Jamie had become my sous-chef, an appointment that kept him busy with finding the *Bat Cave* squeezed in between catching fish and manning the grill.

He started his search with a map. Jamie loved maps. He'd already mapped the island using a quill stolen from a seabird's nest and ink from a reef squid. With cartographic credentials like that on his résumé, a plan of *Four Winds* superimposed on a map of the cave was a snap. But it took him time, and it was three days before he made the breakthrough. The entrance was under the stairs. He removed the wooden paneling and discovered a steel door set in the wall under a layer of plaster and paint. I was his shadow as he levered it open with my pry-bar, dragging it back to the accompaniment of an appropriately eerie grating sound. I lit a coconut oil lamp as we peeked through the doorway. The lamp was our new invention and a vast improvement on Jamie's cave torch, which had left us coughing up engine-oil flavored phlegm for two days straight. So there we were in the doorway, peering beyond, the intrepid Dr. Steiger and his stalwart companion, the lady with the lamp. I edged closer, snaking one arm around his waist as I raised the lamp. There was a flight of concrete steps going down a narrow staircase.

Jamie took the lamp and headed down the steps with me right behind him. At the bottom there was a sharp turn, and I followed him along a narrow corridor with concrete walls and a ceiling so low he had to duck. About ten paces later, we went through another steel door into a room with rock walls and a concrete floor.

"Wow..." Jamie stopped in the middle of the room and swung the lamp around. There were fold-out bunk beds hanging on chains off the walls, bookcases, tables, chairs, two chemical toilets and a washbasin tucked in an annex. Jamie gave me the lamp while he fiddled with a mechanical contraption by the door.

"What is it?"

"An air filter. It's electrical. But if the generator fails—as it might if a nuclear bomb goes off in the neighborhood—then you can wind it manually."

"Holy fuck."

"You got it. Welcome to the Bliss family fallout shelter."

"So that's why he picked this island as far as possible from anywhere."

"Sure. And luckily he died before the Cuban Missile Crisis. He'd have been pissed off big time by that." We chuckled at the irony of it. Charles picking this remote island for his fallout shelter only to have it right next to Cuba, the bullseye in the world's one and only *nearly* nuclear war. "I wonder why they walled it off?" He looked at me, but I had no answer.

He took back the lamp and we kept on poking around, finding a separate utility area with a kitchen, a water tank, a separate generator room with its own oil and air supply, and a larder with shelves of canned goods way past their expiration date. As fallout shelters go, the Bliss family, as ever, had gone first class.

We found another steel door in back of the utility area. Jamie forced it open, and we were standing at the top of another staircase that lead down into a natural cave. Ever since we had arrived on the island, we had speculated about where the murders had taken place. But as soon as we opened that door, we both knew. There were no piles of rotting corpses, no stench of decaying flesh. But we still knew. The walls of the cave were covered in images like a latter-day medieval cathedral, with the faithful depicted as Aztecs attired in brilliant colors. As we walked down the steps, stale air escaped and was replaced by fresh air, with the lamp flame tracking the ebb and flow, its flickering light animating eyes and faces, transforming the congregation into living souls in a game of shadow and light.

We stopped at the bottom of the stairs and Jamie held the lamp aloft. The flame was steadier now, and as he held it motionless, it stretched up towards the ceiling, a bright finger of light revealing the temple that Raymond Bliss had built for his gods. This was his *chef d'oeuvre*, his crypt. At its center was an altar. I recognized the stone table missing from the terrace by its blue tile mosaics. Pieces of it had broken off and were strewn on the floor, and many of the images on the walls were damaged too, defaced with tool marks or smeared with paint.

"Someone trashed the place. Or at least they tried to." Jamie pointed at the pockmarked walls and the piles of rubble against them. "And there's that doorway to the sea cave." He pointed to a bricked off panel at the far end. "Charles built his shelter in the natural cave system, so they had two ways in and out, one from the house and the other from the sea."

"The cave door was an emergency exit?"

"Yeah, and he probably used this cave for storage. It was all about preserving life in Charles's day—"

"Until Raymond turned it into the opposite."

"The new owners must have trashed it, or tried to. Then they realized it was easier to hide it by sealing it off at both ends."

Images crowded every inch of the wall, running seamlessly from one to another like a single body festooned with tattoos. It was a story told in images, a contemporary codex of an ancient cult.

Jamie pointed at the altar. "That's where he must have done it."

We both stared at the transplanted poolside table in silence. It had once been up on the terrace, piled high with food fit for gourmet feasting. Great writers, artists, actors and potentates had all supped their bellies full at this table under a sky of heavenly stars. Then Raymond had dragged it down here and made it the foundation stone in his temple of death, prone bodies stretched out on it, hearts cut from chests still beating, blood tracing patterns in the delicate blue mosaics. Behind the altar, a Mexican Calvary towered on the wall, the crowd rendered as Aztecs, the Roman soldiers as Spanish conquistadors, and on its summit, a single crucifix.

No introduction was necessary.

The corpus nailed to the cross was the same, the round belly and ample breasts, the skeletal arms and legs, the defleshed skull. This was the crucifixion of the Unholy Mother, a graphic rendering of Jamie's crucifix.

"That's why he was so obsessed with you."

"What?" Jamie snapped at me like he'd been in a world of his own.

"Raymond. The *Mendoza Crucifix*. That's why he stole it from you, even killed to get it."

Jamie said nothing, his eyes swinging back to the image towering above him. This place was making me sick and I was desperate to leave. But we only had one lamp and there was no way I was heading back along those corridors in the dark. So I left Jamie in his trance and fell into one of my own, my eyes scanning the defaced images crowding the walls. There were enough of them left undamaged to see that it was an epic retelling of the New Testament, the crucifixion and resurrection re-written for the cult's new players and scripted for its new tenets. Along the wall, beyond the Mexican Calvary, I came across the resurrection scene—the Unholy Mother risen from the grave, carried in a palanquin shouldered by lusty youths. She was portrayed as a macabre Madonna embracing her newborn child in a composition redolent of the Italian Renaissance, but in a style more manga than Michelangelo. Her resurrection had restored her flesh, but she still reeked of death, her bone-white face topped in a fancy hat of brightly colored feathers, her auburn hair tumbling in curls, her eyes white circles in black pits, a maquillage of tombstone teeth framing her lips with a sinister smile. Her baby was feeding at a pendulous breast, looking up at her lovingly, scarlet smudges of blood peppering his shoulders where her pointy fingers held him too tight. Her gnarled hands were drilled with stigmata and still dripping with blood. I couldn't bear to look at it, but I couldn't take my eyes off it.

"Jamie, this place is creeping me out." But Jamie didn't answer. I pulled myself away from the macabre Madonna with her hypnotic allure. There was a pile of debris nearby, smashed relics mixed with chunks of the wall, bits of statues that must have decorated the place before someone laid into it with a sledgehammer. I started poking around in the pile, anything to keep my eyes off those images. "I found something." I dragged it out from under a heavy stone and studied it in the faint light. It looked like a dog. Jamie appeared next to me, holding the lamp aloft. It was a dog, an ugly dog with a vicious snarling face. I pulled it out and swept away the dirt. But as I handed it to Jamie, blood streamed down my forearm. I screamed, tossing it aside.

Jamie grabbed my hand.

"Hold it up." He straightened my arm above my head. "Close your fist." Jamie hacked a strip of denim off his shorts. Blood was oozing out of my clenched fist and running down my arm. Jamie dunked his improvised bandage in the warm coconut oil of the lamp. Then he bound my hand with it. "You're going to be okay."

"It hurts like crazy." Jamie checked the bandage again. The oily cloth had staunched the flow, the faded blue denim shading through red into purple. "What in God's name is it?" Jamie went to pick it up. "Careful!"

"You just have to hold it at the right end." He held up the statue, holding the dog's head between his finger and thumb. But it wasn't a dog. It was a man, a crouching man with the face of a demonic dog. And it wasn't a statue either, it was a knife. The crouching half-man half-dog was the handle, and the razor-sharp phallus emerging from between its thighs was the blade.

"An *ixcuac,* a sacrificial dagger. The blade is rainbow obsidian. It's a kind of glass, fired in volcanoes. It makes an edge sharper than any steel."

He closed his hand around the hilt of the knife and held it like a dagger, point downwards. I lost him at that point, my eyes fixated on the blade, watching as my blood dripped from its point, the flickering light glinting through its stone. My guts heaved in a single spasm with a *whoosh* that echoed around the crypt.

43 - Jamie

It was tough enough looking after a pregnant Kim. But now I had a pregnant, injured Kim to worry about. The blade had sliced her to the bone, putting her hand out of commission and leaving me with long, hard days coping with my chores as well as hers. An underlying disquiet was creeping into our lives too, something on top of the usual island malaise. We were used to that by now, our own strain of cabin-fever, brought on by a lifestyle halfway between a prison inmate's and an impoverished third-worlder's. I thought at the time that it was down to the pain of her injury. But as I was soon to learn, there was much more to it than that. It all came out with a BANG two days after our foray into Raymond's crypt. I was in the smoking room stringing up my early morning catch of fish over a wood fire, when—

Jamie!

As in, *get your ass over here.*

I found Kim on the terrace next to the signal fire.

"Where are the matches?"

I could see a boat with two men in it down in the cove, the din of its outboard fading off the edge of earshot as they headed out to sea. I recognized my sumo friend from Salvation Beach.

"I left them in the crypt."

"So get them!"

"It'll be too late. By the time I get the matches and we get this going, they'll be gone."

"Damn."

I felt it too. We were both running on empty. Survival had worked like a shot in the arm at first, getting us through those tough early days. But now the shot was wearing off. We were tired. We wanted off this island. Kim was pregnant and injured. And if that wasn't enough, we were living on top of a gruesome killing field. I'd been around tombs and burial sites all my professional life, so a few skeletons rattling after lights out were not going to stop me sleeping. But even without the crypt in the basement, *Four Winds* was a new world of creepy. The vinyl 45s, the books and the empty bottles of booze. It was as though the people had just left and would be back at any moment, a terrestrial *Mary Celeste*. It made even me feel bad. As for Kim, she was far more suggestible, and the ghouls in the basement were feeding her data at an alarming rate. Twice she had woken me up in the night to tell me that someone was playing the piano. We had even talked about moving back to Salvation. But we still believed rescue was only days away and the reappearance of my fishing pals only confirmed that.

"I'll get the matches anyway," I said. "But next time, instead of lighting the fire, why don't we burn the house down?"

"The whole house?"

"Why not? We hate the place anyway. Let's kill two birds with one stone. When the next boat shows up, let's light the world's most spectacular rescue beacon and turn this gruesome mausoleum into a field of ashes at the same time. What do you say?"

"What about the owners?"

"They can bill us."

"You could see it for miles. It's true." She wandered over to the terrace wall and looked out to sea where our rescue boat was bobbing in silence on distant waves. "What about the stuff in the crypt? You said that knife was a museum piece."

"They can dig it out of the rubble. We need to get off this island. I don't give a damn about anything else."

She turned towards me, her eyes wary. "I've been wondering about that stuff down there."

"Wondering?"

She stepped closer, reached up to my chest and took the *Mendoza Crucifix* in her hand.

"Where did you really get this? And don't give me that crap about finding it on a beach on Worthless Cay."

"What are you talking about?"

"When I saw that crucifix painted on the wall, I thought it explained Raymond's attack and why he stole it—"

"Makes sense."

She shook her head. "Not even a little bit. Raymond painted that in the seventies when the original was buried under the sea, waiting to get washed up on a beach and found by a penniless student, who'd famously follow its trail and make the biggest archaeological discovery of the twenty-first century—"

"You're reading too much into this. Priest Castillo described the crucifix in a letter to the Vatican—"

"Not in detail he didn't—"

"Raymond must have—"

"You think I'm stupid? I didn't just read your book, pal. I wrote it." She was glowering at me, challenging me. "Whoever painted that crucifix had this cross in one hand"—she held it up to my face—"and a brush in the other. It's that perfect. So how did Raymond Bliss copy it when it was still sitting at the bottom of the ocean a thousand miles to the north?"

"There are a number of—"

"Fuck you, Steiger." She let go the cross and stepped back. "Where did you get that crucifix?" I sank to the floor, my mouth as dry as a dust bowl. Denial had run out of road. I crossed my legs, rested my elbows on my knees and buried my face in my hands. This day was always going to come sooner or later. "Where?" Her voice echoed in the silent, empty space inside me. I slid my face from behind my hands and stared into her stone-gray eyes, the chill wind of resignation sweeping through me.

"Did you ever read about a guy who buys a junk painting at a flea market and it turns out to be a Monet?"

"You bought it in a flea market?"

"I came across it when I was researching the trade in fake pre-Columbian art for my master's thesis."

"But it's not fake."

"I thought it was. And so did the guy who sold it to me. Anyway, I never cited it in the paper. But it gave me the idea for my doctoral thesis."

"About Christo-pagan cults."

"Exactly. And researching that, I came across Castillo's account of a cross with a crucified pregnant woman, dead but alive. So I had it tested in a lab. And no shit. It was real. I was going to sell it. I had a lot of student debt. I was trying to pay it off by working for a treasure hunting outfit in Grand Bahama. So when my contract with them ended, I figured I'd dive a few of my own spots before heading back to the States, then sell it when I got back there."

"So that wreck is not the *Capitana*?"

I shrugged. "It's almost impossible to identify wrecks of that age. You need unique items that can survive five-hundred years of salt water—jewelry, porcelain, precious stones. But you also need a ship's manifest, and the *Capitana* didn't have one. There was too much treasure on board and not enough time to count it."

"I still don't get how you did it."

"Diving off Worthless Cay, I found a clump of silver coins—"

"STOP. Fast forward. How did you get from that dive to being the famous Dr. Steiger?"

"All it took was one lie. According to the assay mark on the coins, they'd been struck in Mexico City around 1560—"

"So, it could have been any Spanish ship. Or even an English pirate who'd stolen them."

"Until I found late Ming porcelain. The Spaniards hauled that across Mexico from the Pacific and shipped it out of Veracruz. The *Capitana* had sailed out of Veracruz in 1564 with Priest Castillo on board. That's documented. *Eureka.* What if I'd found the crucifix along with the coins and porcelain? Three strikes." I stuck up three fingers and counted them off. "The coin verified the date, the porcelain, the port of origin, and the crucifix identified a passenger who was on board. That no-name wreck had to be the Capitana. Of course, I'd need to explain why the crucifix was in perfect condition after being in the ocean for five hundred years."

"So you came up with that hokey *masked in clay* story."

"It fit the narrative. Castillo's private army had put an entire village of cultists to the sword. Slaughter on that scale needed justification. So Castillo was heading to the Vatican with proof of their blasphemies."

"And the clay mask?"

"The crucifix was a monstrous blasphemy. He'd

never cross the Atlantic with it in his baggage. It'd hex the journey. So he'd hide its sinfulness by covering it with clay."

"Then you really sexed up the story by finding it washed up on a beach. That was pure genius."

"That made it a detective story."

"So all your supposed research, years of slogging through codex, Royal Court depositions, church records, ship manifests and bills of lading—"

"Reverse engineered. When you've got the start and finish lines, it's easy to connect the dots."

"But what about the other ships in the fleet? Where were they?"

"Fleets used to split up in storms to increase their chance of survival. They didn't all sink conveniently in one spot."

"And what happened to the vast cache of gold and silver on board the *Capitana?*"

"They found enough to make it plausible. Five hundred years is a lot of ocean currents. Tides, shifting sands and the Gulf Stream. The treasure was bound to be spread over an immense area, unrecoverable in its entirety."

"So you went for it?"

"One simple lie and my no-name wreck became the *Capitana*." My hand went up to the crucifix and I held it up in front of my face. "A find like that brings out the big dogs, governments, museums, investors, major salvors. I was respectable—an archaeologist, not a treasure hunter. I could do a deal with the Bahamas government, get a finder's fee, and be granted what I really wanted. Something worth much more than gold and silver, exclusive media rights. Then I could cut a deal with a TV production company to film the salvage and recovery. I could turn my thesis into a commercial book and sell that too. Whatever they found, I'd make out like a bandit. I was ahead of my time. I saw where the real treasure was, not under the sea but online. Eyeballs on screens. Streaming TV and faked-up reality shows. Fingers poking links on smartphones and flipping pages in a bestseller. That was the twenty-first century treasure I was after."

"I'm in awe." I eyed her warily. She looked more angry than awestruck. "This is world class. You're going to be even more famous than you ever dreamed of. For all the wrong reasons, of course."

I didn't take the bait. There was no way she could blow the whistle. Everything we had was at stake.

"Kim, it was one simple lie."

"And only one man on the planet knew it was a lie, that crazy bastard Raymond Bliss. You stole his crucifix. Or you bought it from someone who did. But how did he get it?"

"The real *Capitana* must have been wrecked here. The northern cays was one theory, but there were others. One account had it wrecked on a cay north of Cuba. The King of Spain issued a warrant to search for it based on information from a sailor who claimed to have been on board. According to him, the survivors had hidden the treasure ashore in a cave."

"So what happened?"

"The search party couldn't find the cave."

"But Raymond did. Then he lost the crucifix."

"These cults had drifters passing through all the time. Someone must have taken it and sold it on."

"He called you a liar and a fraud. He was right. And nobody knew, not even your wife."

"I'm sorry, Kim."

"I don't know what's more incredible, the fiction you sold as fact, or the fact that you faked it. Either way, it's genius. You pulled it off. And you kept it secret, even from me."

"How could I have told you? I was your hero. I was in love with you. I couldn't risk losing you. Anyway, by that time, I believed it myself. You know how that is?"

"What do you mean *I know how that is?*"

"It's just an expression."

She stared at me, her face darkening.

"And so now—coincidentally—you happen on the idea of turning *Four Winds* into a signal fire. *Kill two birds with one stone.* Isn't that what you said? Or was it three? We get a great signal fire, we destroy this hateful place, and we bury under ashes everything it takes to prove you're a fraud. *How convenient.* And then what? We forget about it all?" She waited. But I said nothing. "Do you know what, Dr. Steiger? Or should that be Mr. Steiger? I guess that PhD will be the first thing to go. What really grieves me is not that you're a fraud. It's not even that you lied to me, *your wife.* It's that you're a fucking hypocrite."

"Hey!"

"We light up the house and we bury the evidence. We live your lie. We forget that your entire career, the books, the TV, the money is nothing but a castle built of sand—"

"If this gets out, I'm finished. They'll be lawsuits. We'll both be finished."

"Not me, pal. I'm the poor duped wife. I'm the one who gets to out you. I'll write a goddamn bestseller, *The Scoundrel Scholar: How Jamie 'Seacrets' Steiger scammed me and the world,* by his wife."

"Please Kim, don't—"

"What was it you said? *I believed it myself by that time. You know how that is.* You're right. I do know how that is. You've got a skeleton in your closet and you want it to stay locked up. I don't blame you for that. What I blame you for—you fucking hypocrite— is that you expect me to live your lie, but you won't live mine. You want me stashed in some nuthouse in Switzerland, or locked up in a cage in the States. Don't you think I'm punished enough? I killed my son and I have to live with it."

"You can't compare. I only suggested that out of concern for you and our baby."

"You think history is going to repeat itself? What do you think I am—an animal? What happened could never happen again. I was trying to protect William. I was trying to protect him from you, to stop you and that bitch from killing our family."

Tears were streaming down her cheeks. She swept them aside with a brusque wipe of her bandaged hand.

I stood up and put my arms around her.

She didn't fight it.

"You're right. We have to bury all our skeletons right here on this island. So let's agree to that now. Your confession, the truth about William, it went down with *Kiss the Sky* never to be heard again. William was abducted from *Paradise Found* by person or persons unknown. There will be no Switzerland, no doctors, no cops. The painted crucifix in the crypt never existed. We're going to burn this place down. The *Mendoza Crucifix* was found by me on Worthless Cay. It was the clue that led me to the *Capitana*. There will be no professional suicide. We'll go back to the States after this and take care of each other and our baby. Deal?"

She slipped her arms around my waist and pressed her face hard against my chest.

And that was how it ended.

More or less.

44 - Kim

I woke in the night
The piano again.
I woke up Jamie. He said it was the wind whistling through broken shutters and tugging at piano strings, the wind and my imagination. Maybe he was right. But strange, how it played such a limited repertoire, and only tunes from the sheet music in the bench at its feet. It started up again after Jamie went back to sleep. I tried to ignore it but I couldn't. So I lit the oil lamp and headed cautiously down the rickety staircase to the lounge. Jamie was right. There was no ghost there, no translucent image of Raymond Bliss as a boy, dazzling his elders with his keyboard talents as they gathered around the piano, swilling their potent brews. The keys were at rest, not played by invisible hands. But if they had been, I could not have been more disturbed. Because as I stood there, my eyes on the motionless keys, I could still hear the melody and the voices that rose to meet it, voices in counterpoint to the blues, flushed with bonhomie, weltering in *joie de vivre*. I felt that moment. It was past, but not gone. It was lived again. It was lived in me by all those lost souls.

I hurried back to the bedroom and hid my face in Jamie's chest as he lay on his side sleeping. When I woke up, it was already light and Jamie was pacing around the room. He kissed me and asked me how I felt, and we exchanged pleasantries the way normal people do. But something was different. My invincible knight appeared oddly mortal in the wan dawn light, his face grave, still wearing the shadow of yesterday's revelations. He seemed smaller too, at least five inches I'd say, and that hot pulse of manhood that typically cloaked him like a shield was nowhere to be seen. He tendered—for my approval—his plan to skip our usual breakfast together and go fishing instead, and off he went. He showed up back at the house around midday. But he had no fish. He told me he'd been unlucky and that he planned to try his favorite spots off Salvation Beach after a bite of lunch. I nodded politely, although I didn't doubt that he had passed the morning holed up somewhere in the brush, or floating over a reef, his mind, like mine, rambling along the twisted trails of our lives.

We had a bowl of cold soup made from dried conch and vegetables for lunch. Jamie was solicitous, inquiring into the extent of my morning sickness, unctuous in his concern for my welfare. Beyond that, he was quiet, *pleasant* even—and that's not a word that I would usually use for Jamie—flashing me soft smiles to patch over lulls in our conversation. I wondered how I looked to him. Probably the same. Two bruised hearts dampening down the fires of yesterday's volcanic eruption with studied calm, salving the burns with a fragile but peaceful coexistence. The tectonic plates of our world had shifted. We'd never be the same. Jamie was right. When we had first met, I'd been in awe of him, and the geography of our relationship had been mapped to those coordinates. He was so much more than a great-looking guy. His achievements were an integral part of him, part of what made him Jamie, the Jamie I loved.

So who is the new guy I'm married to?

This new Jamie. The short one. This Cadillac of conmen who'd played the world for a sucker and lived a lie of gargantuan proportions, selling it to college professors, publishers, TV producers, sponsors, and ultimately, to *me*. So if he had shrunk five inches with just me in the know, how far was he going to shrink if the entire world knew?

Right back into his mother's egg.

That was my guess. If this got out, he would fade like a candle flame in a wet mist, shrinking to nothing without so much as a puff of smoke to show it had ever existed. Jamie had lusted after the golden throne of wealth and celebrity and he had ascended to it. But now I had a horsehair thread in my grasp, holding that proverbial sword of Damocles above his head. On the other hand, I was seated next to him on the same throne under the shadow of another sword whose thread he held. We had become the cold-war personified, our mutual destruction hanging by a thread. We were the Humpty-Dumpty couple put back together by Hurricane Nestor, bonded by the challenge of survival on Key Bliss, and now forged into one indissoluble living thing by lies.

After lunch, he headed off. He kissed me on the lips before he left, firm and long, but in no way invitational, more confirmatory. I stood in the courtyard watching him as he made his way south towards Salvation, finally disappearing into the brush without once looking back. I was feeling hopeful despite the deficit column in life's ledger being oversubscribed. Morning sickness was draining me, my nerves were ragged and my hand was painful. I was worn out by the daily grind too, the endless chores—bad enough with two hands and murder with one—and the false alarms, hope crashing into a wall of despair. It was all taking its toll, grinding me down, grinding us both down. We had to get off this island. It was coming. I knew it. I am one of those people who believes that there is a reason for everything. And we would never be rescued until the time was right. That time was now. The last of the hidden truths had bubbled to the surface like a homicide victim dumped in an icy lake who pops up in the spring and calls his murderer to account. To my way of thinking, that was the *why* of all this. And now the truth was out, we would be rescued. It had been painful, but it had worked out. And oddly, I was happy that my husband turned out to be a flawed hero. It made him more human, more on my level. Now there was balance in our lives. I was no longer a planet revolving around my sun. Our new child would live in a solar system with two suns—the way it should be—not a sun and a moon. Jamie and Kim were now equal. We would get off the island. We would keep our vows. Our lies would become our lifeline. That silver chain love song we'd talked about on Salvation Beach came to mind. I still couldn't remember the words. Besides, they didn't fit anymore. Our chain was far stronger than love. It was forged by fear in a furnace of lies. Our chain was stainless steel.

45 - Jamie

When I was a boy, I dreamed of being a warrior. I don't mean a soldier carrying a gun and wearing a uniform with a flag on the pocket. I mean a *caballero*, a man with a horse and a code of honor like a European knight or a Japanese samurai.

So how far do I still have to go?

As I shuffled along the dusty roadway to Salvation, my downcast eyes furrowing the sun-crusted ground at my feet, the answer was forever. I had never been further from that childhood image of a noble knight fit to slay a dragon. I was more like a court jester or a motley fool. I'd been outed, the lie exposed. No longer a closet conman masquerading as a celebrity, now I was a famous fraudster wilting in the spotlight.

When I got to the beach, I didn't have the heart to go fishing. So I sat with my back against my favorite tree, muddling my somber thoughts with memories of my father, my listless eyes scanning the reefs. In my line of work, you get more than a passing acquaintance with the world's great scriptures. But at moments of doubt, I can't say I've ever turned to them for spiritual guidance. When push comes to shove, I heave all that worldly wisdom overboard and pick up the user manual for life that my father gave me when I was a boy. I'd asked him why he didn't go to church like my mother.

"Many of those who go to church on Sunday," he'd said, "cheat on their spouse on Monday. They lie on Tuesday, steal on Wednesday, and murder on

Friday. On Saturday, they usually take a day off and get drunk. So they're good and ready for church on Sunday. I live my life according to my conscience, and that's all I need to hold myself to account."

I was a senior in high school when he passed away. We were on board his sailboat, discussing a trip to the South Pacific. We would never make that trip, and I guess we both knew it. But planning it was a joy all to itself. He'd gone through many surgeries since that stabbing. But in the end, he'd had one too many, and that morning, a post-op blood clot eased him silently out of my life as I was making him a cup of coffee. I inherited his sailboat and his meager savings. I sold the boat, packed my world in a knapsack and got lost south of the border. A woman called Anna found me. She was older, an anthropologist, her mere presence heaving the broken bits of my life into order like a magnet marshaling iron filings to attention. When she went back to Norway, I returned to the US and used the last of my father's money to enroll in college. And that was my inheritance gone. Or so it had seemed. But sitting on Salvation Beach, it was obvious to me that the quiet counsel my dad had given me as a boy was my real inheritance, and equally obvious that I'd squandered it. He'd have been so proud of his PhD son, my bestseller, my TV deal. *But what would he think of me now?* A liar, a conman, an adulterer, a father who'd been having sex with his lover while his son was drowning.

How did it all come to this?

The seduction of fame had been so incremental I hadn't even noticed it. Faking a thesis was hardly a federal case. The facts were fiction, but at least I'd written it. These days, rich college kids routinely hire professionals to write their papers. I was an opportunist. That was all. A crack opened up. Opportunity poked its head out and I grabbed it. Then along came Kim. What was I to do? Tell her I was lying? As for adultery... Excuses trailed off my tongue, but they did little to improve my mood. I'd been determined to get Kim into therapy. But now I'd agreed to forgive and forget. Realistically, I couldn't see Kim as a whistle-blower. She had too much to lose. Then again, if she outed me and turned it into a book, she'd be stinking rich and I'd end up on skid row. My detractors would rejoice—*I told you he was a fraud*—their collective chorus echoing in every corner of social media. Legions of cynical academics would be gleeful. They'd hold parties, and that little prick Walgrave would get a hard-on for a month. I'd have to go into exile, somewhere remote like the Amazon or an uninhabited South Pacific island with seabirds and a few lizards as my only company.

The downside, it seemed, was a bottomless pit.

Even so...

I pondered the options. I could feel my father close by. Something good was happening, a new strength. Just thinking about him was helping me as though we'd set up a virtual hotline between us and he was giving me advice. There were no words or signals on it, nothing articulate. But the message was coming through loud and clear. I gathered up my polespear and headed for the jetty, my backbone stiffening, my hands reaching for the tiller of my life.

We are going to Switzerland. Kim is going into therapy. We'll hire a nanny to watch over our child. If Kim doesn't agree, I'll report her. If she wants to destroy me, she can. Her option. I am ready to lose everything. I will not risk my child's life for even one second.

I strode along the jetty, relishing my conviction, my eyes on the bright horizon. Perhaps I wouldn't have made such a bad knight after all. At least I had finally claimed my inheritance.

I am my father's son.
I didn't see it coming.
We never do.

46 - Kim

By dusk Jamie had still not returned and I was getting anxious. With attempted suicide on my own résumé, I might have considered that a possibility for him. And so I did, but not for long. Jamie had been humiliated. But I could only take my new man analogy so far. Jamie was strong in the most important way a person can be. He could regenerate. It was an instinct to him, and chopping a few inches off his ego was not going to kill it. My real concern was an accident. He'd been distracted, wandering around like a man in a coma. Even at the best of times, he was clumsy and accident-prone and there was always a risk of a shark attack. I stepped outside into the courtyard. The sky was overcast with no moonlight, and a soft rain sprinkled drops on my face. There was no chance of finding him in this light. All I could do was fall and hurt myself. A rumble echoed, distant thunder. Maybe only a shower, but maybe much more. I went back inside and finished the last of the soup before creeping upstairs and falling into a fitful sleep. It was still dark when I awoke and it wasn't nausea that woke me. It was a sound.

The piano? Jamie?

It was neither. It was the storm. Thunder, lightning, and sheets of rain. It was the first time I'd been alone in that creepy mausoleum at night and the noise and the light show were freaking me out. A sudden panic triggered nausea. I fought my queasy guts and won. Then I lit the lamp. There'd be no more sleeping this night. I went downstairs, picking my way on the fragile steps until thunder boomed right over my head. It was so close I ducked and cowered against the wall. Lightning crackled and strobe-lit the lounge. Water streamed from the ceiling and wind whistled through a thousand holes, spinning the fans at hyperspeed and fluttering the sheet music on the piano before picking it up and carrying it away. I cried out and sped down the remaining steps two-by-two. By the time the light show had ebbed, I was scrunched up by the open doorway to the shelter. I peered down into the darkness of its stairway. It was built to withstand a nuclear bomb. I'd feel safe there. Even if I left the doors open, the storm would be nothing but a distant lullaby. There were bunks too. I could see out the night there and set off at dawn to find Jamie. I made my way down the steps and along the corridor. We'd been so curious the day we'd found it, so eager to press on and find the connection to the cave, that we'd spent very little time in the shelter. Jamie had made a cursory check, but I'd been so jittery I hadn't noticed much. It was bigger than I remembered with twelve bunks. I stretched out on one of them and set the lamp on a nearby table. I'd been right about the storm. In the shelter, that thunder was not much more than a whisper. I closed my eyes and planned my morning rescue mission. I knew something had happened to Jamie, but I couldn't afford to let negative thoughts take over.

Salvation Beach.

That had to be my first stop.

Time passed. I couldn't sleep and it wasn't just worry about Jamie keeping me awake. There was something else too, morbid fascination. Our hasty exit from the crypt had cut our exploration short and now Jamie was planning to torch the place. So, with courage and curiosity mounting in equal measure, I made my way through the shelter to the stairs leading down to the crypt. The knife was on the altar where Jamie had left it. I strode down the steps, set the lamp next to it, then turned around slowly, stopping when I noticed writing at the foot of the wall where I'd cleared away rubble to get to the knife. I picked up a tile and used it as a trowel to scrape aside more debris, finding a crumpled piece of paper. I smoothed it out on the altar and held the lamp close. It was a fragment torn from a diary, but there were no complete sentences on it, nothing that made sense. There had to be more of it. I scraped away more rubble, happy to find something to take my mind off Jamie. As I worked, I exposed more writing on the wall. Religious quotations. But I didn't bother with them. I wanted that diary. I'd only seen a few words of it, but enough to tell me that the hand that wrote it belonged to Raymond Bliss. I found four more scraps like the first, lines cut in half, never a complete sentence. But then I found a sheet big enough to have words with meaning—*digging in the cave beyond the mangroves, we found the chest foretold by the Smoking Mirror ... I have it at last ... the crucifix of regeneration is mine.*

Mangroves?

That ruled out the crypt cave. There were no mangroves around *Four Winds*. It had to be a cave on the northwest coast. We'd never explored it. But Jamie had walked around the entire island on his mapping expeditions and he'd mentioned a sweaty coastal stretch of mangroves on the leeward side. Not much of the diary had survived, but enough to prove Jamie right about one thing. The *Capitana* had been wrecked on Key Bliss. For what it was worth, my jumbo fraudster of a husband had lied and blundered his way to the truth about that ship.

I left the paper on the altar and took the lamp back to the wall. My frantic search for the diary had shifted plenty of debris, exposing the base of the wall from end to end. I shuffled along, reading the notations. Every scene had a biblical quote, telling the story portrayed above it.

Behold, I am coming like a thief in the night ... lightning flashes and lights up the sky ... so will the Son of Man be in his day ... then sudden destruction will come upon them as labor pains upon a pregnant woman, and they will not escape.

Bits from the New Testament and some from the Old. But the topic was the same. The Second Coming. That was the message of the crypt walls. I got up off the floor and put the lamp back on the altar.

So the cult's Unholy Mother is—

A loud noise shook me and I stumbled, grabbing the altar to catch myself from falling. I snatched up the knife. No, I didn't make that same mistake. I scooped it up like a pro, my hand tucked under the demon-dog jowl, my fingers wrapped around the god's thighs, his razor-sharp phallus sticking out from the bottom of my fist.

Jamie?

But there was no one. The door had slammed shut. That was all. I went to put the knife back on the altar, stopping when it glinted in the lamplight. I held it closer to the flame and rolled it back and forth. The rainbow obsidian was translucent, streaks of ocher, purple, red and green rippling around islands of dried blood. My blood. I moved the blade behind the flame, turning it into a mirror, and there I was, staring back at me. Tilting the blade this way and that, I played with the image, entranced by my transformation from hauntingly beautiful to hideously deformed. I turned to the Madonna in her palanquin, letting the knife fall to my waist. She was smiling at me, beguiling, seductive, the flickering light animating her face with supernatural life force. I looked down at the knife hanging next to my belly, next to my unborn child.

How pathetic my suicide efforts had been.

Suicide was simple. All you needed was an obsidian blade like this and a pinch of courage. I touched its tip to the skin below my navel and gasped as blood trickled down my belly. I'd barely made contact, not even enough to feel the blade, although I felt its cut sure enough. One stroke would be enough, one deep dig into my belly and it would all be over. No more Kim, and no more—

What shall I call him or her?

I looked up at the New World Madonna and smiled. Blood and pain had cleared my head. The truth was right in front of me. There'd be no more talk of suicide. I understood now why I'd found this crypt, why a new life had been created in my belly. I touched myself with the blade once more, stroking it barely skin deep, making sure the muscle wall of my belly stayed intact. I cut from my navel to my vagina and stood motionless, watching blood drip from my sex to the floor between my legs. Then I reached across my belly and dragged the blade horizontally to make a living cross in blood.

There, it's done.

I dropped the knife, held both hands against my belly and inscribed circles, smearing the blood. This birth was a miracle, a barren woman blessed with child as her vessel had been struck asunder and her heart cleansed by confession. This mural was foretelling my story. I'd been drowned and resurrected. I had sacrificed my son and been guided by the universe to this place. It seemed absurd at first. But why? The Messiah was never going to be born with a halo on his head and a certificate from his father duly notarized by a third party. The prophecy was written in the Bible and echoed on that wall. *The Son of Man will come at an hour when you do not expect him.* So, what type of God should the twenty-first century expect? Had humanity made any moral progress in the past 2000 years? Call me crazy. But answer those questions first. It didn't look crazy to me. What would've been crazy was missing the obvious. The cultists had gotten it right. Death is the womb of life. We all sit at dinner tables every day feasting on death, on plants and animals that were once alive. How could such an intrinsic and fundamental principle of physical existence not prevail in the world of the spirit? There was only one conclusion that made sense of all this. I lifted my bloodied hands up to the Madonna.

I am She.

I am the mother of the returning Son of God—

The lamp flame died. Darkness. I had no matches. No matter. I might have been scared once in the blackness of the crypt, but not anymore. I walked towards the stairs, conscious of each step and where it was taking me. I didn't stumble or fall. Then I climbed the stairs and walked back through the shelter as if I had a map in my head synced with the spirit-powered GPS in my belly. I never put a foot wrong.

It was light when I emerged through the paneling back into the house and set off towards Salvation. The storm was done. Time to find Jamie. I was excited and eager to share my epiphany with him. He was a lifetime student of mankind's search for knowledge. But he'd always been a spectator, never a participant. That was about to change. I was going to punch his ticket to the main event. His career, his celebrity. It had all been a sideshow, a trail leading to this time and place. His destiny was here with me on this island. We would buy it, preserve it, cherish its unique heritage. He would resist at first. But ultimately he would see everything my way. I had never doubted that I was stronger than him. Despite his manly strength, Jamie's life told a woeful tale of weakness, with Jamie cast as a pinball ricocheting off strong women. His mother had been the first. She'd rationed her love, then tossed him aside. Anna, his mysterious college sweetheart, had been next. An older woman, some sort of professor. All I knew about her was that she had inspired his career and apprenticed him as a lover. Then there'd been me, of course. I'd made a man out of him, transforming his idle dreams into wealth and fame. Without me, he'd still have been building castles in the sand. And finally, a dishonorable mention for Sydney Kingston, who'd made him a TV star, who'd turned my loving husband into a deceitful adulterer. So where was Jamie's will in this tale of fame, fortune and failure?

When I arrived in Salvation, I went straight to the beach. By that time the soft glow of the tropical dawn was gone and the sun was flooding the shoreline with light. That was where I found him. He was lying on what was left of the jetty. Its planks and piles had finally given way and then been trashed by the storm. I screeched his name as I crawled on my hands and knees across shards of wet wood. He had to be dead. I checked for a pulse in his throat but I couldn't find any. I panicked, squeezing my face up against his mouth to see if he was breathing. I couldn't tell. I checked his throat again, finding a weak pulse. He was alive, but barely. *Thank God. What if he'd died?* I'd be alone, a pregnant castaway. His ankle was broken and jammed between beams of wood and his head had been ripped open. It was only the trapped ankle that had saved him from getting washed out to sea. I hammered and kicked at the wood and soon cleared enough room to squeeze his foot out.

But how to get him to the shore?

Dragging him back over the busted jetty was out of the question. My only choice was to push him into the water and float him back to the beach. Not so easy. Salvation Beach was protected by reefs. Absent a storm, it was lagoon-like in its calm. But that storm had kicked up a chop and confused waves zig-zagged over the reefs. They weren't so big, but big enough to give a woman my size all sorts of trouble towing a two hundred pound man to the shore. The water wasn't too deep at least, about shoulder height from what I could see. So maybe I wouldn't have to swim it. I'd have my feet on the ground. Reconnaissance done, I clambered into the sea, careful where I put my feet, or as careful as I could be in murky waters muddied by turbulence. The wooden piles had been embedded in concrete stumps and they'd given way too. So the seabed was a mess of littered concrete spiked with wood. Saltwater scorched my ripped belly. It snatched the air from my lungs and left me struggling to breathe. The water came up to my neck. So I'd gotten that wrong, and I'd misjudged the waves too. They were lifting me off my feet and dropping me back on the ground as they rolled on by. That meant pulling Jamie off genteelly was not an option. I'd have to drag him like a sack of coal over the rotten, splintered wood, and that was going to do him no good at all. I tucked my mouth up against his ear. "Maybe it's gonna hurt. But it'll work out. You'll see. I'm going to take real good care of you." My feet found a solid chunk of concrete to leverage against. I grabbed him and kicked off it and we floated free. I wrapped one arm around his chest and swam with the other arm, stroking the water and my legs scissoring frog style. My sneakers got waterlogged in seconds, and that made it hard going, like swimming in mud. I kicked them off and was soon making good progress. After a few strokes, I tried my luck at walking and I was grateful when my feet found sand. The water was at a manageable chest level too. It was all good, until a big wave surged up over my shoulders, plucking me off the sand and dumping me—

I yelped, pain shooting up my leg. My foot was trapped.

And where's Jamie?

Something with big teeth had bitten my foot—it felt like a bear trap—and whatever I'd done with my arms afterward, Jamie had washed away. I ducked under the water. I couldn't see anything with swirling waves kicking up too much sand. So I crouched and used my hands, hoping they wouldn't get trapped too. It wasn't a bite. It was a nail, a long one. It was sticking out of a stump of wood anchored to a slab of concrete and poking right through my foot. I jerked up, breaking the surface and gasping for air. I twisted around, looking for Jamie.

No sign of him.

Waves dragged me this way and that, twisting my anchored foot against the nail. Pain hit my heart and I knew it would burst. I screamed. I was lost. But at least I wouldn't drown. That pain would kill me first. I heaved down air, surely my last, and dropped underwater. Terrified and wracked with sobs, precious air escaping from my lungs, I put both hands on the wood and yanked up my foot as fast as I could like I was ripping off a Band-Aid. As fast as I could still took forever with the nerves in my foot tracking every wrinkle and bump in that rusty nail with a new angle on pain. Bursting back to the surface, I grabbed my foot, sucking down air. The nail was gone, and I knew there weren't any veins or arteries in the foot big enough for the wound to be lethal. I trod water until I caught my breath, barely noticing that my feet were clear of the bottom. I'd been swept further out. I looked for Jamie, picking the top of each wave to scissor my legs and flap my arms to gain a few inches of extra visibility. Nothing, no sign of him. I considered heading back to the wrecked jetty where I could stand up and get a proper view. But in the time it would take me to get back there and clamber onto it, he'd be even further out. Besides, making it out of the rough sea onto the junk pile jetty with no sneakers and a damaged foot was never going to turn out well. Then I saw him. He crested a wave at the same time as I did at least a hundred yards away. I got a lock on his position and started out—swimming breaststroke. My crawl was faster, but I had to stay oriented. In these waves, twisting my head to breathe would have disoriented me. I saw him again about ten minutes later.

Ten minutes!

I'd gotten nowhere. He was even further away. I spun around and let the next wave lift me up to catch sight of the shore. I was hundreds of yards out. Even the junk pile jetty was distant. I spun back towards the sea.

Where was Jamie now?

I bobbed, eyes scanning wavetops every time I

was hoisted up. I thought I saw him once. But it could have been anything, a floating timber from the wrecked jetty. And even if it had been him, and I could make the distance between us, could I make it back? And what if he was already dead? His pulse had been so faint. That hit me hard, my credo echoing back to me loud and clear—*everything happens for a reason*. So in this underwater landscape of sand, rock and jetty junk, a wave had swept me up and dumped me right onto that nail. I'd had Jamie then. We'd been yards from the shore.

Is he meant to die?

One question I didn't need to ask was whether I was risking my own life. That was obvious. And not only mine. However much I loved Jamie, I had to make the right call here. Should I swim further offshore in dangerous seas to rescue a probably dead man at enormous risk to my own life and that of our child, or face the already challenging alternative of making it back to shore alive?

What would Jamie want?

He'd insist I save myself and our child. I sobbed tears in the sea. But when I looked back and saw the shore even further away, I did what any soon-to-be mother would.

47 - Jamie

So here I am, flotsam shifting back and forth across fringing reefs. Lifeless, maybe, but not yet gone, not out of the frame.

It happens to us all. You end up at a certain place and time, and your number gets called. Is there any point in second guessing the trail that led you there?

Does it matter? Hardly.

And yet...

My trail to that pier off Salvation Beach had begun more than a decade earlier in Mexico on a day I'd spent with Anna in search of adventure.

Peyote.

That was Anna's idea. Not for kicks, not for recreation, but for *re-creation*. No theater. No campfire and Bible songs. Anna had written a paper on its ritual use by indigenous people and she was eager to get the first-hand knowledge. Our plan was for a guided spiritual experience, but the reality was more of a psychedelic roll of the dice, *The Electric Kool Aid Acid Test* updated. The drive into the mountains was unforgettable. Jorge, our *guide*, was at the wheel of an old truck taking us to a "safe place" for our trip, a sacred place. The road was steep and skirted a precipitous drop. Jorge lit up a joint, telling us we should abstain to keep our peyote trip *clean*. So there he was, puffing away, one hand or another illustrating some point and the other loosely grasping the steering wheel. Suddenly he braked, the truck skidding perilously close to a vertiginous drop. I looked out of the window. But we were so close to the edge I couldn't see the ground. All I could see was a sheer rock wall fading into the torrid mesa an eternity below us. Jorge was out of the car already, one hand steadying himself on the hood as he heaved up his breakfast in violent spasms. Even the irrepressible Anna was subdued. She gave me a look. This guy had been stone-cold sober when we'd started out in the truck. Now he was puking tortillas and coffee halfway to Kansas, and all he'd done was take a few hits from a joint. This, evidently, was what the local weed did to you. We, on the other hand, had munched our way through a shopping bag full of peyote whose effects were still pending.

No words were necessary.

Skidding to the edge of the abyss turned out to be a prophetic metaphor for the experience that ensued. Most of it, I would never recall. The part I remember was the part I spent with Anna, hidden by a bush in the shelter of an overhanging cliff. It was as if I was seeing a naked woman for the first time, her sexuality radiating power and funding a limitless passion within me. Lost in lovemaking, I was weaving in and out of consciousness when I tumbled back through time and traveled a strange but somehow familiar journey. I made it to the tune of a heartbeat. Then the heartbeat faded and light burst my eyes open. I took a rasping breath, cried out and stared at a world of faces looking down at me. I was alive. I was born. Cynics will dismiss this experience as a hallucination. More kindly doubters might call it a dream. But I knew what it was. I had recalled my journey from my mother's womb to the world of men. I had borne witness to my creation. Some cellular memory, coded deep beyond the ken of my everyday consciousness, had opened its doors, summoned forth by an elixir of magical plants and the taste of a woman. I had traveled the path of life from nothingness to existence.

Predictably, our arrival back on earth came with a bump. Jorge was gone and so was our money and our backpacks. We were quiet and forlorn as we wandered hand in hand off that mountain. Pathetic figures, no doubt. But we were infinitely richer too. Anna wrote me once or twice from Norway. Her adventure days were over. She settled down, married a high-school sweetheart and had a kid. I changed too, choosing a career in archaeology and knuckling down to years of study. Partying became a thing of the past for me, ditto playing the field. From this point on, the women who shared my bed were no longer disposable like condoms to be tossed in the trash. I wanted one woman, not a merry-go-round of half-women. Two paths, one professional and one personal, opened up before me as I walked off that mountain. The first had led me to the *Mendoza Crucifix*, the second to Kim, and both paths had come to an abrupt end on the pier off Salvation Beach.

So here I am, flotsam drifting in the ebb and flow.

Is this the end?

All my life I had studied the origins of humankind, its religions and philosophies, its theories of living and dying. Now I was about to put all that to the test, or debunk it once and for all. If it was the end, all the world's religions agreed. There had to be something left over, some part of me to hold to account. A flicker of consciousness had to remain, something beyond the reach of medical science, a subtle body invisible to scientific tools that only measure gross matter and energy.

My spirit?

I couldn't say.

Yes, I was still there. Not the way I was. But something remained. If not my spirit, then what? My will? I'm not talking about the legal document. That had been drawn up by lawyers way back. My estate would pass to Kim, the mother who drowned my son and left me to the same fate. But what of my child in her belly?

What future awaits it?

Lulling between worlds, I latched on to something as real as anything I'd ever known—let's call it my will—and I swore an oath on it, knowing with certainty that, dead or alive, my battered flesh and broken bones would bear witness to it. *I swear before all the gods and antigods that roam here in this place between heaven and hell. Somehow, I will save my child.*

48 - Kim

Sitting on Salvation beach, feet drawn up to my butt, elbows on knees, head hanging between my thighs, I watched my tears plop one by one, dissolving in splotches of wet on the sand. So lost was I that the voice came to me as a dream at first, another hallucination, another voice in my head, nothing to get worked up about.

"Are you okay?"

I didn't look up. I was too caught up in my thoughts to be distracted by hallucinations. Besides, I couldn't bear the sight of the sea here, the place where I killed my husband. I kept telling myself it hadn't been like that. I hadn't killed him.

But could I have saved him if I'd tried harder?

That was a question I couldn't answer. I kept telling myself I'd done the right thing. I might have been killed too. I had to save our child. Reasonable excuses, all of them. So why was I not convinced?

Ghosts.

They were haunting me. They'd latched onto me in the crypt and a few were still hanging around. The big one I'd gotten rid of. Hiding from the storm in a blood-soaked crypt, that Mother of God/Second Coming epiphany had been so real. But the shock of losing Jamie had ripped it to pieces. I was not the Mother of God. I was a frightened woman in a world she'd never understood since that night spent with her dead father hanging over a lake of ice. Fear and pain had contaminated that crypt like radioactive fallout after a bomb. The walls, the altar, that knife, they were all embedded with evil, and I'd been a Geiger counter perfectly tuned to its frequency. So that madness was gone. But I was still struggling with minor ghosts, the whispering kind. They'd shown up in the waves, when I'd been cradling Jamie, skipping notions through my head.

Jamie's promise.

They'd whispered it over and over.

I'll forget your bad if you forget mine.

When Jamie had said it, he'd meant it. I didn't doubt that. But promises were not hardy perennials. They were desert blooms. True, I had his professional head under a guillotine. But what if he stopped caring? He'd planned to teach college. Imagine that—the famous Dr. Steiger surrounded by fawning female students. How long would it be before one of them joined in the pinball game of his life? If he were dead, there would be no question marks, no talk of Switzerland, therapists, or jurisdictions. My motherhood would be safe, my rights unquestioned. I would also be rich. I didn't have to *do something* to achieve all that. All I had to do was *nothing*. In the waves, I hadn't thought it through like that, all cold and calculating. That wasn't me. But ghosts don't have to speak in whole sentences to deliver a message. And sitting on Salvation Beach, tears rolling into the sand, I was replaying their whispering in my head, and the choice I'd made out there was getting grayer and grayer.

"We're coming ashore. Okay?"

I looked up. A man was waving from the deck of a catamaran, its shallow draft breezing over the reefs. Next to him, a woman was peering at me through a video camera. I was rescued. The big day had come. I should have bounced up and hollered, "Yippie!"

But my first thought was *what a state I must look*. At least I wasn't naked. I had my skirt on and my flotsam sneakers, the left foot—the one I'd impaled on the nail—swathed in rags and squeezed in a shoe two sizes too big. I waved back and stood up.

Is it real?

It wasn't until I was on the boat, drinking wine and tucking into a ham and cheese sandwich, that I got my answer, and it hit me with a wallop.

It's over.... It's all over.

The rich food, the wine and the euphoria of it all left me lightheaded, and for a while, Jamie's death and my soul searching were forgotten. My saviors were Paul and Janis Taylor, a retired couple from Chicago. And how lucky was I? Janis was a Doctor and Paul a nurse. They'd met in the hospital where they'd both worked, and after thirty years of marriage, this was their dream trip. They'd gotten lucky too, missing Nestor by long enough for the islands to have recovered, but close enough to have the still-empty seas to themselves.

So there I was, talking, drinking, eating, and plenty of all three. Yes, drinking. I hadn't shared with them the good news about my pregnancy. As medical professionals they'd have nixed that offer of a glass of wine without a second thought. And of all mothers-to-be, I was one who knew more than most about fetal alcohol spectrum disorders and the increased risk of a miscarriage. I could say that in my excitement I forgot I was pregnant, and there was an itsy-bit of that. But the real reason was certainty. I knew in my bones that this time I was never going to have a miscarriage. I could have skated downhill on my belly and still been sure of that.

Those first days after my rescue, I was in a dream state with things I'd taken for granted—a shower, shampoo, toothpaste and mouthwash—transformed into voluptuous luxuries. The boat was a floating hospital in terms of medical supplies, and my saviors soon had me patched up. Meanwhile, along with his duties as captain, Paul videoed me as Janis ministered to my needs, firing questions about my great adventure. They'd set up a vlog to share their once-in-a-lifetime trip online and I was a bonanza find. Not only did I have a great story, but I was desperate to talk. I'd been marooned on a desert island with only my husband for company and not even that for days. So I talked, and all the time the virtual tape was rolling. The big question came up early, way before the reality of being saved had hit me. *What happened to your husband*? I said he was lost at sea. Then I burst into tears, which pretty much ended that line of conversation. If you're going to be snippy about prepositions, then technically he was lost *to the sea,* not *at sea.* But what the hell difference does a preposition make? To my mind, that was not a lie. Except it was. But what was the alternative? A lengthy discourse about the ruined jetty? I'd barely set foot on the boat when Janis noticed the cross on my belly. Given my state of dress, that was hardly surprising and needed an explanation. The jetty came to my rescue. It had collapsed beneath me, and writhing in the nail-infested debris, I had sustained wounds that by chance resembled a cross. That was how I'd gotten the foot injury too. All that was already on tape. So what was I supposed to do? Edit my earlier account to include Jamie. Explain how I'd dragged my husband from the jetty to the sea where I'd abandoned him. Would the world understand I'd had no choice? Would they agree? Better to duck the whole thing and make life easy. So that's what I did.

By the time we reached Georgetown, I was well-fed, rested and thoroughly debriefed. Janis had clothed the quasi-naked castaway with her own wardrobe, and since she was a plus size woman, that meant I was now dressed in fashionably baggy jeans and shirt. I was desperate to get some clothes that fit and make arrangements for my journey home. Janis and Paul handed me an envelope with a thousand dollars in crisp twenties—part of their emergency cash fund—and I picked up the clothes I needed to tide me over on a whirlwind shopping trip. I also made a few calls. My bank was first on the list. And after bouncing between managers, I had cash wired to the local Western Union and arranged for new plastic to be sent to a Nassau hotel. I was keen to get back to California and pick up the broken pieces of my life. But before I could leave the Bahamas, I needed a passport. I also needed a few days of pampering and recovering and enough me-time to stop my world from spinning. So I booked a VIP suite at a five-star hotel in Nassau. They had a world-class spa and I was planning on getting every treatment on offer. I said goodbye to Janis and Paul in a tearful farewell, then headed for Exuma Airport in a taxi, clutching a tiny bag containing all my possessions.

Know what a stringer is?

Most people don't, but I'd worked in the media and I recognized him for what he was as soon as I saw him pace across the lounge toward me. The giveaway was his smile, his I-want-something friendliness when he greeted me, and the calculation in the casual once-over he gave me. He was in his 30s but already run to seed with all the hallmarks of a failed hack. Foreign correspondent. That had been the dream. But this was the reality, marooned on the ex-pat trail, praying for a hurricane, a coup, an assassination, or a live shooter in a shopping mall. Nothing doing there. But he did have me. With forty minutes to wait for the plane, I was cornered, so I gave him an interview. But I was careful, no longer the dumb motor mouth I'd been in the days following my rescue. I made sure every word was in sync with what I told the Taylors. Even so, I was alarmed about how much he knew already. It was all up there on their vlog, he told me. That and what else? I had to get to a computer and a phone. I had to catch up. Information is a virus and, like any smart virus, it mutates as it travels from host to host. So what did this look like from the other side? As the interview progressed, his questions looped back to topics we'd already covered and that made me twitchy. He was trying to trip me up to see if I was lying. He must have sniffed something that made him suspicious, a discrepancy. But what?

My speculations were interrupted when my flight was called, and I was still wondering when the door closed on the plane and we were on our way to Nassau. But by the time we landed, I'd moved on. The prospect of staying in a luxury hotel with everything I needed was now just a taxi ride from the airport. Simple enough. Or so I thought. But waiting for a cab—

"Delighted to see you, ma'am." I spun around. "My condolences on the loss of your husband."

Detective Inspector Rolle was standing right behind me, his unexpected arrival giving me a jolt. *Delighted*? He was on his own with that one.

"You waiting for a taxi too?" I said.

He smiled. But I hadn't meant it to be funny. I'd meant it to be snide. My memories of this man were all sour.

"No ma'am. Since your husband passed in the

jurisdiction of the Bahamas authorities, there is some paperwork to attend to. This is normal in cases where a person goes missing at sea. A loss that's not uncommon in the islands. How long will you be staying with us?"

As little time as possible, I almost said. But I bottled it up. My spleen was pointless. Of course there'd be paperwork. Why was I fighting a battle that didn't exist?

"About five days."

"Yes, you'll need to get yourself organized. New travel documents and so on. Did you contact the embassy?"

"Not yet. I plan to go in the morning."

My taxi came. I declined his offer of a ride to my hotel, but agreed to stop by the station to sign off on the paperwork. An hour later, I was lounging in a Jacuzzi, bubbles up to my nose, the fragrance of sweet oils soothing my soul.

The next day, I visited the embassy first thing and left with an emergency US passport. I shopped for clothes in a department store, ate a light lunch and at three in the afternoon I presented myself at the police station, eager to get this over and done with. A female police officer in a uniform introduced herself as Sergeant Wilson. She led me into a room and fetched me a coffee. I say room rather than office and that fact troubled me. I'd expected to be shown to a desk piled with papers where Rolle would be staring at a computer and tapping on a keyboard. But this one was empty save for a long table bolted to the floor. Cameras were mounted in corners where they'd get a clear shot of everyone sitting at the table, and a big screen on one wall finished the furnishings of what was a lot more like an interrogation room than an office. I noticed all this, but I wasn't too concerned. I was in that room voluntarily, and I could walk out of it as easily as I'd walked into it. I sipped my coffee and waited. Minutes later the sergeant returned with a laptop. She opened it and was setting it up when Rolle entered and closed the door. He had papers tucked under his arm. He thanked me for coming, then sat down next to his sergeant and fiddled with the papers, making sidelong glances at her computer.

"Is this going to take long?" I said.

Rolle shook his head. He wasn't smiling now and nor was the sergeant. She was done at the keyboard. Now she was staring at me with fierce eyes like someone might look at a serial killer, one who'd eaten her victims.

"Sergeant," Rolle said.

She hit a few keys and the screen on the wall lit up.

I cried out, and if they'd punched me in the chest, I couldn't have meant it more.

Jamie.

He was sitting in a hospital bed, his face so thoroughly patched that he was barely recognizable. He wore a hospital smock, bandages clearly visible beneath it, tubes running in and out of his mummified arms. Despite the minimal amount of him on show, there was no mistaking who it was. Those eyes drilling into me said it all.

I turned to Rolle, eyes narrowing, a blood rage flushing my face with heat and locking my jaws tight. *Here comes the big bang.*

Why didn't you tell me? Why did you lie? Why are you—?

I choked on the words unsaid, my brain clicking on and my anger fizzing to nothing. Tears welled, and a swirl of emotions made me dizzy—happiness,

Jamie's alive! confusion, *how can he be?* fear, *what's with all this theater?* I held onto the table, knuckles turning white.

"Why?" I said.

"Here, take a sip." Rolle pushed the coffee towards me. "Dr. Steiger can't hear us yet. We're still setting that up."

I ignored him, my eyes back on the screen, questions backing up so fast I couldn't count them. But then a voice swept them all aside. *Amazing Eric.* I'd long ago dismissed him as a charlatan. But now his words came back to me, along with the creeping nausea I'd felt during the séance. *The sea gives him up.* Not William, but Jamie. *The Sandman saves his child.* Not William, but...

My hands fell to my belly. How could he say it so right and I hear it so wrong? A whimper slid between my lips and my hands trembled. I locked them together, fingers intertwined, writhing as if to escape.

Rolle turned to his partner. "Are we connected yet?" She nodded. "Go ahead."

She picked up a sheaf of papers from the top of Rolle's pile. "This is a warrant. It authorizes me to place you under arrest."

Rolle leaned across the table, his face softer now. "Dr. Steiger made a statement implicating you in the death of your son. Did you confess that to him ... in the storm?"

I looked from the screen to Rolle. "Can he hear me yet?"

"He can't help you. But you can."

I was catching up, the shock fog clearing. This was trouble. But how much? I'd reported on plenty of trials back in my news days and there was something hokey about all this.

A confession? On a sinking boat in the middle of a hurricane?

"Shouldn't I have a lawyer? Aren't you supposed to tell me that? I walked in here of my own free will and I can walk out again."

"If you try, I'll arrest you," Wilson said. "And any chance you have of squirming out of this will be gone."

Squirming?

Evidently that was a bit much even for Rolle. He raised his hand, telling her to back off. If she was playing the bad cop, she was doing one hell of a job. Rolle turned toward the screen. "Dr. Steiger, are you there, sir?"

"I am."

"Are you good to speak?"

"I am."

It was Jamie's voice, but then again, it wasn't. Something different about it, a hard edge. And monosyllabic and muffled though it was, that voice told me a lot about why I was sitting in that room. This was the Jamie I had to deal with now, the one who'd recently returned from a roundtrip to hell.

My chair screeched as I spun it towards him. "We had a deal. Remember?" Jamie stared on but said nothing. "If you talk, I talk." I was doing this all wrong. I had an audience and cameras catching every blink of my eye. But all that faded away. There were only two of us in that room, me and my husband. Yes, I was overjoyed to learn he'd survived. But that was all swept aside by—

"Kim," Rolle's voice pulled me up sharp. He'd never called me that before. "You need to talk less and listen more."

"Let her stick her head in the noose." The sergeant was still pinning me with her eyes, trying to get a rise out of me, but that was never going to happen. She looked the type to break my arm "accidentally" while arresting me, and no way was I going to give her that pleasure.

I ignored them both and went back to Jamie. "I love you. I'm so happy you're alive. But damn you for this. Why should I keep my word when you didn't? If I talk, you can kiss goodbye to—"

"Go ahead." Jamie's mouth was a pink slit between bandages. "I expect you to."

"But why?"

"Your last line ... remember?"

"My last line when?"

"*I'm going to take real care of you.*"

"So?"

"Before you dragged me off the jetty and dumped me in the sea, making sure you'd pulled me far enough out to catch the current and get swept away."

Rolle and the sergeant were sitting back, eyes transfixed on me. I looked back and forth between them and Jamie. Everyone was expecting me to speak, but I'd been struck dumb. *Not even close* was all I could think of, but I couldn't even get that out. In the end, my back-and-forth settled on Detective Rolle and his partner. Tears were rolling and I left them to it, vertigo spinning my head. I was falling, my world a bottomless pit.

"That's an attempted murder charge right there." Rolle leaned across the table toward me. "On top of William's homicide."

"Do you have any idea where you're headed here?" Wilson picked up the baton as Rolle leaned back in his chair. "Murderers ... your new roommates. Women who've killed with knives, guns, their bare hands. Their victims were men and women who got in their way, and plenty they just didn't take a shine to. But kids?" She shook her head. "Child killers don't make out well on the hard-core block. They're prone to accidents."

"Sammy." He waved his hand again, quietening his pit bull. "The sergeant here has four kids. But she makes a good point. There are women in those institutions who wouldn't give you the benefit of the doubt—"

I leaped up in my seat and my chair fell back. The sergeant was on her feet in an instant but Rolle grabbed her arm. I swirled around, looking up at Jamie. "I nearly died. What I did for—" I gave up on words and stuck my foot up on the table. The sergeant broke away from Rolle, and she was at the end of the table heading my way when he barked something at her. I didn't even hear what. But it stopped her. I yanked off my left sneaker, then tossed the white sock at Wilson. I clawed at the dressing I'd painstakingly applied that morning. Then I jerked my ankle up to give them all a good view, but especially Jamie. "A six-inch nail did that. It went right through. I didn't let you go. I was nailed to a slab of wood and concrete. We were all going to die. You, me, and our baby. You want to arrest me for attempted murder? Do it! My lawyer will rip your case to pieces. As for my confession, was that under oath? It's his word against mine."

"No, it's not," Rolle said. "Dr. Steiger's account— your confession—matches other evidence. The missing paddleboard, and the tracks you left in the sand when you dragged it down to the sea. The medical forensics—"

"Medical what?"

He turned to Wilson. "What did that doctor call it?"

"Dissociative amnesia." She roamed her eyes back

and forth between Kim and Rolle before continuing. "A memory gap"—she pulled out some notes and glanced at them— "linked to overwhelming stress caused by a traumatic event like killing your own child. In your case, it's consistent with—"

"That's enough." Rolle stopped her. "And there's the glass on the beach. In your account, you didn't even mention that young couple, the Smiths, who described your state of mind as *very disturbed*—"

"You interviewed them?"

"As for the attempted murder charge, Dr. Steiger's account rings true to me when you add it to..." He flicked his hand at Wilson, and she spun her laptop around towards Kim. "That journalist you spoke to in Exuma didn't waste any time in filing his story." I read the headline, my fight back over. REALITY TV STAR LOST TO NESTOR'S FURY. It had already gone national. By tomorrow it would be all over the planet. With the slip-up I'd made on the catamaran out there already, I'd had to stick with it. "According to your account, Dr. Steiger was floating in the ocean for over a month and survived. How's your lawyer going to argue that away? Jurors will know you're a liar. Why would they believe anything else you say?"

Wilson spun the laptop back her way, breaking my stare. But I'd seen enough. Yes, I'd need a lawyer, not for fighting the charges, but for saving my life. If this went wrong, I'd end up in a penitentiary. I had no illusions about that. I'd barely survived in the free world. In jail, I'd be a goner, and the biggest threat to my welfare wouldn't be the hard cases on murder row. It would be me. So then and there, I stopped caring, caring about anything except my baby. I looked up at the camera. "I killed William. I tried to kill myself first, but I couldn't... I couldn't abandon my son. So I went back for him. Then I came to my senses and I tried to make it to the shore. I hit my head somehow and got washed up unconscious on the beach." I turned to Jamie. "But you, I did everything I could to save your life. I swear it." I held my wrists out for the sergeant. "That's it. Arrest me. You've got it all on camera."

"Inspector, please." Jamie's voice was sharp, commanding. "We need to speak."

Rolle stood up, glanced at his sergeant and tapped one ear. "Audio." He headed for the door and Wilson hit a few keys. She nodded confirmation as he reached the doorway. Then he was gone.

We waited in silence with me winding the dressing back on my foot and Wilson staring at me. In the end, she broke the silence. "We'll get a medic to take care of that for you."

I nodded, grateful, less for the promise of medical attention, than the softer tone in her voice. Maybe I wasn't going to get that arm broken after all. I squeezed my foot back in its sneaker and looked up at the screen. Jamie was talking but no sound was coming through on our end. "Who rescued him?"

"Two locals."

"Fishermen?"

"So-called. Let's say part time. When there aren't any cruisers to sell pot to."

"How long was he—?"

"In the water?" I nodded. "Less than twelve hours. The waves had beaten him on the reef and something big had taken a few bites out of him."

"I was still on the island then. Why didn't someone—"

"He was in a coma. No ID. He was listed as a John Doe. One of the guys who pulled him out of the water had helped himself to that crucifix. So the hospital had no clue. And what with his change of appearance, his castaway beard and beaten-up body, nobody linked him to that famous reality TV star lost way back in Hurricane Nestor. It was only after you were rescued and the news trickled out that the local guy realized the crucifix was too hot to sell and came forward. That was a few days ago. About the same time as your husband was making sense."

I looked back at the screen. They were having quite a conversation with Jamie's pink-slit lips working overtime. "What's going on here?" I said, nodding at the screen.

"No idea."

"Why is it taking so long?"

"They set up two feeds. Your husband's side of it is being piped to another room too."

"Is there someone else watching?"

"The prosecutor, maybe. But I didn't see her around today. Maybe they wanted a private chat room. Who knows?"

Jamie was waving his hand, hammering home some point. I stared at those pink slits. But I'm no lip reader.

What are they saying?

49 - Jamie

"Not a chance," Rolle said. "Get that idea out of your head."

I rubbed my eyes. Thinking straight was close to impossible. How many pills had they given me? How many shots? I'd lost count. But their side effects, topped off with physical and mental exhaustion, were an easy tally. Total confusion. I fixed my eyes back on the screen. Rolle was in an interrogation room, identical to the one where they were holding Kim. He was sitting at the end of a long table and as far as I could see, he was alone.

"That foot injury looked real to me and she didn't have it when I left her. She didn't try to kill me. I got that wrong. She tried to save me."

"Okay, I'll drop the attempted murder charge. But that's not what you're asking me."

"Is the prosecutor there with you?"

"She couldn't make it."

"How does she feel about putting a pregnant woman in the dock, one who was suicidal at the time and—?"

"The prosecutor will do her job. She won't do it with a smile, but she'll do it."

"Kim tried to save William. She came to her senses in time and turned back to the shore. I believe that."

"Murder is murder. The accidental nature of the death changes nothing. The issue is intent. On the beach, she planned to kill herself and William. That makes it premeditated murder. Her account of what happened subsequently doesn't change that."

"But there's diminished responsibility."

"They'll take that into consideration."

I was banging my head on a brick wall here.

"I'll bog you down, Rolle. Appeal after appeal. I'll take it all the way to the Supreme Court." I waited. He wasn't going to like this. "All the way to the Privy Council in London." I was right. That got to him. His eyes flared. I'd overstepped. A mistake. I needed this guy on my side. He said nothing, stone-faced. I continued, anger dampened, voice soft. "Does the prosecutor know about that case in California? How it all fell apart."

"Different jurisdictions and none of my concern. My job is to bring murderers to justice, not deliver the judgment."

"Justice is doing it my way. Kim is already in jail, the open jail of her own conscience, and she'll never be paroled."

"I'm sorry, Dr. Steiger." Rolle stood up and made for the door.

"Inspector." My voice stopped him. "At our lunch in Miami, you said you'd solve this case or take it to your grave. So, congratulations. You told me why you'd never give up on it too. It was because you remembered my face on the night I lost William. And something else." Rolle waited, but he had to know what was coming. "The real reason was that it stuck in your craw. So what's your best guess here? Is your version of justice—putting Kim in jail—going to change that?"

He waited, thoughtful, his eyes dropping away from mine. Then he looked up, shaking his head, and walked out the door.

50 - Kim

An age passed with Jamie just sitting there, staring at the screen, his lips motionless. I wanted to read his face, but the dressings made that impossible and I didn't dare guess. Why was it taking so long? Where was Rolle? Jamie hadn't said a word for at least fifteen minutes. I was about to ask Wilson when the door opened and the detective walked in, nodding to Wilson as he made his way to his chair. Moments later, we were back in conference mode.

"Kim," Rolle said, "this is where you get to take a long breath and decide what's best for you, your child, and your husband." He left that there for a while and I took his advice. "Your husband has made a proposal, and after speaking with the prosecutor..." He turned to Wilson. No choice about that. The look she was giving him had to be burning a hole in his face. He nodded some reassurance, then put his attention back on me. "This can all go away if you agree to certain terms. That emergency passport you picked up this morning. You hand it over to me now. You agree to stay in the jurisdiction of the Bahamas until you give birth. When you do so, Dr. Steiger will become the sole guardian of the child. You will have no further contact with that child. But you will be free to return to the US and resume your life."

"And never see my child again? Forget it. I'll take a shot in court."

"Tell her inspector," Jamie said, "the whole deal."

Rolle hesitated. Evidently, this was the part of it he didn't go for.

"If you agree to undertake treatment at a facility chosen by Dr. Steiger—he has suggested a clinic in Switzerland—and your treatment there is successful, meaning that two independent experts are satisfied that you could never pose a risk to your child. He will allow you reasonable visitation rights."

"You got lucky," Wilson said. "That prosecutor, she never wanted any part of this. If it was me, you'd—"

"Sammy." Rolle cut her off and leaned towards me. "You'll get to be a mother again. What you were going through that day—your state of mind—those things don't matter a damn. Only facts matter. Your son died, and you caused that. You can't blame your husband for this now. He's the father. He has a duty to protect his child. This is one hell of a second chance."

I looked up at Jamie, my face all tears, sniffs, and pucker. I held his eyes in mine, long and lingering, then nodded twice.

Epilogue

<u>Montreux, Switzerland - April 2017</u>

Jamie looked over the hedge and down into the street, watching a white hybrid with a black roof parallel park. He turned to the child churning the pedals of a tricycle on the terrace behind him and said, "Guess who's here?"

The girl flashed a look at him, bright blue eyes under blonde bangs, and the tricycle bundled to a halt, toppling over as she leaped off it. She ran to her father at the hedge and he scooped her up with one arm, pointing down at the car.

"Mommy," she said as Kim stepped out of the vehicle and locked it.

Kim looked up and waved, and they waved back as she crossed the empty road. It was her first visit, the first of the new regimen following her discharge from the clinic. Jamie had bought a garden-level duplex in Chernex, a village just outside of town. This was the place that her daughter Chantal called home, a far cry from her own modest apartment, but close enough to make the journey in minutes.

The two years after Chantal's birth had been brutal. Kim had complied and cooperated. She'd had no contact with her daughter and she'd gone through the motions at the clinic. But none of that meant she agreed with the rules or any of the treatment she was getting. The doctors and nurses weren't on her side. In her mind, they ranked somewhere between probation and corrections officers. Either way, they weren't her friends. That wasn't a considered opinion, more of a feeling, and it got in the way of meaningful progress until something brittle snapped inside her. From that day on, self-acceptance had paved her road to recovery, with faith in her treatment and sincerity towards her doctors riding roughshod over cynicism and anger. She'd been introduced to her daughter in a closely monitored reunion and weekly visits at the clinic had soon followed. Just an hour at a time, but a glorious one for mother and daughter. Now here she was, a year later, knocking at the door of the place her daughter called home.

On the other side of that door, Jamie picked up Chantal and sat her on his hip, then opened it.

"Right on time," Kim said, glancing at Jamie but not meeting his eyes. All her attention was on Chantal. She held out her arms and Jamie gave her the child. Chantal hugged and kissed her mother as Jamie waved her in and shut the door behind her. That was a comfort for Kim. She'd been ready for a hand-off at the door and a quick rundown of the rules, the when, where and how of her twice weekly visitation allowance.

"We've got a view," Jamie said. "Here, take a look." He led her into an open plan living and dining room, a big one with a family size dinner table. Glass doors made up the far wall and opened onto a patio with a metal table and chairs backed by a lawn. Beyond the hedge at the end of the garden, a townscape of rooftops swept down to Lake Geneva and the mountains beyond.

"Beautiful." Kim took it all in, sweeping her eyes back and forth, the whole Swiss package, mountains and lakes.

"The sun goes down right there." Jamie pointed across the water. "The sunsets are unreal."

"I bet they are."

"I'm not sure if you'll need this." Jamie reached for a stroller leaning against the wall and opened it up. "It's multi-terrain. Check out these wheels."

"No." Chantal shook both fists. "I'm not a baby."

Jamie looked at Kim, eyebrows raised.

Kim pulled her head back to get a better look at the tiny lady with the big spirit who was writhing with indignation in her arms. "I'm with you, girl," she said. "Three years old ... better get those legs working."

"So what's the plan?" Jamie hadn't wanted it to sound authoritative. But it did. And that registered on Kim's face momentarily, before she recovered her smile. She'd known the question was coming, the holding to account. She was on probation after all.

"The *petit train*," she said, referring to the toyland train that shunted up and down the lakeside promenade. She turned to Chantal. "Would you like that, a train ride with mommy by the lake?" Chantal grinned and patted her cheeks with both hands. "Then we'll take a walk in the park." Kim finished her accounting, giving her husband all her attention.

"And no ice cream." Jamie wagged a finger at his daughter, hoping to lighten the mood. "Because today's our pizza day. She'll be very persuasive and use several clever ploys to get around that prohibition. So watch out for that."

"I get it. Pizza and ice cream on the same day. That's a no-no. Mommy agrees."

Kim headed back into the lounge. It was time to go. They had a train to catch, albeit a dinky one on rubber tires. She put Chantal on the floor and took her hand.

Following her, Jamie said, "I'll order the pizzas for five thirty, so—"

Kim stopped and turned a little too quickly. "I know the rules. Four hours on the dot. I get four hours with my daughter, twice a week." She tapped her wrist. "I've got a brand-new Swiss watch. I won't be late. I promise you."

Jamie nodded. That hadn't come out right either. He'd wanted that comment to end on a much more positive note. He opened the front door, but not wide enough to let them through. He picked up Chantal and hugged her, then held her to the side and put his hand on Kim's shoulder. It was the first time they'd touched in years. Then their eyes met. That was new too. He slid his hand behind her neck and pulled her closer. Her body braced with resistance at first. Then her face softened and she pulled him in to her. They kissed, with wide-eyed Chantal staring on and bursting into giggles when they slid apart. Kim took Chantal from Jamie's arms. Their daughter was still bug-eyed, her head flashing back and forth between them. Jamie opened the door wider, and as they stepped through it, he said, "Kim." She swung around. "They do that two-for-one thing here like in the US. The pizzas, I mean. That's way too much for the two of us. If you're not busy later, maybe you could join us. We could eat at that table out on the terrace and watch the sunset."

Kim stared, insides churning, raw feelings kindling hope. She couldn't get the words out. So she turned to her daughter. "Pizza with mommy and daddy, the three of us. Would you like that?" Chantal nodded to each of them in turn, her face solemn, before bursting into giggles and clapping her hands.

"Enjoy the day," Jamie said, "and take good care of our girl."

Kim smiled. "With my life," she said.
Jamie didn't doubt it for a single instant.

(This story was inspired by a real-life tragic incident. See the next page for details.)

About this Book
(Warning: Spoilers)

This story and all of its characters are fictional, but much of it was inspired by actual events.

In 1985, Fumiko Kimura went to the beach in Santa Monica, California with her four-year-old son and six-month-old daughter. With her children in her arms, she walked into the sea and kept walking. According to media reports, she was suffering from depression following the discovery that her husband was having an affair. Some college kids dragged her out, still holding both children. All three were barely alive. They were rushed to A & E, where both children died, but their mother survived. She was put on trial for murder, provoking an outcry and a heated public debate. In the end, the charges were reduced to manslaughter, and Fumiko spent one year in detention. The sadness and horror of that event shocked me. I resolved then to one day write a story, exploring the theme of survival, with a tragedy like that at its heart and hope at its end.

The history and geography of the Bahamas gave me a rich and fascinating canvas, so I fictionalized much of the story based on real events or people. Christian beliefs and rituals have often fused with pagan religions in this region, although *El Culto de La Madre Impia*, its rituals, beliefs and symbols, such as the *Mendoza Crucifix*, are fictions created by me. The description of the *ixcuac* is adapted from a sacrificial dagger in the British Museum. Ragamoffyn Island and Worthless Cay are fictional, but all the other islands and locations are real. My 1564 Tierra Firme Fleet is fictional too, although its circumstances and fate mirror those of the New Spain Fleet of 1563, whose *Capitana* was lost in a storm, possibly in the Jumentos. The efforts referenced here to recover my fictional *Capitana* are based on recorded attempts to find the *Capitana* of the 1563 Fleet. There were many Caribbean storms in the 2013 season, but only two minor hurricanes. Nestor was the next name-in-waiting that year, but it remained unused. It was recycled in 2019 as Tropical Storm Nestor. I had already written an early draft of this book by then and I liked the name, so I kept it. Hurricanes usually exhibit typical behavior, but they can spring surprises like Nestor. In 1983, Hurricane Alicia went from a tropical depression into a category 3 hurricane in thirty-six hours, and in 2004 Hurricane Jeanne made a complete loop before heading north, characteristics I attributed to my fictional storm.

I am grateful to the authors whose works I consulted while writing this story and especially the bloggers and social media users who shared their personal experiences.

Enya Wolf
January 2023